# HEREAFTER

# HEREAFTER

## ⟡TARA HUDSON⟡

HARPER TEEN
An Imprint of HarperCollinsPublishers

HarperTeen is an imprint of HarperCollins Publishers.

Hereafter
Copyright © 2011 by Tara Hudson
All rights reserved. Printed in the United States of America.
No part of this book may be used or reproduced in any manner
whatsoever without written permission except in the case of brief
quotations embodied in critical articles and reviews. For information
address HarperCollins Children's Books, a division of HarperCollins
Publishers, 10 East 53rd Street, New York, NY 10022.
www.epicreads.com

Library of Congress Cataloging-in-Publication Data
Hudson, Tara.
    Hereafter / Tara Hudson. — 1st ed.
        p. cm.
    Summary: Amelia, long a ghost, forms a strong bond with eighteen-
year-old Joshua, who nearly drowned where she did and who awakens
in her long-forgotten senses and memories even as Eli, a spirit, tries to
draw her away.
    ISBN 978-0-06-202677-4 (trade bdg.)
    [1. Ghosts—Fiction. 2. Future life—Fiction. 3. Near-death
experiences—Fiction. 4. Good and evil—Fiction. 5. Family life—
Oklahoma—Fiction. 6. Oklahoma—Fiction.] I. Title.
PZ7.H867Her 2011                                      2010045622
[Fic]—dc22                                                  CIP
                                                              AC

Typography by Erin Fitzsimmons
11  12  13  14  15   LP/RRDB   10  9  8  7  6  5  4  3  2  1
❖
First Edition

*To Robert. In an instant. In a heartbeat.*

# HEREAFTER

*Chapter*
## ONE

It was the same as always, but different from the first time.

It felt as if my sternum was a door into which someone had roughly shoved a key and twisted. The door—my lungs—wanted to open, wanted to stop fighting against the twist of the key. That primitive part of my brain, the one designed for survival, wanted me to breathe. But a louder part of my brain was also fighting any urge that might let the water rush in.

The black water seized and scrambled and found

purchase anywhere it could. I kept my lips pressed together and my eyes shut tight, though I desperately needed sight to escape this nightmare. Yet the water still entered my mouth and my nose in little seeps. Even my eyes and ears couldn't hold it back. The water wrapped around my arms and legs like shifting fabric, tugging and pulling my body in all directions. I was buried under layers and layers of slippery, twisting fabric, and I wasn't going to claw my way free.

I'd struggled too long, fought too hard, and now my body was weakening from the lack of oxygen. The flail of my arms toward what I assumed was the surface became less exaggerated, as if the invisible fabric around them had thickened. I literally shook my head against the urge to breathe. I shouted *No!* in my head. *No!*

But instinct is a slippery thing, too—ultimate and untrickable.

My mouth opened and I breathed.

And as I always did, except for the first time I'd experienced this nightmare, I woke up.

My eyes remained closed and I continued to gasp. This time my gasp brought hysterical gulps of air, but not the brackish water that had flooded my lungs and stopped my heart during that first nightmare.

Now the air was useless, purposeless in my dead lungs. I nonetheless felt a dull joy at its presence: although my heart no longer beat, the air meant I was no longer drowning.

Still, I felt a little silly for being afraid. After all, it's not like you can die twice.

And I was already dead, that much was certain.

It had taken me awhile to accept the fact, perhaps years—time became a very uncertain thing in death. Years of wandering, confused and distracted by every sight and sound. Screaming at passersby, begging them to help me understand why I was so lost or even just to acknowledge my presence. I could see myself—bare feet, white dress, and dark brown hair that had dried into thick waves—but others couldn't. And I never saw another person like myself, someone dead, so there was really no point of comparison.

The nightmares were what made me finally see, and accept, the truth.

At first nothing in my wandering existence brought back memories of my life, nothing but the elusive familiarity of the woods and roads I wandered.

But then the nightmares began.

I would suddenly and without warning fall into periods of unconsciousness. During them I would drown again. Only after the first few nightmares did I see them for what they were: memories of my violent death.

So the memories of my death had returned. Yet only

a few memories of my life came with them: my first name—Amelia—but not my last; my age at death—eighteen—but not my date of birth; and, of course, the fact that I'd apparently thrown myself off a bridge into the storm-flooded river below. But not the reason why.

Though I couldn't remember my life and what I'd learned in it, I still had some vague recollections of religious dogma. The few tenets I remembered, however, certainly hadn't accounted for this particular kind of afterlife. The wooded, dusty hills of southeastern Oklahoma weren't my idea of heaven; nor were the constant, narcoleptic revisits to the scene of my drowning.

The word "purgatory" would come to mind after I woke from each nightmare. I would play out my horrific little scene and then I would wake up, gulping and sobbing tearlessly, in the exact same place each time. It wouldn't matter where I'd been wandering when I went unconscious—an abandoned railroad track, a thick grove of pines, a half-empty diner—my destination was always the same. And each time the nightmare ended, I would wake in a field. It was always daylight, and I was always surrounded by row upon row of headstones. A cemetery. Probably mine.

I never waited around to find out.

I could have searched for my headstone maybe. Could have learned more about myself—about my death.

Instead, I'd pull myself up from the weeds and dash for the iron gate enclosing the field, running as fast as my nonexistent legs would carry me.

And so it was with my existence: a montage of aimless wanderings; an occasional word spoken to an unhearing stranger; and then the nightmares and subsequent hasty escapes from my waking place.

Until this nightmare.

This nightmare had started the same. And, just as it always did, it ended with a terrified awakening. But this time when I finally opened my eyes, I didn't see the sunlight of a neglected cemetery. I saw only black.

The unexpected darkness brought back the terror, the frantic gasping. Especially since, after what would have been only one beat of my still heart, I recognized my location.

I was floating in the river again.

My renewed gulps, however, didn't drag in muddy water that surrounded me. My body was still as insubstantial as it had been before this nightmare. It floated, unaffected by the drag and pull of the angry water. This time things were different, although the dark, twisting scene looked almost the same as it did in each of my horrible dreams.

Almost.

Because this time I wasn't the one drowning.

He was.

*Chapter*
TWO

My first impression of the scene was wrong. The water wasn't entirely black. Faint light shimmered above the surface—moonlight, maybe; it was too grayish to be sunlight. Below me two muted yellow beams seemed to rise from the depths of the river.

No, not rise. The beams pointed upward, but they were retreating. I spared a quick glance at them. They came from a huge, dark shape just below me. The shape—a car, its headlights beaming into the darkness—floated downward with an eerie slowness.

I shook my head. I didn't really care about the car; my attention was riveted on the boy illuminated in its headlights.

His body had shaped itself into a kind of *X*, arms floating limply upward and sneakered feet dangling. His head hung down, but I could tell his eyes were closed.

This boy didn't flail or struggle, and I had a sudden, sickening realization. The boy was unconscious. Not the kind of unconsciousness that torments the dead, but the kind that kills the living.

If he didn't wake up, this boy was going to drown.

Without another thought, I swam to him as fast as I could. When I reached him, I could see his face fully. He was young, no older than I was when I died. His face looked peaceful in its stillness. He was strikingly handsome. I could see that, even under the water. His dark hair floated above his head almost lazily, considering the current. An involuntary and silly image sprang to my mind: his outspread arms resembled wings. Useless wings, at that. I wondered, almost idly, whether my arms had resembled his when I died.

My thoughts, then, were as sudden as they were fierce. This boy couldn't die. I couldn't watch him die. Not here, not like this.

I began to grasp at him, frantically trying to pull at

his clothes and his limbs. To drag him to the surface. I tugged at his long-sleeved shirt and his jeans, even at his dark hair.

I pulled and pulled, but of course nothing happened. My stupid, dead hands couldn't touch him, couldn't save him. It was like struggling in the water on the night of my death—not a damn thing that I did would have any effect on the outcome. I was impotent, ineffective, and never more aware of the fact that I was dead.

Soon I started weeping my tearless sobs and pressed both my hands against his chest. As we sank deeper into the river, I became acutely aware of something: the sound of his slowing heartbeat.

As far as I knew, I possessed no supernatural senses whatsoever. Although some of my human senses had survived my death—my sight and hearing, obviously—I could no longer smell, taste, or feel anything in the living world. My remaining senses hadn't dulled, but they certainly hadn't improved, either.

So the sound of his heartbeat shocked me. I shouldn't have heard it so well, but I did. Even with a foot of water between us and with my no-better-than-human hearing, I could hear his heartbeat as clearly as if I'd pressed a stethoscope to his chest.

I wondered whether this had something to do with death. With *being* dead. Perhaps the dead could hear one of our own approaching, racing toward us. Or slowing toward us, in his case.

The boy and I continued to sink; and as we did so, his fragile heart beat unevenly toward its end. Each thud came slower than the one before it, until finally—

His heart stuttered once. Twice. And then I couldn't hear it anymore. A tiny bubble escaped the corner of his lips and floated upward.

I screamed. I screamed as I did in the first flush of death, angry and humiliated at my own lack of power. I screamed and slapped my useless hands against his chest.

At that moment his eyes opened.

He looked to the left and the right, taking in his surroundings. Then he looked at me. He looked right into my eyes.

I froze. Could he . . . *see* me?

He smiled, and then suddenly reached out his hand to place it upon my cheek. I felt his skin, warm on mine. Without thinking, I put my hand over his. His smile widened when I touched him.

He *did* see me.

He saw me, he saw me, he saw me.

My still, unbeating heart soared. And then so did his.

His heart—the one I'd just heard dying—stuttered, and stuttered again. The renewed beat sounded slow and uneven at first, but quickly it began to steady itself.

He looked down at his chest and back up at me, eyebrows arched in surprise at the sound coming from within him.

Then he coughed. The motion shook his whole body and sent bubbles flying out of his mouth.

He began to kick and flail. As he flailed, I realized I could no longer hear his heart. It was silent, at least to me. Yet he was thrashing about, fighting against the dark water. He continued to cough violently as his lungs spasmed back to life. Through the churning water, I could see his expression. He looked angry, terrified, and desperate.

I recognized that look. I had once *felt* that look. This boy was alive. He was alive, and he didn't want to die.

"Swim!" I screamed at him suddenly. "Up! Out!"

He didn't look at me, but he began to scissor his legs and grab at the water above his head as if he were climbing out of a pit. Unlike my efforts on the night of my death, however, his struggles worked. He began to float upward, toward the surface of the river.

I'd never felt a wave of relief like this. Not in a million nightmare-wakings. Not in a million of those gasps that proved I was no longer drowning.

"Up!" I screamed again, this time with joy.

He continued to claw his way up, not once looking

back at me or at the sound of my voice as I followed him effortlessly. Perhaps to him I was once again other, different—dead. For the moment, I couldn't have cared less. He would live. He wouldn't die in this cold, wet pit like I had. That was more than enough.

It felt like an eternity until he broke the surface of the river, but he did. In the night air, he choked and sputtered and gasped, flapping his arms against the water as if he were trying to fly away from it.

I floated beside him, entirely unaffected by the current or the churning his movements had created. When he sucked in a huge breath of air, I actually laughed aloud and clapped my hands together. Then I clapped my hands over my mouth. I'd never laughed. Not once since my death.

"Josh! Josh!"

The unfamiliar voice startled me. Someone had called out across the river to us. Well, to the boy anyway. I turned away from him, almost unwillingly, and saw a cluster of figures on the riverbank behind us.

"Josh!" a girl's voice screamed. "Oh Jesus, Josh, please! Someone help him!"

I turned to the boy, who was still coughing and flailing.

"Josh?" I asked. "Are you Josh?"

He didn't answer.

"Well, Josh or not Josh, I know you're tired. God

knows I know. I know you probably can't hear me, either. But you've got to swim toward those voices. Do you understand?"

For a second he didn't react. Then, with painful slowness, he began to move his arms. The movements didn't exactly qualify as swimming, but they were enough to start pushing his body through the water.

As he got closer, the screams from the shore grew louder. In them I could almost make out a rational thread of conversation concerning the plan to pull him out of the river.

But really, I wasn't listening to the people on the shore. I was watching the boy swim, closer than I'd ever watched anything in my existence. I found myself praying for the first time since my death. Praying that he made it safely to the shore; praying that he didn't give up and let the current take him.

"Please," I whispered as I followed him. "Please, let him make it."

This boy proved much stronger than I ever had. For several more agonizing minutes, he fought his way through the current. Finally, he was close enough so that someone was able to grab his arm and half swim, half drag him to the shore.

Cries of both joy and fear rose up from the crowd that had gathered on the grass embankment and the bridge above us. A man, the one who had pulled the boy from the water, stretched the boy out upon the muddy red riverbank. As I rose out of the water and walked onto the shore, I could see the man flutter his hands over the boy's body, checking for some sign of life.

The boy instantly rolled over, coughed once, and began to vomit water. Audible sighs of relief rose up from the crowd. Their faces were illuminated by headlights from the cars parked in a jumble on the grass as well as on the bridge. The onlookers' expressions varied from tense to excited to scared.

"Josh. Josh," they called like a chorus.

They all seemed to know his name.

It was then that I noticed the multicolored flash of lights coming from the emergency vehicles that had formed their own sort of crowd behind the bystanders on the bridge. Within what seemed like only seconds, two uniformed paramedics had made their way down the embankment and knelt beside the boy, doing their own, more effective sort of fluttering over him. Within less than a minute after that, the boy—my boy, if I was honest in my suddenly possessive thoughts—was placed on a gurney and hoisted across the bank, then up toward an ambulance. The crowd surged forward with the paramedics, and I lost sight of him.

That should have been the end of the ordeal. Yet I

couldn't stand still. I couldn't watch strangers take away the only living person to see me. My boy. My Josh.

Determined, I pushed through the crowd. They couldn't see or feel me, of course, but I still had to fight to find a clear path.

By some miracle I made it through. I shoved in between two figures and suddenly found myself at the side of the gurney just as the paramedics began to raise its wheels so they could slide it and its passenger into the ambulance.

I leaned over the boy. He looked pale in the moonlight, his face gaunt and drawn. For some reason I had to hold back a sob.

"Josh?" I moaned, unsure of what to do. Unsure of everything.

He opened his eyes then. Dark-colored eyes—too dark a color to identify at night. He looked at me and held my gaze in the moment before the paramedics moved him out of my sight, possibly forever.

"Joshua," he croaked, his voice rough from the river water. "Call me Joshua."

Then the gurney was shoved into the ambulance, the doors slammed shut, and he was gone.

I stood there on the riverbank, motionless. Some of the onlookers remained after the departure of the ambulance, milling around to discuss what I could only assume was the near tragedy. I barely noticed when the last member of the crowd left and the last set of headlights disappeared into the darkness of the night. I wasn't really paying enough attention to hear or see anything going on around me.

What I saw instead were his eyes, looking right into mine. What I heard was his voice . . . talking to me? Yes, I'm sure he'd been talking to me. No one had asked him to identify himself as they loaded him into the ambulance. He'd had no reason to give his name to anyone but me. Most of the crowd seemed to know him. Maybe they'd known him all his life. Maybe they'd sensed, as I had, how important he was.

Of course I knew his importance now. I knew it deep in my suddenly very awake core. I knew nothing about him—not his age, his last name, the way his voice would sound if it spoke my name. But I knew things had changed for me. They had changed forever.

*Chapter*
## THREE

**T**wo days passed.

Their passage, although probably not remarkable to the living, was extraordinary to me. I'd never really had a reason to count the passing days. The sun's rising and setting had no effect on me except to obscure my vision at night. I didn't need sleep, and my lack of company in daylight didn't change at sunset. When the nightmares had begun—wrenching me from wakefulness into unconscious terror and then unfamiliar daylight—I'd lost the will to mark time altogether.

Until now.

Now I couldn't stop counting each lonely moment as it passed.

On the first night, while I watched the ambulance drive away, I'd thought fleetingly of following it on foot. But I'd ultimately rejected the idea. Even though I could travel instantly through space and time in my nightmares, I hadn't discovered a way to do so while awake. I still moved at a normal human pace, and I could probably walk for years before I found the hospital where the ambulance had taken the boy.

It hadn't occurred to me until after the last car had left the riverbank that I could've snuck into an empty backseat, maybe gone with the driver to the hospital . . . and then what? The idea of stowing away with a living stranger on the slim possibility that I would end up at a hospital, wandering lost through its corridors in search of another stranger—well, I felt silly and irrational just imagining it.

Of course, milling around the scene of my death didn't seem very rational, either.

From the bank of the river, I'd watched as police barricaded the gap in the bridge above me. I'd looked on as a wrecking crew, completely oblivious to their audience of one, towed the boy's sodden car from the water. While these activities took place, I hardly questioned my desire to stay here—really, who wouldn't be interested in such things?

But after the activity had ended, each subsequent moment I'd spent at this site made me feel more and more foolish.

For a while I'd tried to justify my need to linger. I told myself that I just needed some time to reorganize my thoughts before I began wandering aimlessly again.

Deep down, however, I knew the truth. I knew the real reason I didn't leave this river.

I didn't *want* to wander aimlessly anymore. I wanted to wander with a very specific aim. I wanted to wander to *someone*.

Someone who had nearly died (or actually died; I couldn't be sure) in this river. Someone who, in doing so, had changed me irrevocably.

There were signs, other than my unwillingness to leave, that a change had taken place. First, there were what I came to think of as "flashes." I would be walking through the woods beside the river, or along the bank, and a flash would happen. An image—bright and colorful, and full of smell and taste—would flash across my mind and then disappear as fast as it had arrived.

Like my nightmares, the flashes occurred unexpectedly. But instead of terror and pain, the flashes brought something infinitely more appealing: what I could only assume were memories of my life before death.

Nothing significant had appeared yet: a black ribbon fluttering in the wind; the sound of a tire squealing on pavement; the earthy smell of a spring storm. No people, no names, no fleshed-out scenes to give me some clue as to who I was or why I'd died. Nor did I really experience the tastes and smells. The things that occurred in the flashes were more like ghosts of those sensations. But they were enough.

However little I saw, I became more and more certain that these images were *mine*. My memories from life, breaking free of the fog that death had wrapped around my mind.

And it was because of him. Because of his eyes on mine. Because of his hand upon my cheek, placed there as naturally and easily as it would have been had we been made of the same stuff. Skin, blood, bone. Breathing, seeing, touching.

The mere memory of his skin on mine made me tingle. But not some fleeting, imaginary tingle—this was a sensation. An actual, physical sensation. And the next, most miraculous, change in my new existence.

The first time I'd felt something had occurred on the night of the accident. While I stood on the riverbank watching the lights of the ambulance fade, I'd become aware of an odd, pins-and-needles sensation in the soles of my feet. I stared down at them, confused and afraid. Suddenly, I could feel the mud between my toes and the tickling of the dry grass upon my bare feet. Then, just as abruptly as it had begun, the sensation had ended.

The event had stunned me, to say the least. For so long I'd been desperate for a waking, physical sensation. I'd wanted to feel something, anything. Yet I could place my hand on an object, press myself against it, and it would never matter. I felt nothing. Nothing but a dull pressure that prevented me from going further.

My afterlife had proved all the supernatural stereo-types wrong. I couldn't walk through walls or float amorphously from room to room. The living people who came close to me didn't walk through my body but instead seemed to move unthinkingly around me, as though I were just an obstacle in their path.

The only thing I could feel, could affect, was myself. I could touch my hair, my dress, my own skin. After a while this exception provided me no comfort. Actually, it became more of a big, hideous joke: I was trapped in a prison of one. It was as if I existed in my own little dimension, unseen and unheard by others but maddeningly aware of my surroundings.

I have no words to describe the way that made me feel: not only invisible, but also without the power of smell, taste, even touch. Then, how to describe the way I felt when I realized my only physical sensations occurred in the nightmares through which I reexperienced my death?

Or, alternately, how to describe the touch of a hand on my cheek after so long?

Not only was the touch itself extraordinary, but it had also opened some sort of floodgate of sensations.

In the two days following the accident, and at the strangest moments, I would feel things from the living world. Such as the rough bark of the blackjack oak tree against which I'd leaned, or a tiny drop of rain when a brief shower had passed over the river. These feelings came and went quickly, outside of my control.

Yet I found I could control one of them: the little thrill in my veins each time I thought of his skin. This thrill bore a haunting similarity to a quickened pulse in my wrists and neck, so I sought ways to replicate it as often as I could.

I was thinking of his skin again when another flash occurred. Without warning, a scent overwhelmed me, capturing me completely. I froze where I stood, smelling a cluster of late-summer blackberries that clung to a bramble along the tree line. I leaned closer to them, breathing in their smell, tart and overripe under the noonday sun. Although the scent soon vanished and the numbness began to creep back over me, I laughed aloud.

This was the second laugh of my afterlife, and I wanted more of them. Without another thought, I dashed up the steep, grassy embankment to the bridge.

*Bounding tall hills in a single breath. Or no breath at all. Super Dead Girl.* I laughed again, feeling giddy as I arrived at the top of the hill and began to stride across the grass.

When I crossed the shoulder to the road, however, I froze, one bare foot on the pavement and one on the grass, arms out in an imitation of a trapeze artist.

*High Bridge Road.*

The words whispered like a threat in my mind, and I immediately had an urgent desire to get away from this place. I could feel a gnawing at the back of my mind, an itch creeping up and down my skin.

Did I sense the stirrings of another nightmare? No, this felt like an entirely different kind of foreboding, one I'd never before experienced.

I shook my head. I was being ridiculous. After all, I was dead. What could be scarier than me?

I forced one foot off the grass and the other farther onto the pavement. My legs moved almost involuntarily, and each step along the shoulder of the road sent unpleasant tingles up my spine.

*This is stupid,* I thought. I straightened my back. I refused to skulk on the side of the road like a dog with its hair on end.

"Move it," I commanded myself aloud. I strode forward with purpose, albeit still a little stiffly. Each step unnerved me further, but I didn't slow until I made it almost halfway across the bridge.

I only stopped when I reached the jagged gap in the waist-high metal railing to my right. Yellow police tape and a few wooden sawhorses stood between the gap and the road, ready and willing to keep absolutely nothing from plummeting off the bridge. The torn railing hung out over the edge of the bridge on both sides of the gap, swaying lightly in the breeze. His—Joshua's—car had torn a hole at least six feet wide into the railing before flying into the river.

I shivered from the very idea of the crash as well as from the sound of his name in my head. Wrapping my arms around my body, I spared a timid glance at the ground. Streaks of black rubber crisscrossed the pavement where his tires had made a futile attempt to keep him from going over the edge.

It was then I heard the scream, a terrible, pealing sound that shrieked from behind me.

I actually jumped up in the air. An expletive, one I didn't even know I knew, flew out of my mouth as I turned to face the sound.

Only then did I see that the horrible noise hadn't been a scream after all. It had been the sound of tires squealing to a sudden stop. Only ten feet away from me, a black car parked, and the door opened.

Without thinking, I relaxed. My ghostly instincts kicked in and told me there was no need to run, no need to fear anything. Because if it drove a car, it couldn't hurt me. It couldn't even see me.

But, obviously, my instincts had forgotten the one exception to this rule, even if my heart hadn't.

A boy climbed out of the driver's side of the car and slammed the door shut. From his profile I could see he had full lips and a fine nose with just the slightest curve in it, as though it had been broken once but set well. He had almost black hair and large, dark eyes. When he cast those eyes on me, I absently mused that he was a much healthier color than when I'd last seen him.

"You! It's you!" he cried, pointing right at me.

Without another thought, I turned and ran.

## Chapter FOUR

I was just full of foolish impulses lately. There he stood, the boy about whom I'd been thinking—obsessing, really—for the past two days. Yet I ran, as fast as I could, in the opposite direction. Had any of my adrenaline still existed, it would have burned in my legs as I fled.

Apparently, and as I'd suspected, my ghostly instincts had become as strong as my living ones had been. Ghosts weren't meant to be seen, no matter how much they wanted to be. Anything to the contrary was cause enough to run away, and fast.

At least those would have been my thoughts were I capable of any. But at that moment I was only capable of blind terror. Fear buzzed in my brain, and it nearly blocked the voice that rang out from behind me.

"Stop! Come on, stop! Please."

It was the quality of the voice that did it—low, and still a little hoarse from the river water he'd swallowed. Hearing the break in it, I felt a little ache right in the middle of my chest. Just a small, inconspicuous, and completely incapacitating ache.

I skidded to a stop, almost at the other end of the bridge. Ever so slowly, I turned around to face him.

"Thanks," he called out roughly, settling back on his heels. From his stance he looked as if he'd just been about to take off after me.

I gave him one tense nod. There was a noticeable pause, and then he asked, "So, will you come back here?"

I shook my head. *No way.*

Even this far apart I could hear him sigh.

"O-kay." He dragged out the sound of the *O* as if he was taking the seconds of extra pronunciation to deal calmly with a frustrating puzzle. "Then . . . can I come over there to you?"

I frowned, not indicating an answer one way or another. I guess he took my indecision as a yes, because he began to walk toward me. He kept his steps intentionally slow, and he held his hands in front of his body in the universal gesture of "I won't hurt you, wild animal."

"I come in peace," he called out, and I could see him grin just a little. The grin was all at once wry, and sweet, and cautious.

So I couldn't help but grin right back.

The boy dropped his hands and smiled fully at me. And, with that, the little ache exploded in my chest like a bomb, warming every limb.

Warmth. I felt warmth. Really felt it, just like I'd felt the touch of his hand in the water. My smile widened.

"Does that smile mean I can keep walking toward you?"

"No," I said quietly.

He stopped moving, surprised by my words, or maybe just by the sound of my voice. "Really?" he asked after a moment.

"Walk over to the grass," I instructed.

He frowned, knitting his dark eyebrows together. "Why?"

"I don't like this road. I want to go back over there." I jerked my head in the direction of the embankment I'd only recently left.

He kept frowning, but that grin twitched at the corners of his mouth again.

"O-kay." He gave me a thoughtful look, holding my gaze. The message was clear: I was the frustrating puzzle with which he was calmly dealing.

Then he smiled, closed lipped and dimpled like a little boy, and gave me a quick nod. He shoved his hands in the pockets of his jeans, turned on one heel, and began strolling back to the embankment.

Slowly. Too slowly. Swinging his legs in an exaggerated, deliberate way. I sighed loudly.

"Could you hurry up, please?"

He laughed, still walking away from me.

"You have a way with giving orders, you know that? Not a master of the casual chat, are you?"

*Given that you're the first person I've talked to in God knows how long since my death . . .*

Aloud I muttered, "You have no idea."

I could tell he'd heard me because he hesitated just a little. Then he kept walking forward, minus the mocking swing of his legs. After he'd gone about ten feet, I began to follow him. I walked even slower than he did, trying to think, think, *think* of what I was going to do, or say, when he stopped.

Blessedly, he kept going, past the black car and past the end of the bridge. Then onto the grass of the embankment. I was worrying so deeply about our upcoming exchange, I didn't notice when he stopped and turned toward me. I looked up in time to jerk to a stop just a foot from him, within touching distance.

Terror raced through me. I could have run into him. If that had happened, I would have either felt him, skin against glorious skin, or I would have felt nothing but the numbing, impossible barrier. Either way, he surely would have realized something was wrong and do exactly what he should: get away from me.

"So," he began, casually enough.

"So," I responded, my eyes going to my bare feet. I felt ashamed, terrified, excited.

"I'm Joshua."

"I know."

"I thought so."

The humor in his voice made me look up, finally meeting his eyes. As I suspected, his eyes were very dark, but not brown. They were a strange, deep blue—an almost midnight sky color. I was certain I'd never seen eyes that color before, and they had a disconcerting effect on me. I felt even more flustered just staring into them.

I was suddenly, uncomfortably aware of my own appearance: the tangles in my hair; my deathly pale skin; my hopelessly inappropriate dress with its strapless neckline, tight bodice, and filmy skirt. I probably looked as if I was headed to some sort of dead girls' beauty pageant. For the first time in a very long time, I wished I had access to a mirror, whatever good it would do someone who couldn't cast a reflection or change clothes.

He didn't seem to notice my discomfort, however. Instead, he looked right into my eyes and grinned at me, although his expression had lost some of its amusement. He looked more speculative now, as if he knew there were mysteries between us. Questions.

"So," he started again.

"You already said that."

"Yeah, I did." He laughed lightly and looked down at his shoes, absentmindedly running one hand through his hair and then leaving it on the back of his neck.

There went my little ache again, flowing out of my core like a pulse. That absentminded gesture—the guileless sweep of a hand through his hair—was utterly endearing. He looked so vibrant, so alive, that the words spilled right out of me.

"You want to know what happened, don't you?"

I recoiled from my own words, blinking like an idiot. *Stupid, stupid, stupid.*

"Yeah, I do. I really do." He dropped the hand from his neck and stared at me more intently, the playfulness entirely gone from his eyes.

*Crap.*

"Well, that's a matter of opinion, Josh," I said aloud.

"Joshua. Joshua Mayhew," he corrected instantly. "But

my name's not really important right now."

Deflect. I had to deflect, and fast, so I blurted out the first question that came to mind.

"Why am I supposed to call you Joshua if everyone else calls you Josh?"

"You're not everyone," he said bluntly. "Anyway . . ."

He knew I was stalling and meant to lead me back to the original trail of conversation, that much was clear. What was less clear was whether or not he meant any flattery by his words.

"Um . . . ," I floundered, and did something I hadn't done since my death: I fidgeted. I grabbed at my skirt and began to twist it. I had no idea where to go from here.

Neither did he, it seemed. He watched me worry at my skirt and then he stared at my face until I eventually met his gaze.

"What's your name?" His question was soft, gentle. He wasn't trying to lead me back to the conversation. He really wanted to know.

"Amelia."

"What's your last name, Amelia?" His voice wrapped so well around my name, I flustered out yet another stupid answer.

"I don't know my last name." Or, at least, I'd never felt brave enough to try and find it in the graveyard.

He blinked, taken aback.

"Huh. Where do you live?"

"I don't know that, either."

Disarmed. I was completely disarmed. That was the only reasonable explanation for my stupidity.

"O-kay." The long *O* again. He wasn't as playful with the sound this time.

He stared down at his canvas sneakers, frowning and digging the toe of one shoe into the grass. He shoved his hands back into his pockets and rolled his shoulders forward, a reflexive gesture that made him look boyish and sweet. After a few more silent moments, he looked back up at me.

"You know, we have a lot to talk about." His eyes, serious and urgent, met mine. My little ache curled out even farther in my chest as he continued. "I would have come and found you sooner, but they wouldn't let me out of the hospital. Apparently my heart may have . . . Well, I may have . . . died, a little. In the water."

He tilted his head to one side, clearly gauging my reaction. I shivered, but I didn't look away. I probably didn't look too surprised by his choice of words, either. After all, I was there when it happened. My face obviously answered some unasked question of his, because he nodded again.

"So," he went on, "after I got out of the hospital, I

started asking around about you. But nobody saw you that night. Not my family, not my friends, not even the paramedics. Not only did nobody see you on the shore, but nobody saw you in the water with me. Which I find weird. Because you *were* in the water with me, weren't you?"

I bit my lower lip and nodded slightly.

"I knew I didn't imagine you. Well, maybe when I was, you know, *dead.*" He said the word as if he was afraid of it. "But not after. Not when I swam to the surface or when I made it out of the water."

Still biting my lip, I shook my head. *No. You didn't imagine me. You saw me.*

"I practically had to steal my dad's car to get out of the house today, and I came right here—to the scene of the crime. And here you are."

"Yes," I whispered, totally lost for a clever response. "Here I am."

"So," he whispered back, "we have a lot to talk about."

"You already said that."

He laughed, and the sound surprised us both. Then he nodded decisively.

"Well, here's how I see it, Amelia. We don't have to talk now. I have to get the car back to my dad soon anyway, since I've spent the whole morning stalking you. Besides, this doesn't seem like a conversation you want to have, especially in this place. Can't say that I blame you." He glanced quickly at the hole in the railing, shuddered, and then looked back into my eyes. "So, tomorrow I'm going to be at Robber's Cave Park. Do you know where that is?"

Stunningly, impossibly, I nodded yes.

I knew the park. I suddenly knew it as well as I knew my first name, and I knew the direction of the park from where I stood now. I knew it from memory, a genuine one that hadn't flashed into and out of my mind but just . . . was.

What was this boy doing to me?

"Okay, good. I'm going to sit at the emptiest park bench I can find. I'm going to be there at noon, because, unfortunately, I'm healthy enough to go back to school tomorrow. I think I can talk my parents into letting me skip fifth period—play the sympathy card with them—but noon's the earliest I can get there. So I'm going to go to the park. And I'm going to wait for you."

"And if I don't show?"

He shrugged. "I'll respect your privacy. Or I'll pursue you all over the earth like I've been trying to do since they let me out of the hospital. Probably the latter."

I should have been afraid. I should have run away again, hid until the years passed and Joshua became an old man and the fog wrapped around my dead brain again.

Instead, I smiled.

He gave me a slight nod, grinned, and walked past me back to his car.

"Till tomorrow," he called out with one small, backward glance.

I watched him walk away, once more unsure of everything. But when he opened his car door, my incapacitating ache curled again. My impulses, it seemed, were still doing unfamiliar things to me, because the ache seemed to have incapacitated everything but my big mouth.

"Joshua?" I called out, a slight hitch in my voice.

"Yeah?" He spun around immediately. I could swear he looked expectant, maybe even eager.

"What do I look like to you?"

He tilted his head to the side, frowning.

"What do I look like to you?" I repeated urgently, afraid that if I didn't talk fast enough, I would have time to realize how absolutely, mind-bogglingly stupid I sounded.

Joshua smiled. He answered me, so quietly I almost couldn't hear him.

"Beautiful. Too beautiful for people not to have noticed you the other night."

"Oh." The little sound was all I could manage.

He stood up straight then and cleared his throat.

"So . . . um . . . I'm going to leave before I say anything else that makes me sound like an idiot. Tomorrow?"

I nodded, stunned. "Tomorrow."

Joshua, too, nodded. Then he got into his car and reversed it back off the bridge, giving wide berth to the gap in the railing. With one quick, final spin, the car pulled away, disappearing from sight around a curve.

*Chapter*
FIVE

Hours can pass like years when you wait impatiently for something, especially something you crave and dread in equal measure.

What I craved, in a manner so intensely I nearly ached from it, was to see Joshua's face and to hear his voice. Wandering and dreaming of him, I'd never imagined Joshua would be able to see me and talk to me again, much less that he would want to. I hadn't anticipated how much I would want it too. How much my longing to be seen, and specifically by him, would intensify each time I was.

But seeing him again meant telling him the truth.

Sitting on the riverbank after Joshua left, I felt certain I wouldn't be able to lie to him the next day. Not if my completely ridiculous behavior on the bridge proved any indication of my ability to deceive him. If I saw him in the park, and we spoke, I would undoubtedly tell him everything: what I'd seen under the water, and what I really was. Which, in turn, would undoubtedly drive him away from me.

So even if I went to the park, I probably wouldn't see him again afterward. Presuming this, I had to ask myself what would hurt worse: the numb loneliness of invisibility or the aching loneliness of an outright rejection from the living world? I knew the awful boundaries and depths of the former, but I had no idea how excruciating the latter could, and likely would, be.

Following this line of reasoning, I came to a decision about my course of action the next day. I wouldn't go. I would hide. I would protect my dead heart from anything worse than numbness.

And I would probably feel miserable about it for years. I lay my arms across my knees in a posture of defeat.

That's when something made my head jerk upward and then made me jump up into a crouch on the grass. At first I couldn't be sure what made me react this way. When I tried to glean some clue from my surroundings,

I noticed that the sun had nearly set while I sat feeling sorry for myself. It threw a fiery glow across the water and cast deep shadows into the woods.

Yet it wasn't the dying sunlight that had frightened me. It was instead the thing that contrasted so sharply with the burning light of the sunset: a bitterly cold wind that now lashed across my bare legs and through my hair.

I'd been experiencing so many unexpected sensations lately that perhaps I shouldn't have been so alarmed by the wind. But I was.

Late summer was not the season for a freezing wind. Worse, nothing around me had ruffled in the wind—not the tall grass on the bank or the needles of the nearby pines. The wind came from the wrong direction, too. It didn't blow off the water behind me or down the wide alley that the river made through the woods. It came directly from the shadowed tree line in front of me.

Realizing all of this, I actually felt the hairs on my arms stand on end. I couldn't help but raise my forearm to stare at the goose bumps there, marveling at the revival of my long-dead fight-or-flight response.

Without warning, the wind became a gale, whipping my hair across my face and obscuring my vision. I stumbled backward, knocked off balance by its force. It howled out from the trees, and my hands flew up to protect my ears from the sound. Then, just as suddenly as it had appeared, the wind stopped. The bank became deathly still.

My hands still covered my ears, and I'd unknowingly squeezed my eyes tightly shut. I'd curled almost completely over, clutching my bent knees together with my elbows.

"Hello, Amelia."

A male voice floated silkily out from the tree line. I remained curled over and opened only one eye, refusing to believe I could actually hear someone speaking directly to me. Someone other than Joshua.

"Do you hear me, Amelia?"

I opened the other eye and straightened myself slowly, still keeping my hands over my ears as if they afforded me some protection from this stranger's voice. I couldn't seem to force my vocal cords to work. He sighed impatiently, obviously waiting for me to provide him with an answer.

"Really, Amelia, you're being terribly rude."

"E-excuse me?" I managed to stammer.

The owner of the voice clicked his tongue in admonishment. "Still rude."

His tone broke through the terrified frost that had begun to creep over my skin. I felt myself flush with the warmth of anger, as though I were able to blush from fury.

"You can see me, but I can't see you. Don't you find

*that* a little rude?" I demanded.

He laughed, a smooth sound that didn't do much to dispel the skin-crawling feeling. "Oh, I suppose I could remedy that problem, if you wish."

The tree branches directly in front of me stirred as something crept out from behind them. I could tell that, whoever the speaker was, he moved deliberately, possibly to put me at ease and keep me from bolting from this place. It wasn't a very effective tactic, because I could feel the twitch of impending flight in my muscles.

Before I made the final decision to run, however, the owner of the voice stepped out of the gloom of the woods and into what little sunlight still filled the bank.

I knew instantly that he wasn't a living being, although at first I wasn't sure why. As I stared openmouthed at him—another action he would likely find rude—I noted all the details of his appearance. He looked about my age, or maybe just a few years older, but he wore strange, wild clothing: an unbuttoned black shirt, its sleeves rolled up to reveal metal cuffs on both his wrists; impossibly tight jeans slung low on his hips; and several necklaces bunched together on his bare chest. Beneath the ashy blond hair that fell in messy curls to his shoulders, he looked terribly pale. As if someone had scrubbed all the color from his face.

Despite his pallor, I supposed you might call him

handsome. Sexy, even.

The contrast of his skin against the darkness, however, gave away his otherworldliness. His skin was too bright, too unaffected by the dying sunlight. It had its own, nearly imperceptible glow in the dark, reflecting neither sunlight nor moonlight but illuminated by his very nature. Like a black-and-white photograph that had been given a slight sheen and then centered in front of the darkened scenery. Out of place and otherworldly, just like me.

"What are you?" I breathed.

"You know exactly what I am. I am what you are. The better question, Amelia, is *who* am I?" He halted his approach, folded his arms over his bare chest, and smirked at me.

So I was right. He *was* a ghost. A ghost of whom I wasn't growing any fonder. I threw back my shoulders and raised my head high.

"I don't think I'm really interested, but thanks anyway."

"Funny girl. Of course you're interested."

"And why is that?"

"Because I'm the first of our kind you've ever seen."

I stifled a gasp. How could he know that?

I thought briefly of retorting that it didn't matter anyway, because he certainly wasn't the first person to see me. Yet some protective instinct told me not to mention Joshua. To keep the very thought of Joshua out of my head, if possible.

The other ghost was too sharp—he noticed my pause and narrowed his eyes.

"I can understand your shock, Amelia. I've been watching you for years, keeping my distance. You've never seen me, and I've never noticed you encounter any of our kind. Unless you've been sneaking around behind my back." He smiled, showing off a slightly chipped front tooth. The effect would have been charming were he not so creepy.

"But . . . how do you know my name?" I asked.

"Well," he said, "you spent a lot of time screaming it at the living, didn't you?"

I felt myself retch.

This ghost, this dead thing, had been watching me—for years? If so, then all of my private moments had been exposed to him. Shared with him.

I came to another, quick conclusion: if he'd been watching me, then he'd let me wander, utterly lost and alone, for God knows how long. He'd left me without a guide or a friend, amusing himself with my humiliation and loneliness. How cruel did someone have to be to silently watch another's suffering for so long?

Anger sparked within me, glowing like a small coal in

my core. I found myself suddenly grateful for the implication that this ghost apparently hadn't seen Joshua and me together.

"Why haven't I ever seen you?" I tried to speak evenly, carefully choosing my words to reveal as little as possible.

"Well," he said, "you've always been too lost, too blind, to know I was there, sometimes right at your side. Except for those odd times when you disappeared all at once and I had to hunt for you afterward."

I exhaled quietly in relief. He couldn't follow me into my nightmares. Strange that I would now appreciate the solitude they afforded me. Luckily, he didn't notice my change in expression but instead continued to explain himself.

"You have to know, Amelia, it was quite the momentary surprise to see you turn around tonight. You see, the wind you just felt is . . . well, a kind of supernatural announcement of my entrance. My calling card perhaps." He smiled, almost proudly. "You've always been too unaware to feel the wind, just as you've never seen me before. But now you do."

"Yes," I said flatly. "Now I do."

He sighed. "Then I'm obviously left with a dilemma." He paused, apparently waiting for some sort of audience participation from me. I stared at him in silence, willing myself not to glare outright.

"My dilemma, Amelia, is a complex one: what do I do with you now?"

I winced. "What do you mean?"

He sighed again, intentionally drawing out the drama of the moment. "I've grown pretty fond of watching you stumble along. But now that you're awake and aware, I can't really let you wander around anymore. Rules are rules. So, like I said: what exactly do I do with you now?"

I resisted a strong urge to scream at him that he wouldn't be doing anything with me, *ever*. Now I wasn't the least bit angry that he hadn't pulled me from the fog and explained my nature to me. I had nothing but a foul taste in my mouth at the very thought that he'd been so near to me at all. Instead of expressing these thoughts, however, I responded quietly and calmly.

"What's your name?"

"In life my name was Eli."

"And in death?" I couldn't hold back the trace of scorn in my voice.

"Eli will do just fine," he said.

"I think I have a solution to your dilemma, Eli."

"Wonderful. Would you share it with me?"

"Well, Eli, the way I see it, I can feel that wind now. It's not one of those things you can easily hide, is it?" I smiled sweetly but tried hard to make sure my derision was as thinly veiled as possible. "So it stands to reason that you won't be able to watch me unannounced any-more, right?"

Eli frowned deeply. I could tell he had no glib reply, no way to circumvent my logic. Inside, I shouted a silent cheer. Apparently, there were no loopholes that might allow him to continue to watch me unseen.

After a long pause Eli sighed and smiled. I could have been imagining it, but his smile looked much less cocky than before.

"Yes, Amelia, you're right. You'll always be aware of my visits from now on."

"Great. Since we've got that settled, I'd appreciate it if you'd limit those visits from now on, too."

A shadow seemed to pass over his face. "What are you saying, Amelia?"

"I'm saying that I know what you can 'do' with me, Eli," I said, faking a bright grin. "And what you can do is leave me alone. Permanently."

Instantly, Eli's frown deepened and lifted the curl of his lip until he looked like an animal baring its teeth. I half expected him to growl; and, involuntarily, I flinched.

He obviously read the fear in my reaction, because his sneer widened into a sharp grin. He looked no more pleasant for the change.

"As you wish," he murmured. And miraculously, he spun around to leave, stomping through the pine needles piled upon the ground. But before he crossed into the tree line, he stopped and turned around to face me. He folded his arms over his chest, the wicked grin still plastered on his face.

"I won't follow you again, Amelia. There's no point, really." Eli lowered his head to stare up at me, his eyes hooding over. "But you'll come find me soon enough, I can promise you that. You have no idea what we are— what *you* are. But I do. So I'll simply leave you with a warning. A little taste of the place where you truly belong. The place where you'll eventually be trapped, now that you're awake, if you don't seek my help."

As Eli uttered the last few words, I felt a sudden chill, sharper and more piercing than any I'd felt before. Unlike the wind announcing Eli's arrival, this cold wasn't directed or brief. It was all around me, as if the temperature on the riverbank had instantly dropped at least thirty degrees. I gasped from the shock of it, and my breath puffed out visibly in front of me.

I was so transfixed by the chill that I almost didn't notice when my surroundings began to change, too. Before I understood what was happening, the riverbank darkened. Within seconds it appeared as though the sun had disappeared entirely, taking with it all the light and color.

At first I thought the bank had plunged into total darkness, but that wasn't right at all. Everything around me had become a cold, deep gray everywhere I looked.

I stared back at Eli, who seemed perfectly at ease in this new environment, his arms still folded casually across his chest. In the charcoal darkness, his pale skin looked brighter, even more unnatural.

"What . . . ? Where . . . ?"

My whispers couldn't shape themselves into real questions. In response, Eli chuckled darkly but didn't answer.

He stared intently at me for a moment longer and then his eyes began to dart to my right and left, as if seeking something beside me. Without thinking, I turned to catch a glimpse of whatever seemed to have distracted him.

That's when I saw them: the clusters of strange, black shapes moving along my peripheral vision. Like enormous moths, or shadows, twisting and flitting just outside my line of sight. I whipped my head from one side to the other, trying to get a solid look at them. But each time I turned my head, the shifting black shapes would move with me and out of sight.

I whirled around completely, turning my back to Eli and facing the river. And in that moment, I forgot all about the shapes still dancing at the edge of my vision.

Only minutes ago a normal river had drifted behind me, greenish and brown in the late-summer sun. Now, even in the gray darkness of this place, I could see a dramatic change had overtaken its waters.

Something floated in this version of the river, but certainly nothing as benign as water. Between the banks of the new river, a thick liquid moved past me. It looked like tar, so inky and black that I could barely see the signs of movement along its surface.

It *did* move, though, drifting sluggishly toward High Bridge. Slowly, I turned my head toward the bridge; but before I could take in its new form, I found my attention riveted to what lay beneath it—to the place where the dark river seemed to lead.

There, beneath what may or may not have been High Bridge, an enormous blackness gaped. If it were possible, this expanse was even darker than the gray riverbank, darker than the river itself. The top of the expanse brushed against the underside of the bridge, and the bottom of it pawed at the water and the nearby shoreline. Peering into the darkness, I couldn't see an end to it; I couldn't see one speck of light in all that black.

It was the darkest point in an already dark world.

It almost seemed to pulse beneath the bridge as if it were some living, breathing beast waiting for something. For me maybe.

I managed, with great difficulty, to pull my eyes away from the chasm beneath the bridge and stare down in horror at my feet. My toes were inching, of their own will, toward the river—drawn by some unseen force to the water. With no small amount of effort, I yanked my feet away from the river's edge.

I whirled back around to Eli, truly scared now. More scared than I'd ever been before.

"Where am I?" I finally managed to ask.

"You really want to know?" he whispered, his eyes glowing with what could only be malicious delight. I nodded mechanically.

In reply Eli rolled his head around, gesturing to our bleak surroundings. "This is part of the hereafter, Amelia. This is where dead spirits are supposed to go. While you were lost, I kept you safe from this place. But now, only one thing can keep you from ending up here forever."

I raised one eyebrow. I had a feeling I knew what that "one thing" was. He confirmed my suspicions as he went on.

"Without me, Amelia," Eli insisted, "you'll be trapped. Without me, you'll spend eternity here, unable to move between worlds at will. So now you see why I know, beyond any doubt, that you'll seek me out again. All you have to do is call for me on High Bridge . . . and you will, soon."

Despite the terror crawling over every inch of my body, I rankled at Eli's words. At his implication that I needed him, that I couldn't avoid this foul place without him. Even now I had enough sense to suspect his motives, and to remind myself that this dead young man hardly resembled my concept of a guardian angel.

I straightened my back, as much as I could, and met his gaze squarely.

"We'll see, Eli," I murmured. "We'll see."

Now it was Eli's turn to raise an eyebrow. Obviously, he hadn't expected this small display of courage. Instead of reprimanding me, however, he gave a final, amused nod and spun around once more to disappear into what used to be the woods.

If sharp, cold winds announced Eli's arrival, then the opposite evidenced his departure. For a long second it felt as though a vacuum had sucked away everything, including the cold wind. I didn't feel anything—no chill, no gale, not even myself. I'd never felt so numb in my entire existence. I choked, clutching my hands to my throat.

Then, almost as quickly as it began, it was over.

The soft greens of the riverbank shimmered and reappeared around me, and the late-summer air swam gently back into my lungs. Gasping, I collapsed onto my hands and knees on the grass.

*Chapter*
SIX

That night I didn't mark the passage of time with uncertain pacing as I had the day before. Instead, I marked the time in absolute stillness, crouched on the riverbank, my eyes never moving from the spot in the woods where Eli had disappeared. I remained motionless as dawn broke over the tops of the trees. I kept my hands pressed hard into the grass, ready at any moment to sprint away if I felt another gust of that cold wind.

Finally, reluctantly, I stirred. Inch by inch I raised

myself out of my uneasy stance, never taking my eyes from the trees in front of me. I spared a glance upward, trying to gauge how long I'd crouched against the unknown. I blinked at the light in surprise.

Although thick gray clouds covered most of the sky, I could see the occasional ray of sunshine break through, halfway between the east and west horizons. It had to be nearly midday.

While I waited, almost an entire day had passed without Eli's return. Without a return of the dark, terrible world he'd shown me.

Before me the woods remained just that: normal, living woods, with normal, living trees. I spared one glance over my shoulder. The river, once again a murky green, flowed rapidly toward High Bridge, beneath which lay nothing but the river itself.

I willed my body to relax and then stretched each limb in turn. The effort was needless, since my dead muscles hardly had any reason to cramp, even when held in one position for many hours. Still, the gesture seemed appropriate. I wanted to feel my new resolve in my body as well as in my mind—my resolve to never allow Eli to control me.

This resolve felt important—essential, even—because I suspected I would meet him again. Though Eli promised he would stay away for a while, he'd also said that there were many things about him and our kind that I didn't know or understand, things he would inevitably tell me. His words certainly had the ring of threat to them, especially when delivered in the awful place he'd shown me.

Yet, although ignorant of my ghostly nature, I was no longer ignorant of some things. I didn't doubt that the next time the wind cut across my skin I would know Eli was there. He couldn't take me back to that dark place without me first knowing he was present. There was some comfort in this knowledge.

I couldn't promise myself I wouldn't be waiting, watching, dreading. But I refused to stay by this river anymore. Because I didn't want to let fog, or fear, keep imprisoning me.

And because it was almost noon, judging by the position of the sun.

Yesterday I'd decided not to meet Joshua again. I'd had every intention of hiding, and letting the confusion take me back. After Eli's sudden appearance, however, I had no intention of ever going back into the fog. I intended to stay as awake and alive as possible.

And Joshua made me feel very much alive. He was the reason behind all of this change, this newness. The reason I'd woken up from the fog.

I couldn't explain it, any more than I could explain

why I'd wandered lost after death, or why I didn't now. But the new desires that had filled me after Joshua's accident hadn't changed. They'd grown stronger, more acute. Even more than the first moment I saw him, I wanted to be near him. I wanted to feel him, maybe, just once more. Anything, even the sight of him running away from me when he learned the truth, would be worth the risk.

Now I sensed a new purpose to this day. I stared at the river and its bank one more time, drinking in the image of the green water and the summer-yellowed grass. This was the scene of so many of my changes: life to death . . . and maybe back to a sort of life again? Maybe. It was worth trying to find out.

"See ya," I said aloud to the water.

And I began to run, bare feet flying across mud and grass, then pavement, leaving the river and High Bridge Road far behind me.

I reached the park with only a little time to spare. A clock sitting atop a large wooden platform outside the park entrance read 11:50.

I slowed my pace until I was almost strolling up the cedar-lined road that led to the picnic area. Although I'd run for miles, I wasn't winded or even ruffled. Still, I began to fidget, smoothing invisible wrinkles from the skirt of my dress and running my hands through the thick waves in my hair. I felt . . . jittery. I guess a case of nerves could survive even death.

I nearly turned back, my previous resolve shrinking. My future hinged on Joshua and the outcome of our conversation. I felt this in my core, and I suddenly couldn't fathom how I'd decided to face him with such bravado.

But my feet were traitors. Or more loyal, depending on one's perspective. They kept marching me down the road, through a parking lot and a thin grove of pines, past a cluster of empty benches, and to the only occupied one.

Joshua sat, not on the bench but on the concrete table to which the bench was attached. He stared to his left, into the woods surrounding the picnic clearing. His profile—square jaw, high cheekbones, and full lips—made me shiver as a wave of desire and fear washed over me. I watched his black eyebrows pull together while he continued to study the forest. Perhaps he was thinking I had, in fact, stood him up.

"Hey, Joshua."

Although I'd all but whispered, his head jerked toward me. Then a huge, radiant smile spread across his face. He jumped off the table and strode toward me, one arm lifted as if he intended to touch me.

Instinctively, I took a quick step back.

He stopped and frowned.

"Uh . . . sorry. Too enthusiastic?"

*God, no. I just wasn't ready for this to end before it starts.*

"No," I said aloud. "Just . . . unexpected."

He laughed. "Sorry. I probably looked like a golden retriever or something. Big, dumb dog. But this was a little unexpected too, you know?"

"How so?"

"You showed up. Unexpectedly." He half smiled, and the ghost of a dimple tugged at his cheek.

I found myself smiling back a little too. "I aim to please."

"Then mission accomplished."

"Oh."

*Brilliant, Amelia,* I screamed in my head. Death had obviously not improved my vocabulary. Joshua's half smile crept a little farther upward, possibly a sign of his amusement at the flustered look on my face.

Unfortunately, our banter wasn't going to last forever. He swept one hand back to the table like a maître d'. "A quiet park bench, as promised?"

I sighed. No putting this off any longer, so it seemed. "Yeah, I guess it's time."

Joshua's eyebrows knit together as I strode past him to the bench.

"Look," he said, "I'm not going to conduct the Spanish Inquisition or anything."

"I know," I said flatly.

I sat down, feeling the pressure of the bench but not really the bench itself, and folded my hands in my lap. Joshua turned toward me but made no move to sit. I stared down at my lap and tried to ready myself for the inevitable ending. But there was something I needed to know first.

"Before we get into explanations, can I ask you a question?"

"Anything."

I looked up to see him shove his hands into the pockets of his jeans and tilt his head to one side. Judging by his stance, he was probably more than a little bewildered by my behavior, so I asked my question carefully.

"Did you . . . intentionally drive off the bridge?"

"Ha." He barked out a sort of laugh. "Not exactly."

It was odd, but I thought he sounded almost embarrassed. I too tilted my head and raised one eyebrow, encouraging him to continue. He laughed again, a little sheepishly, and a flattering blush spread across his cheekbones.

"The only thing I did intentionally was take a stupid shortcut."

I kept my eyebrow raised, so Joshua continued.

"I was following a bunch of my friends to a party. For some crazy reason I decided to take a shortcut across High Bridge Road by myself. I have no idea why I did. My family practically forbids me to drive over the bridge since it's such a death trap. Anyway, right before I crossed on to High Bridge, I thought I saw something in the river. I was distracted; and when I looked back at the road, I saw something dart out at me—a deer or a bobcat, maybe; it looked so black, I couldn't be sure. I swerved to miss it and then my car spun out across the bridge. I must have hit my head on the steering wheel, because I really don't remember any part of the crash after that. Thank God I'd rolled down the windows. I guess that's how I got out of the car before I sank with it."

"And your friends got there so fast because . . . ?"

He gave an embarrassed shrug. "Because I . . . um . . . had the beer in my car."

As he finished, I exhaled slowly. I was grateful that at least one of my theories behind our interaction was wrong: suicide wasn't our commonality; it was only our mutual deaths, however brief his had been.

"Would it be weird, Joshua, if I said I'm glad?"

"Why, because I like beer?"

I smiled slightly. "No, because you didn't mean to drive off the bridge."

He laughed. "Then that's not weird at all. I wouldn't

exactly *choose* High Bridge for my exit scene, you know?"

I gasped.

Seeing my strange reaction, he spoke quickly, almost apologetically. "Sorry. I'm . . . Look, I don't know what I'm saying. I'm not trying to upset you or anything. I guess . . . I mean . . . you really don't have to do this. To tell me anything, that is."

"But I do," I said, unable to keep the misery out of my voice. "I don't really think I have a choice, if I ever want to talk to you again. If you'll even want to talk to me, afterward."

"Why wouldn't I want to talk to you?"

His gentle tone, and the implication in his words, made me meet his gaze. With his strange blue eyes locked onto mine, I felt the little ache ignite again in my chest.

"You won't want to talk to me because I'm going to tell you the truth."

"And the truth will make me . . . what? Decide to shun you?" He grinned and raised one eyebrow, obviously skeptical.

"Something like that," I murmured.

"I find that hard to believe," he said as he momentarily broke our eye contact to walk over to the bench and finally sit beside me.

"Actually, you're probably going to find what I'm about to tell you hard to believe. But it's the truth."

He clasped his hands and leaned closer to me, placing his elbows on his knees before raising his eyes back to mine.

"Good. I want to hear the truth, Amelia."

Inexplicably, my breath quickened. A pulse, one I knew I didn't have, began to race through my arms and along my neck. I could swear I felt heat from the nearness of his body—heat that threatened to turn into a blush on my unblushable cheeks. The kind of heat that could make me do or say just about anything. Words started to fall from my mouth almost before I thought of them.

"You said you saw me under the water, right?"

"Yes."

"And you're the only person who saw me at all?"

"Yes." He kept his voice patient, calm. My voice, how-ever, trembled as I continued.

"Well, I think you saw me because . . . well, because you were dead."

He frowned again. "I know I was dead, at least for a few seconds. But I'm not sure I'm following you."

"You couldn't see me at first, right? Not before you . . . died."

The more I spoke, the less I could breathe. Joshua seemed to be struggling too with where I was heading. He responded slowly, methodically, as if he needed to hold tightly to reason in this conversation.

"Amelia, I couldn't see you because I was unconscious before my heart stopped."

"No. Well, you *were* unconscious. But that's not the only reason you couldn't see me. Even if you were conscious, you still wouldn't have been able to see me. Not yet anyway."

"Huh?" His frown deepened, and he leaned away from me.

Suddenly, I couldn't stop the flow of my words. It was like pulling a piece of thick tape from my mouth. I wanted to rip it off, tear through my explanation, so I could breathe again.

"I have a theory, sort of. I can't be sure, but I think I can't be seen unless someone is, well, *like* me. That's why the people on the shore couldn't see me, and that's why Eli can see me. Because he's like me."

"Who's Eli?"

I was in such a hurry to get the truth out that I'd lost control of the things tumbling from my mouth. "Sorry," I moaned. I dropped my head into my hands and squeezed my eyes tightly shut. "I'm not making any sense, am I?"

Joshua's response surprised me. He didn't sound frustrated, or even confused. Instead, his voice was hushed, intense.

"Amelia, I'm trying very hard to understand this. I

know something . . . strange has happened. Is happening. I'll believe your explanation. Just go slow, okay?"

My eyes flew open and met his. His eyes were lovely, and serious; they reminded me of the night sky. I tried to shake the distraction of them from my head so I could focus on this horrible conversation.

"Joshua, I have no idea how to say this."

"It's okay. It'll be okay."

I turned away from him, staring at but not really seeing the patch of red dirt in front of us. When I spoke again, I did so slowly. Painfully.

"I think you saw me, and you can still see me, because we have some sort of—I don't know—magical or spiritual connection. You're *like* me. Or you were, at least for a moment."

Joshua's eyes narrowed. "And by 'like you' you mean . . . ?"

"That you died."

The word "died" hung heavy in the air between us, like an ax waiting to drop.

Joshua's forehead wrinkled as he tried to make sense out of my words, tried to follow the convoluted path I'd laid. He may not have connected all of the pieces yet, but he would. As each second passed, I could see it happening, piece by piece. He would rip off the bandage at any moment, would either call me a lunatic or—worse—believe me.

"Okay," he started haltingly. "You and I have both died? Me in the river, and you sometime in the past?"

"Yes. In the same river, actually."

"Wow." He blinked in surprise but then composed himself again. "So you're saying this 'connection' is the reason I was the only one who could see you? Some sort of magic, or something?" He said the last words uncertainly, as though he were trying out a strange new language.

"I think so." I bent my head down toward my lap again.

"And the connection exists because you died?" he asked.

I only nodded.

"And you came back to life, like me?"

A heartbeat or two passed, and then—

"No, Joshua. Not that part."

For a while there was only silence. Then I heard him suck in a sharp breath. Here it was—the moment. The finale. I finished it off with nothing but a whisper.

"You see, Joshua—I never did come back to life."

At the worst possible moment, I had one of those new, unpredictable sensations. I could suddenly feel the warm breeze against the skin of my legs and arms. The air felt charged, electric, like the gray sky would tear open and let thunder and lightning and all hell break loose around us. Goose bumps rose on my arms. Real goose bumps, like the ones Eli had inspired.

I couldn't look up at Joshua's face, but I could hear him stammering, making incredulous little noises. Then he became very quiet and still. This stillness lasted for possibly a full minute before he spoke with an unnatural calm.

"Amelia, are you trying to tell me you're . . . ?"

"Dead." I spoke immediately. It felt wrong to delay the inevitable any longer.

"Dead." He repeated the word without any inflection.

Another heartbeat passed and then, unexpectedly, Joshua leaped off of the bench. He spun around to face me. I stared up at him, undoubtedly wild-eyed and frantic. His face, however, was expressionless. He wore a sort of mask—hiding terror, anger, disbelief, hatred? I had no idea.

I couldn't stand it. I couldn't stand the frozen look on his face, the look I'd put there with the truth. He thought I was crazy, or he knew I was dead. Whichever conclusion he'd made, I would certainly lose him, however little I'd had him.

In this moment I felt impossibly and utterly alone. Alone for eternity probably, and now painfully aware of what I would be missing.

"I'm sorry," I moaned—apologizing to him, to myself,

to who knows who—and clasped a hand over my mouth.

I was so lost in sorrow for myself, I almost didn't notice it: something on my cheek. Something warm and wet, trailing its way to the corner of my lips. Without taking my eyes from his empty face, I touched one finger to the edge of my eye. I pressed the fingertip to my lips. It tasted salty.

A tear. My dead eyes had shed a tear.

Something about that single tear must have stirred Joshua, because his frozen expression suddenly melted. His eyes and mouth softened.

"Amelia." His voice was rough, and it broke. My name had never sounded more beautiful.

Joshua reached out to me, moving his hand as if to cup it around my cheek. Without giving a thought to anything but the ache that raged inside me, I leaned into his gesture.

Nothing could have prepared us for the moment when his skin once again touched mine.

*Chapter*
SEVEN

I shouldn't have been surprised. My world had changed the first time he laid his hand upon my cheek—there was no reason why it shouldn't change when he did it again.

Yet when his hand cupped my face for the second time, we both gasped and jerked away, stunned. My fingers involuntarily flew up to the burning spot on my cheek, and likewise he grabbed his right hand with his left.

Our actions may have looked protective, even defensive, to an outside observer. For me, however, they were anything but.

The moment his skin brushed mine, a current shot through my entire body, from my scalp to the tips of my fingers. The current made the ache in my chest, and the tingles that raced along my spine each time he looked at me, seem like low-burning cinders. My heart, my brain, my skin—all of it was momentarily engulfed in flame, a flame lit only by the spark on my cheek.

I'd never felt anything so exhilarating. Not in death . . . not even in life. I knew it, deep within my core.

Joshua stared at me, rubbing his hand. He continued to breathe unevenly, as though he'd just run a long distance. Then, still gasping, he smiled. Hugely.

"What," he managed to choke out, "was that?"

"I have no idea." And I began to laugh. "Want to do it again?"

"Hell, yes," he growled, and lurched forward to grab my hand from my lap.

As it had been with my cheek, we didn't make perfect contact. Not exactly. I couldn't feel the texture of his skin or the force of his fingers gripping mine. I felt the old, familiar pressure that always came when I tried to touch something from the living world. But I didn't feel numb; the fiery shock came again, just as strong and fantastic as before, and there was nothing numb about it.

We simultaneously pulled back our hands, gasping again.

"What . . . what does that feel like to you?" I finally stuttered.

"Like fire. In the best possible way. You?"

"The same. Good." I shrugged, almost sheepishly. "Very good."

"I'm pretty out of breath," he confessed with a grin.

"Me too." I laughed. "Which is saying something for someone who doesn't really need to breathe."

He stopped smiling and cocked his head a little to the side. I immediately regretted my words. Stupidly, I'd jerked us out of the moment and back to the topic at hand. I shook my head, furious with myself.

*Might as well quit playing around and get it over with,* I thought bitterly. I took a deep breath to steady myself and cut right to the chase.

"So, Joshua, here's the part where you run screaming into the night, right?" I paused to stare around at the clearing, lit up by the overcast daytime sky. "Metaphorically, that is."

"Amelia, do you see me running?"

I leaned back, startled. "Well . . . no."

"And why would I run?"

"Because any sane person would think I'm either crazy . . . or dead."

"I don't think you're crazy." He kept his voice even, and quiet.

"Huh. Um. So." I couldn't get my brain to form a logical sentence.

"So," he went on to finish my incoherent thoughts, "the way I see it, process of elimination leaves only one conclusion."

I kept my lips shut tight and studied his face. His midnight blue–colored eyes were wide and a little stunned. He looked as surprised as I felt by this turn in the conversation. Yet he sounded completely serious, maybe even . . . accepting? I shook my head, bewildered.

"You *believe* me?"

"I guess so."

"You believe I'm . . . dead? A ghost?"

Joshua blew out a long breath and ran his hand through his black hair.

"Yeah, I kind of think I have to," he said with a shrug. "I mean, I don't have an explanation for the river. How you were underwater with me, but you weren't drowning. How you were on the shore—looking pretty damn dry, by the way—but no one saw you. And how it feels when I touch you. I mean, unless you are alive. And you have gills, and you're invisible. And you're electrified."

I shrugged back. "I don't know. Maybe I am."

He smiled—an unbelievably casual gesture, considering the topic. "You mean you don't know if electrification is a common trait for ghosts?"

I stared at him, openmouthed. Was he *joking* about me being dead? "Um . . . no, Joshua, I have no idea what is or isn't a common trait for ghosts. This is my first . . . ah . . ."

"Haunting?" he offered.

I snorted. "Yes, this is my first haunting."

"Then I'm flattered."

"Joshua," I said, rubbing my forehead, "you're taking this awfully well."

He sighed, still smiling, and walked over to sit beside me again on the bench. Tingles, like little licks of the flame I'd just experienced, raced along the side of my body closest to him.

"You know, I've heard ghost stories all my life. Especially ones about the bridge, from my grandma. I've never believed any of them, of course. But like I said before, I kind of have to now, don't I? Because otherwise I'm crazy, and I'm talking to a beautiful, electrified, *imaginary* girl."

"I swear I'm not imaginary." An uncontrollable grin spread across my face. "I would know if I was imaginary, right?"

He laughed, rubbed his palm down the length of his thigh, and then raised his hand up toward heaven as if to ask the sky that same question. "Who knows? Maybe we're both crazy. But I'd like to think I'm not just talking to myself on a park bench."

"Well, you probably look like you are, you know."

"Huh." He frowned. "I hadn't really thought of that." He glanced around the clearing, looking relieved at the emptiness of our surroundings. "We're going to have to be kind of careful about that, aren't we?"

"We are?" I sort of croaked the question. "We're planning on future conversations . . . and in public?"

"Of course." He shook his head impatiently and then abruptly switched gears. "So, am I really the only person who can see you?"

"The only living person," I qualified.

"What about other dead people?"

His question, and the fact that I had absolutely no idea what rules governed this situation, gave me a disconcerting jolt. Because I knew of only one other soul who could possibly know the answer—Eli. Eli, who could clearly see me, and who I could now see, too. Eli might be able to tell me every "how" and "why" about what was happening between Joshua and me. But I mentally shook my head firmly against the idea of contacting him. I made an internal vow never to fulfill Eli's prophecy that I would seek him out voluntarily. Nor would I let Joshua know about Eli if I could help it.

"I'm not so sure about that one," I answered cautiously. "I haven't had a lot of experience with that."

"Hmm." Joshua pondered my response briefly. I expected some kind of follow-up question, one that would certainly be harder to answer; but he asked me something entirely different.

"Just out of curiosity—why did you ask me what you look like? When we were on the bridge yesterday."

I wasn't prepared for that question, either. I covered my mouth with one hand. "God, Joshua, do I really have to answer this one?" My words came out muffled, and dripping with embarrassment. But he just stared at me expectantly, so I sighed and dropped my hand. "I guess it's because I have no idea what I look like."

He blinked. "Seriously?"

"Um, yeah."

"No reflection?"

"No, not that I've ever seen. I mean, I can see some of myself without a mirror." I gestured down at my clothes and then up at my hair. "I just can't remember what my face looks like. I think I sort of . . . forgot."

"Wow," he breathed.

"I know." I sighed again. "Incredibly embarrassing, right?"

Joshua didn't answer me. Instead, he sat in complete, motionless silence, thinking who knows what. I was too mortified to speak, and he was staring at me in an intent way that, of course, unnerved me further.

Finally, he broke the silence. "I wasn't lying yesterday when I said you're beautiful."

*Wow.*

"Oh," I said aloud, and suddenly found something very interesting to study on the filmy, tulle overlay of my skirt. I spared a quick glance up at him and found him grinning at me.

"Should I go on?" he asked.

I could swear I heard an almost playful tone in his question. I shrugged as casually as possible, considering I simultaneously wanted to jump up and down while giggling *and* disappear into a hole in the earth.

"Your hair, it's dark brown and wavy," he said nonchalantly, as if he were cataloging the inventory of a store. "You're pale, but you've got some freckles on your nose. Your eyes are really green, like the color of the leaves. And your mouth . . . well, your mouth is . . . pretty."

If I could have blushed, I would have.

"Oh," I repeated. One syllable seemed to be all I could muster right now. Joshua studied my face and, possibly seeing my discomfort, grinned.

"Now, your dress makes an interesting statement," he teased.

I sniffed, trying not to feel wounded. "So, let me get this straight: I have a pretty mouth and an ugly dress? I'll tell you what—if you can find me the ghosts of someone's tank top and cutoffs, I'll get right into them, I swear."

Joshua grinned wider and shook his head. "No, the dress isn't ugly." He gave my figure a quick scan of appraisal and then added, "Far from it, actually."

"Oh," I said again. My eyes dropped right back down to my dress. Once more I wished it covered a bit more of my skin. I wondered what kind of girl I'd been to pick out a showy outfit like this: someone bold and confident; someone flashy and mean?

Joshua, however, obviously wasn't as bothered by my clothing as I was. He chuckled quietly and leaned back against the table with his arms folded across his chest. We sat that way for a while, him in a casually amused pose and me with my eyes glued once more to my skirt. The issue of whether or not I wore a sexy dress was the least of our worries, and I knew it.

Eventually, Joshua leaned forward again.

"So what else should I know about you?"

I couldn't seem to pull my eyes away from my skirt. "Well, how about this: I can't feel anything I touch. Except you, apparently."

"What? You can't *feel* anything?"

"Nope. Not this bench, those trees—nothing. I can't even open doors."

"But what about people? I mean, you and I obviously—"

"I know," I interrupted. "I have no idea how to explain what just happened between us. You're the first person I've ever tried to touch, but I'm pretty sure I wouldn't be able to feel anyone else. Not like . . . well, you and me, anyway."

"Any guesses as to why that is?"

I shrugged. "I don't know. Maybe it's like what I said earlier, about you being able to see me. Since you were dead for a little while, maybe you can see ghosts *and* you can sort of touch them. And maybe a connection like that can wake up a ghost's senses, too. At least a little."

"Maybe," he mused. After a few seconds he added, "That's kind of a sad statement on the afterlife, though, isn't it? That you can't feel anything unless someone else dies, too?"

I nodded vigorously, still staring at my dress. Once again Joshua didn't respond but instead fell into a thoughtful silence. Eventually, I peeked up at him, just in time to see what I thought might be a rare dark look pass over his face. It stung me, that look—as if Joshua might have finally reached the crucial moment when he realized how crazy all of this really was. But instead, he just shook his head and gave me a sympathetic smile.

"You know, Amelia, being dead must really . . . suck."

I barked out a surprised laugh. "Yes, Joshua. It does, in fact, suck."

We chuckled together. In our laughs, I could hear the strange mix of relief and tension. Then Joshua furrowed his eyebrows and rubbed his hands together.

"So. . . ."

He dragged the word out awkwardly. He sounded cautious now, maybe even afraid to continue. From the tone of his voice, it seemed as though he wanted to ask me something but wasn't sure how to go about it. I met his eyes and nodded in encouragement.

"Whatever you want to say, Joshua, just say it."

He cleared his throat and then blurted out the question. "How long have you been dead?"

I frowned, trying to form an explanation that wasn't scary. "I'm not sure about that one, either. A while, I think. There was a lot of aimless wandering for an awfully long time. I've found it pretty hard to keep track. I'd have to guess it's been . . . years? At the very least."

Letting out a low whistle, Joshua muttered the word "years" under his breath.

"At the very least," I repeated.

"And you really can't remember anything?" He sounded skeptical again.

"Nope. Well, nothing but my name."

"Not where you grew up? Not who you parents were?"

"No."

My voice cracked a little with that answer. I hadn't thought about that until now—the fact that I'd probably had a family, once. A family I'd loved, or one I didn't even want to remember? Maybe, like the information on my tombstone, the details of my former home life were better left a mystery?

Luckily, Joshua didn't seem to notice anything unusual in my response, because his questions kept coming. And soon they drew me out of my dark thoughts with surprising ease.

We went on like that for a while, him as interviewer and me as interviewee. Some of his questions were serious and sad (did I remember my childhood home), and some were pleasantly inane (did I ever own a pet iguana, because his sister did, for about two weeks before their parents made her get rid of it). My response to every question was inevitably negative, mostly because I didn't remember the answer.

But strangely, each question made me less depressed about my lack of memory. I began to feel as if I said the word "no," not because I'd lived the sad life of the waking dead, but as part of some verbal game I was playing with him; as if I would only provide him a "yes" when he asked the right question.

With each question my smile began to grow. Before

long Joshua's face reflected mine, as if my enthusiasm for this game was infectious.

"Do you remember which flavor ice cream you liked best?"

"No." I laughed. "I don't remember if I even liked ice cream."

He prepped for his next question by frowning and resting his chin on one fist for dramatic effect. "Do you remember your school mascot?"

"Nope. I don't remember school at all. So there *is* something positive about being dead, right?"

He started to chuckle, then abruptly jerked upright as though he'd been pinched. Checking his watch, he swore under his breath. He jumped off the park bench and began to run toward the parking lot. If I weren't so confused by his sudden behavior, I might have laughed when he skidded to a stop and spun around to face me again, kicking up a dramatic cloud of red dirt.

"Come on," he yelled, and turned to run back to his father's car. Without thinking, I obeyed the order and ran after him.

As he fumbled to unlock the driver's side door, I cleared my throat.

"Um, Joshua? What's wrong?"

"We're going to be late."

"For what?"

He ignored my question. "Lunch is over in about ten minutes."

"And?" I asked, growing a little frustrated with the mystery.

"And we're going to have to break about forty-seven traffic laws to get there on time."

"To get *where*?" I threw my hands in the air, completely baffled.

"Class."

The word was muffled as he ducked into the driver's seat. Within seconds he threw open the passenger side door in front of me and leaned out.

"Come on," he repeated.

"Come . . . to school? With you?"

"Of course."

The idea made me almost rock back on my heels in shock. I wanted to argue the logic of this with him, especially the possibility of going anywhere in public together. But the urgency in his expression told me he wouldn't be open to debate. So I too spun around rapidly—facing him, then the familiar safety of the woods, then him again.

"No time to think, Amelia. Just get in."

"But," I protested weakly, "I don't even remember how to ride in a car!"

He grinned and patted the seat.

"It's like riding a bike, I promise."

"I don't remember how to do that, either," I grumbled, but I slipped into the passenger seat and let him lean over to pull the door shut beside me.

*Chapter*
EIGHT

Death may have stolen my old memories of riding in a car, but it certainly couldn't take away my new ones. The farther Joshua drove, the more my initial fear of the ride, and the events to follow it, began to melt away.

As Joshua's borrowed car flew along the steep, curved roads outside the park, I shifted forward in my seat until I'd nearly pressed myself against the dashboard. I watched the dense green woods rush by us in a panorama outside the windshield.

Although I was unable to experience the physical sensation of sitting in the car, I didn't feel the least bit sad about this. I felt untethered, and impossibly fast— as though I were flying. I gripped the edge of the seat beneath me, and, incredibly, the sensation of its rough leather scraped against my fingertips.

"Hey, Amelia?"

Joshua's worried voice broke into my thoughts, and the feel of the leather instantly disappeared.

"Yeah?" However much I enjoyed looking at him, I could barely tear my eyes away from the road long enough to give him a sidelong glance.

"I'm not trying to tell you what to do or anything, but would you please scoot back? The way you're sitting, you're putting a lot of faith in my driving."

I laughed. "Well, it's not like I can fly through your windshield."

From my peripheral vision, I saw him frown deeply. The image of his car floating to the bottom of the river flashed into my mind. I shook my head at my own stupidity.

"Sorry," I muttered. "Bad joke."

"It's okay," he answered with a faint smile. "But . . . all the same, you're making me nervous."

"Sorry," I repeated, and I slid back into the seat.

I kept my eyes glued to the blurred scenery outside

the windows. Still, I itched to lean forward again, so I grabbed the seat to hold myself in place and tried in vain to revive the sensation of leather against my skin.

Eventually, the woods gave way to a small town. The road wound through a sort of main street dotted with small buildings and scattered pines. A painted wooden sign along the roadside welcomed us to Wilburton, Oklahoma.

The town reminded me of a vaguely familiar photograph, one that I'd seen a long time ago but couldn't place now. Had I passed through this particular town in my death? I'd never really taken much note of the places where I'd wandered. I couldn't be sure, and the uncertain familiarity made me squirm in my seat.

Too soon, Joshua slowed to a few miles per hour. Next he pulled onto a side road, one lined more heavily with pines. When the trees thinned, a set of low buildings appeared. As Joshua pulled into a parking lot, I could see a few students milling around or making their way into the corridors between the buildings.

"Made it." Joshua sighed in relief. He parked the car, then unbuckled his seat belt and reached into the backseat to scavenge for his schoolbag.

I remained focused on the redbrick buildings in front of us. I took in the sight of the flat white roofs, the dark purple benches on the lawn, the faded metal signs that proclaimed GO DIGGERS! in block letters. Something about the buildings itched at me—something I couldn't put my finger on. . . .

"Good ole Wilburton High School. Shall we?"

The nearness of Joshua's voice made me jump in my seat. He stood beside me but outside of the car, with one hand holding the frame of the passenger side door and the other gripping the bag that hung from his right shoulder. In my concentration, I hadn't even noticed him leave the car or open my door.

"Um. . . ."

I began to twist the fabric of my dress, suddenly nervous again. Before Joshua, impending contact with the living world would have saddened me. Now Joshua's awareness of me (and honestly, Joshua himself) had made the depression slink back to a remote part of my brain.

Yet the sight of those buildings, and the creeping sensation they gave me, made me a little scared. And more than a little fused to my seat.

"Move it, Amelia. You're making me look crazy, standing by an empty door." Joshua's words may have seemed harsh, but his voice was playful. Although my indecision was certainly going to make him late for class, he simply smiled and held out one hand for me.

It seemed as though my bravery could stretch itself out a

little farther, because I grabbed his hand and stepped out of the car. Immediately, a fiery shock jolted up my arm.

"Oh!" I cried out, and dropped his hand. As he leaned across me to close the passenger side door, he managed to gasp and laugh at the same time.

"More of that later." He chuckled. "Now for school. Just follow me."

He actually winked and then strode quickly past me. A smile—formed half from embarrassment, half from excitement—crept onto my face, and I followed behind him toward one of the smaller buildings. As we walked, he spoke through clenched teeth without looking back at me. I assume he did so to keep from appearing to everyone else as if he were talking to himself.

"You all right back there?"

"Yeah, I think so," I said, mirroring his volume even though I didn't need to. "This place just looks so . . . familiar. I feel as if I remember this school; but I don't know why, or from when."

"Huh. That could be . . . interesting." He was silent for a moment and then, in an unsure tone, he whispered, "Will you be okay with this? I mean, I sort of forced you into it, didn't I?"

He sounded so genuinely worried, I had to stifle a laugh. Apparently, he hadn't thought to ask me what *I* wanted until the last possible second.

Aloud I said, "I'll probably be all right."

As I stared at his back, broad and strong beneath his light gray shirt, I impulsively blurted out my next thought.

"Anyway, it doesn't matter where we go, because I just want to be wherever you are."

Upon hearing my words, Joshua froze with one hand on the door he was just about to open. Looking at his back, I bit my lower lip in frustration. Was I really such a moron that I'd make a proclamation like that without being able to see his response?

I could see Joshua's hand flex against the doorknob, so I readied myself for the worst: he would tell me my very presence here was a risk, just as I suspected; he would scold me for touching him in public and would then suggest that I wait outside for him . . . or go away completely.

But, of course, I misread him again. Instead of fleeing from me, Joshua reached one hand behind him and, still facing forward, squeezed my hand. Then he jerked the door open wide and stepped into a classroom just as a bell rang out across the lawn behind us. I saw him clench and unclench the hand that had touched me, possibly in response to the same fire sizzling in my fingers. I took a deep breath and slipped into the classroom before he pulled the door shut behind us.

I guess I wasn't prepared for the change in scenery, because I began to blink furiously against the sudden dimness of the room. To be fair, I didn't have much after-life experience with poorly lit high school classrooms, and I absently wondered if my pupils still expanded in the dark.

Joshua's loud cough pulled me out of this reverie, fast.

The cough was obviously a warning, because an elderly woman stood right in front of me, her face mere inches from mine. Her yellowed face matched her wispy hair as well as the yellowed whites of her eyes.

Which were looking directly into mine.

Frantic, I turned back to Joshua, who had frozen in front of the first row of desks. I whipped my head back to the woman, tensing every muscle. Was she another once-dead human who could now see me, like Joshua could? Or another malevolent ghost, like Eli?

A second look into her eyes told me all I needed to know. The eyes didn't focus fully on mine but instead gazed past me and at Joshua. She squinted, her vision possibly obscured by my form but not enough so as to make me visible to her. The woman looked through me like one looks through a wisp of smoke: distracted by it, without really being fully aware of or concerned by it. When she spoke, she confirmed my assumptions.

"Mr. Mayhew, has your brush with death given you permission to waltz in whenever you please?"

"No, ma'am, Ms. Wolters. I thought I made the bell?"

She frowned, allowing deep lines to pull her mouth into a droopy sort of scowl.

"The bell signifies the start of class, not the time for your entrance. Now take your seat."

"Yes, ma'am," he mumbled. Ducking his head, Joshua moved quickly down the aisle and slid behind an empty desk—his, I presumed.

A burly, red-headed boy, sitting at the desk next to Joshua's, clapped him on the back and whispered, "Should have skipped sixth period, too, dude." Joshua just nodded tensely.

Without another glance at me—or through me, really—Ms. Wolters circled behind her own desk. I caught Joshua's gaze and ran a hand across my forehead, mouthing, *Whew*. He gave me the faintest smile of relief and then began to pull books from his bag.

In that moment I realized I was standing in front of a room full of living people. I suddenly recalled the stereotypical adolescent nightmare: standing naked in front of a classroom of your peers. I certainly wasn't naked, and these living beings weren't exactly my peers; but I still felt horribly exposed. I had the unpleasant sensation that the students were all staring right at me even though most of them just looked bored as they watched their teacher start to write on the chalkboard behind me.

Only then did I realize I hadn't been around this many members of the living world, and all in one place, since my death. So many breathing, blushing, heartbeating people made me nervous. Made me curl protectively into myself.

I glanced up at Joshua. He too was staring around the classroom with a look of wonder. After he analyzed each classmate, he turned his eyes back to me. *Wow*, he mouthed. I frowned at him, confused. Ever so slightly, he rolled his head in a circle, gesturing to the entire classroom, then nodding emphatically back at me.

I understood. He was coming to the conclusion that he really was the only person who could see me. In the park, he'd listened to me and believed me . . . in theory. Here, the theory had been put to the test. A test that proved I was invisible—a *ghost*.

I nodded in confirmation. To underscore his sudden realization, I spoke aloud, "Weird, huh?"

No one but Joshua looked up at me. *Wow*, he mouthed again, and grinned.

That grin spoke in full paragraphs, telling me exactly what Joshua thought about his new friend's state of being. The grin set off the warm little ache in my chest, a welcome sensation in the face of my insecurity; the grin was all the reassurance I needed.

Braver, I smiled back. I put one hand in front of my waist and bowed to my bored, unaware audience, then clapped loudly as if to thank them for their kind attention to my performance. Still, no one looked at me.

A brief memory entered my mind: that of my own voice, screaming at unseeing strangers, just after my death. Something about that remembered anguish, in comparison to this moment, made me inexplicably light-headed and almost giddy. I began to pace back and forth in front of the classroom, folding my arms behind me like a general.

"You're probably wondering why I called you all here today," I intoned in my deepest boardroom voice.

Joshua snorted and shook his head. "Weirdo," he said aloud.

"What was that, Mr. Mayhew?"

Ms. Wolters's shrill voice cut across the room as she spun away from the chalkboard. Joshua coughed and hacked, trying desperately to cover his error.

Unfortunately, some of his classmates, including the big, red-headed boy next to him, mistook Joshua's actions as the intentional mocking of their teacher. They began to laugh, joining in the supposed fun. Ms. Wolters, believing herself to be at the receiving end of some unheard joke, stood as straight as the piece of chalk she now gripped. Her glare looked no less than murderous.

"Mr. Mayhew, since you seem to have such a keen grasp on this material, please come to the board and tell us what the order is for this differential equation." She practically spat out the words.

Joshua shot me a panicked look. It was painfully clear from his face that differential equations weren't exactly his specialty.

"Oh, God," I moaned. "I'm so sorry. I'm a moron."

He shook his head slightly, trying to tell me no despite the fact that I'd obviously gotten him into trouble. He slid out of his seat and walked sluggishly to the chalkboard, hardly looking at Ms. Wolters as he took the chalk from her thin hand.

I hurried to his side, fluttering my hands uselessly. I stared up at the complex math problem in front of him, only to see it was a tangled mess of numbers and letters and symbols. *Oh no*, I thought as I struggled to keep my eyes in focus while staring at the equation. Just looking at all the $d$'s and $3$'s and $x$'s and $y$'s, I felt my breath start to mirror Joshua's in rapidity.

He stared at the equation on the board too, his face a total blank. He seemed pretty smart . . . but maybe not this smart. Not without some warning. Not in the face of this monster problem.

"Crap," I said out loud. I had no idea what to do. Out of the corner of my eye, I could see Ms. Wolters smirk at Joshua, whose hand had pressed the chalk to the board just under the equation and now held it there motionless. The teacher's smug face infuriated me. I turned back to the problem and stared at it intently, determined to do something, anything.

Nothing . . . nothing . . . nothing.

And then—

"Three," I shouted. "Joshua, the highest derivative is $d^3/dy^3$—the third one. So the order is three."

He shot me a sidelong glance with one eyebrow raised, and then scratched the number *3* on the board. The ghost of a smile skittered across his face when he turned to Ms. Wolters, but he kept his voice meek.

"I think the order is three, ma'am."

Ms. Wolters' mouth gaped open like a trout. When Joshua reached out to give her the stick of chalk, she mindlessly took it and slipped it into her pocket.

"Well . . . um . . ."

As she sputtered at the front of the classroom, Joshua walked back to his seat, deliberately strutting. I walked beside him, cramped close to him by the narrow aisle. We passed a sandy-haired boy who sat in the desk in front of Joshua's, and the boy reached out one fist into the air. Joshua lifted his left fist and bumped it against the other boy's.

Using that moment as a distraction, he reached out his right hand almost imperceptibly and brushed his fingers against mine. The flame in my hand was thank-you enough.

*Chapter*
# NINE

After school ended, Joshua drove us back to Robber's Cave Park and directed me to our bench. Once seated, Joshua leaned against the edge of the concrete table, resting both elbows behind him on the tabletop. I sat quietly beside him, one leg crossed beneath me, the other propped up and cradled to my chest with my arm. We didn't speak for a while, probably because I was concentrating on anything but him. Mostly, I tried to ignore the incredulous smile he would occasionally turn up at me.

I had a feeling I knew what he was thinking; and, to my deep embarrassment, I found I was right when he finally spoke.

"So, Amelia—do you remember when exactly you became a math genius?"

I glued my eyes to the tree line and did my best to shrug casually. "I wasn't . . . I'm not a genius. I probably just studied. Like you should be doing right now."

Joshua laughed. "I do study. I have a three point eight GPA . . . until Ms. Wolters finishes with me anyway. And what's with the false modesty?"

I made a petulant little noise and turned around to glare at him. He smiled with feigned innocence, possibly pleased to get a rise out of me, and to get me to look at him, finally.

"Humph." I whipped my head back to the tree line, fast enough to send my hair flying around my face. For a few more moments, we sat in near silence, except for the sound of Joshua chuckling softly. He started to make a dramatic show of coughing, as if he had to do so in order to cover his laughter.

The coughing was the last straw. I threw my hands up in protest.

"I'm not falsely modest, okay?" I cried. "I have no idea if I'm a genius. Obviously, I know differential equations. But I have no idea how, or why. Anyway, maybe I have a terrible vocabulary . . . or I can't grasp geography . . . or something." I trailed off weakly, losing all steam at the end of my quasi defense.

Joshua began to laugh outright. "You're cute when you're angry, you know that?"

"Ugh," I moaned, wrinkling my nose in disgust. Well, at least a little disgust. "That's patronizing, Joshua."

More laughter, and then: "See? Good vocabulary. 'Patronizing' has four syllables."

Despite myself, I laughed out loud too.

Soon enough I forgave his teasing. For the rest of the afternoon, however, I made sure to keep almost the entire conversation focused on him, diverting his questions to get as much information about him as possible.

I learned that he'd just turned eighteen in August (it was currently late September, and a Monday—I couldn't get over this new awareness of time, mostly because it was previously so absent) and that Joshua lived with his parents, his grandmother, and his sixteen-year-old sister, Jillian.

I pressed him about what he did for fun, and he reluctantly confessed to his place as a center fielder on the school baseball team. When I pushed the subject, Joshua spoke about his athletic ability with modesty. But I could hear the pride in his voice when he speculated that a baseball scholarship, coupled with his good grades, would probably pay his way through college.

"It's not my absolute favorite thing in the world," Joshua said, "but I do like playing. College ball couldn't hurt my chances of becoming a sportswriter, either. Besides, I don't think my folks are looking forward to paying tuition at two colleges, at the same time."

"Jillian wants to go to college too?"

"She'd better," he nearly growled. I leaned back, surprised by the fiercely protective look now on his face. I arched my eyebrows to demand some kind of explanation. Joshua sat forward, resting one elbow on his knee and gesturing in the air with his free hand as he spoke.

"Jillian . . . well, Jillian is kind of a pain in the ass right now. She's just as smart as the rest of us, maybe smarter. She's almost like you when it comes to math." He gave me a quick, sly smile, and I looked down at my crossed leg—an unsuccessful attempt to hide my pleased embarrassment.

"But," he went on, "it's really important to her to . . . blend in, or something."

"Not to you, though?"

I couldn't help but ask. Joshua didn't seem offended, because he just laughed.

"Nope, not to me. I do fit, which is the ironic thing. But within reason, I'm going to do what I want without worrying about what other people think."

"Like talking to an invisible dead girl?"

"Exactly." Joshua grinned, but then the corner of his mouth quirked up in thought. "You know, this might actually have something to do with Ruth."

"Huh?"

"My grandma Ruth. She's the one who told me ghost stories about the bridge when I was a kid. She's into all that communing-with-the-spirits stuff . . . she and a group of old ladies from around here."

I balked. "What, like a coven?"

Joshua frowned. Clearly, the fact that he had a ghost-obsessed grandmother hadn't really struck him as relevant until now. He pondered the thought for a moment and then shook his head, albeit a little indecisively.

"I don't think so," he said. "I *do* know they believe in a lot of unbelievable things. I guess I always thought they were full of it . . . until today."

Joshua gave me an appraising look, and I ducked my head again. I understood his look well enough: *I* was one of those unbelievable things.

Shakily, I asked, "Do you think she'd have a problem with me? With my . . . existence?"

Joshua shook his head again, looking slightly more assured. "No way. Even though Ruth believes in ghosts, it's not like she can see them. Besides, she'd probably just be excited to know I proved all her theories right if

I told her about you."

My laugh heightened in pitch, betraying the apprehension I suddenly felt about this topic. "Well, let's just agree you're not going to give her a Ouija board anytime soon, okay?"

Joshua must not have noticed my anxiety, because he laughed, too, and settled easily against the concrete table. He was right about his grandmother, of course; my performance in his classroom, unseen by anyone but him, proved it. Yet this seemed like a good moment to change the subject from the supernatural, so I launched into another series of questions about his life.

We continued talking long enough for the gray clouds to clear completely from the sky and then for the subsequent blue to shift into pinks and purples. As the sky changed, Joshua spoke a little about his friends, but mostly about the things he loved: horror movies I'd never seen and musicians I'd never heard of (surprise, surprise, so long after my death), but also literature. When he mentioned how much he liked Ernest Hemingway, an immediate response leaped out of my mouth before I even had time to ponder it.

"Ugh, I hate the way Hemingway writes."

"Huh? I thought you said you couldn't remember anything about yourself?"

"I can't. I don't," I floundered. "But . . . I think . . . I do remember not liking Hemingway."

In reaction to the very name of the author, I had another one of those strange flashes. Suddenly, an image was bright and clear in my mind: a book in my hands, a thin paperback collection of short stories I read while sitting cross-legged in the grass. Summer sun lit up the memory, brighter than the one now setting upon Joshua and me.

I struggled to shake myself from the reverie; and when I did, Joshua looked at me expectantly, almost excitedly. I went on, frowning from the effort to recall the details of the flash.

"I remember . . . I actually *remember* reading this short story . . . something about a woman and man having this awful conversation while he's dying on safari. Anyway, I remember thinking, 'This is *not* for me.'"

We were silent for a beat, and then he blew out one heavy breath. "I guess I'd have to question your literary judgment but . . . well, I'll be damned, Amelia."

"Yeah." I paused and then, reverently, added, "Dude."

Joshua laughed and reached absently to brush his fingers across the back of my hand, which I'd laid on top of the bench. The sudden burn on my skin was familiar now—no less fantastic than it was earlier today but a little more expected. And very welcome.

I shivered at his touch, and, inexplicably, the edges of

my vision began to blur. At first I thought the shiver had done something to my eyesight. But I quickly realized the change in my vision had nothing to do with my shaking.

Judging from the abrupt shift in my surroundings, I was having another flash. This flash, which followed so soon on the heels of the last one, seemed to have pulled me into some nighttime setting.

Now I knelt in the grass, huddled over a cold, metal object. A small telescope, I think, propped up on short, tripod legs. I couldn't really focus on the telescope, though, because my face was tilted up to the night.

Above me, the sky was the kind you could only find in a place almost devoid of man-made lights. I could see the stars—all of them at once, it seemed. Millions of them washed across the sky, glittering and flickering in the darkness. I wanted to gasp from the impossible beauty of them, but the flash wouldn't let me; apparently, whatever memory I was experiencing, I had no control over it.

I'd resolved to enjoy the view for however long it lasted when a noise from behind startled me.

"Focus, Amelia," a female voice cautioned. "You aren't going to get a science credit if you don't at least *try* to finish your work."

Beyond my control, the flash-me sighed. "Yeah, yeah,

Mom. And if I wasn't homeschooled, class would've been over about six hours ago."

My thoughts raced. *My mom? I was talking to my mom?*

I wanted so badly for the woman to continue speaking, for the flash to keep going, I felt almost physical pain when it ended, shimmering and fading around me until the afternoon sunlight flooded back into sight.

Now I was free to gasp all I wanted.

I dragged in a ragged breath, one that must have frightened Joshua, because he immediately spun around to face me.

"Amelia?" he asked. "What's wrong? What happened?"

I shook my head. "I . . . I'm not sure. I think I just remembered something else."

"What?"

For the briefest second, I thought about lying to him. I had the inexplicable urge to keep this memory all to myself, to hoard it away like some secret. But looking up into his midnight blue eyes, the moment passed. I didn't want to keep anything from him; I wasn't even sure I could.

"My mom," I answered. "I remembered my mom, I think."

He flopped heavily against the picnic table, obviously stunned. "What do you mean? Did you see her?"

"No, I just heard her voice."

"Huh," he said, staring blankly out into the tree line. "I think I'm a little confused by how this 'remembering' thing works for you, Amelia."

"You and me both," I muttered, looking down at the bench.

Concentrating on the cracks and imperfections in the concrete beneath me, I tried to recall what I'd heard: the tenor of my mother's voice, the flavor of her words. Were we fighting in that memory? Had she been angry with me, or I with her?

When I looked up at Joshua, I realized he had turned back to me and was waiting for some further response.

I sighed and shrugged. "Honestly, Joshua, I have no idea how I'm remembering all this stuff. Or why. I kind of think it has something to do with you, actually."

Joshua blinked. "Me? Why?"

"These flashes of memory—I never had them before I met you. And now I'm getting them more and more. Twice, just now, while we were talking. So . . . I think maybe *you* might have triggered the memories some-how."

Joshua pondered the suggestion for a moment and then he broke into a huge grin. "Well, that's a good thing, right?"

I bit my lip, frowning. "Yeah, I guess so. It's just a lot

to take in, you know?"

"Definitely," Joshua murmured. I could tell from the glow in his eyes, however, that he wasn't really thinking about how this was a lot to take in; he looked . . . excited. Thrilled, in fact. He confirmed my suspicions with an emphatic nod. "No matter what, Amelia, you have to admit it's still pretty cool."

"Cool?" I raised one eyebrow.

"Yeah, you know—cool. Kick ass. Awesome. Et cetera."

In spite of myself, I laughed. "Joshua Mayhew, the sunny optimist?"

Joshua grinned. "Always. Which means we need to celebrate."

"And how exactly are we going to do that?"

Smiling wider, Joshua didn't answer. Instead, he pushed himself into a standing position and turned to face me.

"I, for one, have to get to dinner at the Mayhew house, since I'm at least an hour late."

"Oh," I said, frowning.

I'd completely forgotten about his need to return to a family at the end of a day. Or his need to eat, honestly. These things were necessary for him. And he obviously needed to leave to do them. The ache in my chest curled at the thought of watching him drive away, but I tried to keep the sound of it out of my voice.

"I guess . . . I'll see you tomorrow, or something? We'll celebrate then?"

A strange look passed over Joshua's face, one I couldn't place. As he had when we'd spoken yesterday—was it really only yesterday we'd had our first full conversation?—he ran one hand through his hair and left it on the back of his neck.

After a moment of awkward silence, I realized what I was missing: Joshua looked shy, even embarrassed. Bold, confident Joshua Mayhew actually seemed *nervous* about something. He stared at me for a moment and then must have gathered up the courage to ask one, halting question.

"Actually, I was thinking you might like to come over tonight to meet my family?"

I blinked, unsure of what to say. I didn't even want to mention how little I wanted to "meet" his grandmother, despite her inability to see me. Slowly, I stumbled through my answer.

"Joshua . . . well, I'd love to. But isn't this a little . . . fast? Considering they can't really meet me back?"

Joshua ducked his head down, but not before I saw him flush a deep pink.

"Yeah, you're probably right. Too fast," he muttered, trailing off at the end. His eyebrows drew together as a small, embarrassed smile tugged at his lips. Kind of a flattering look on him, really.

I bent slightly forward to watch his face for a moment longer. He couldn't seem to meet my gaze; and, for some reason, his discomfort made the little ache in my chest curl pleasantly outward. I took a quiet breath for courage and then asked, "Are you worried about *my* opinion of your family?"

"The other way around wouldn't make much sense, would it?"

"No," I said. "It wouldn't. But are you afraid I'm— what?—not going to like them?"

"No, you don't seem like the type. I'd still like to know your opinion, though. I . . . I have a feeling it's going to matter."

He said it like a confession, as if the words had some underlying meaning. He didn't have to explain that meaning, though. I felt exactly the same way.

"Well," I said, giving him a quick, bright smile. "Let's go form my opinion then."

B y the time Joshua pulled his car off the main road and onto a rough gravel path, the sun had finally set. The sky—at least the part I could see through the branches of the tall pines—had varied itself from a dark navy in the east to a pale, pinkish violet in the west.

I found myself suddenly grateful for the deepening of the shadows around us; they provided ideal cover for my growing discomfort. I felt as if I was about to take some kind of test. Not that I was afraid of seeing the Mayhews per se; even the witchy grandmother didn't really worry me.

But Joshua would undoubtedly be watching me, gauging my reaction to everything I saw. More importantly, I knew he wouldn't be able to communicate with me while his family was around. No sidelong glances, no whispers, no notes. He would have to deal with my presence very carefully, as if I wasn't there at all.

So, ultimately, I would probably spend the next few hours in an intimate family scene, and I would basically do it alone.

Before I had time to feel truly sorry for myself, the car looped around a corner and a large house came into view. I'm not sure what I'd expected. Maybe some modest Oklahoman ranch house or one of the new brick-and-stone monstrosities that had begun to pop up all around this area. Whatever image I had in my mind, and whatever worries I'd been previously nursing, they all evaporated in the face of the lovely old home that rose before us.

The house was green clapboard, with white-railed porches that wrapped entirely around its first and second stories. At every gable and eave, between every free stretch of wood, were windows: huge bay windows framed by swoops of curtain; tiny, round windows promising only a tantalizing fraction of a view; stained glass windows exploding with color. From every window shone a warm glow that contrasted charmingly with the dusk that now settled over the house. Even in the pleasant violet gloom, I could make out the shape of the garden through which Joshua now drove—clusters of rosebushes, wisteria vines, and dogwood shrubs tangled in a gorgeous chaos around the house and the cottonwood trees surrounding it.

This was a fairy-tale home.

I didn't even bother to shut my mouth while Joshua parked behind the house. After closing his own car door, he came around to open mine. When he offered me his hand, I took it, as much to steady myself as to feel his skin. Normally, my entire focus would have been centered on the contact of our hands. My attention, however, was elsewhere.

I shouldn't have been surprised that the back of the Mayhew house would be even more marvelous than the entrance. Still, my mouth gaped farther when I took in the sight of the lawn stretching out before me.

The thickets of pine and cedar, so ever-present in southeastern Oklahoma, had been trimmed back to form a kind of wall around the Mayhews' yard. Within the backyard, enormous maples and cottonwoods dotted the lawn, their branches lacing into a sort of dome overhead. Through the leaves I could just make out a few glimpses of the night sky.

Winding through the yard and around each of these trees was a stone walkway. But this wasn't your average back patio. The stones, which were various shades of blues and grays in the dark, branched all around the lawn into twisting, almost labyrinthine paths. Some paths meandered around the yard and then back into each other, while others broke into sets of steps, leading to iron-railed platforms. In a few places, paths turned into covered bridges, canopied with heavy wisteria vines. Underneath the elevated portions, a thick sea of ivy and flowering plants swelled up from the ground.

At the far end of the yard stood a wooden gazebo, its walls enclosed by a ring of tall cypress trees. The entire scene was illuminated from above by huge white lanterns hung on sturdy electrical wires stretched between each of the trees. The lantern light nearly hid the flicker of hundreds of late-summer fireflies that hovered in the dark tree line surrounding the yard.

"Dear God," I breathed aloud.

"Yeah." Joshua nodded. "My mom owns a landscaping company. She really knows what she's doing, doesn't she?"

"You could say that."

Joshua turned to me with a half smile but then frowned a little. Staring at me, he knitted his eyebrows together.

"What?" I asked sharply as a wave of self-consciousness washed over me. "Why are you looking at me like that?"

"Do you know you sort of glow in the dark?"

"Oh. That." I looked down at my hand, still locked in his, and then back up at his face.

Light from the lanterns above us brightened some of Joshua's features, while the darkness of the night shadowed others. My skin, however, looked exactly the same as it had during the day, unaffected by the change from daylight to darkness. It was something I was used to, and the reason I'd immediately recognized Eli as a ghost: the flat, unreflective nature of our skin against the dark. To me, Eli had looked like a black-and-white image against a three-dimensional one. To Joshua, I apparently looked like I glowed.

I shrugged. "I guess it's a ghost thing. Creepy?"

"Little bit," he confessed, but he did so with a smile. I sighed, once again grateful for his seemingly endless ability to accept all the strange things about me. I didn't get the chance to express this gratitude, though, because the sound of a slamming door made us both jerk our heads toward Joshua's house.

A small, darkened figure now stood on the highest platform of the patio. I could see from its silhouette that the figure was a woman. In the bright light from the house windows, she appeared backlit, her features obscured by shadows. I could tell from her stance—hands on hips, back rigidly straight—that, whoever she was, she wasn't terribly happy.

Immediately, I dropped Joshua's hand and hunched my shoulders, suddenly feeling like a child who'd been caught doing something bad by someone else's mother. When the woman spoke, however, I knew I wasn't the child about to be scolded.

"Joshua Christopher Mayhew." The woman's voice was high and delicate, but right now it sounded strained from worry. "Do I even need to ask if there's some valid explanation for why you're so late?"

"No, Mom," Joshua groaned, looking down at his sneakers.

"And do I even need to tell you that we were this close to filing a missing person's report on you?"

"I'm not *that* late," Joshua mumbled, so quietly that the woman on the porch couldn't hear him. More loudly, he said, "Yes, Mom. I'm sorry, Mom."

Then he sighed and began to trudge forward. I followed him, ducking my head.

"Is she always like this?" I whispered, even though Joshua's mother couldn't hear me and Joshua couldn't answer me.

He surprised me by whispering back through gritted teeth, "My grandmother's worse—think pit bull.

A really mean one."

I gulped lightly and shook my head. As if I needed another reason to be afraid of Ruth Mayhew.

I'm not sure whether Joshua's mother heard his unflattering description of his grandmother, because, without another word, she spun around on one heel and marched to the back door, opening the screen door and then letting it slam behind her with bouncing thuds.

Joshua gave me a sheepish glance before leaping up onto the porch and crossing to the door. I followed quickly, as if I too had been ordered inside. Joshua reached the screen door first. He caught it midbounce and held it open, turning back to me.

"My parents' names are Rebecca and Jeremiah, by the way," he whispered as I approached him.

I laughed, jittery. "Got it. So even though they'll be too busy screaming at you, and they can't hear me anyway, I'll at least be able to address them properly?"

Joshua rolled his eyes but still gave me a quick grin. Then he stepped through the doorway and waved for me to follow suit. With a gulp, I crossed the threshold and let Joshua shut the door behind us.

Once inside, I walked several paces behind him, down an unlit hallway. Watching his darkened form ahead of me, I experienced a moment of almost overwhelming nervousness. I'd already opened my mouth to tell Joshua

*Thanks, but maybe some other time* when we passed through an archway and into yet another fantastic scene.

The Mayhews' kitchen sprawled before me, well lit and pleasantly cluttered. The entire room was paneled in a warm, red-colored wood; and jars and gadgets covered every inch of its seemingly endless counter space. In the center of the huge room sat a small wooden island over which various pots and pans hung from the low ceiling beams.

The room looked as though it stretched across the entire width of the house, running from the north-facing bay windows in front of us to the large window box on our left. Underneath that window, a man and a young girl stood at a sink full of dishes, laughing.

Jeremiah and Jillian Mayhew, I guessed.

Across from them, Joshua's mother had just walked over to the center island, and she began sorting through the dishes stacked on it. For a moment her sleek black hair covered her face; but when she glanced up at the sound of the laughter, I could see her lovely features and bright hazel eyes. Her eyes sparkled happily for a moment before landing on Joshua. When they did so, they sharpened.

"So, prodigal son," she said. "What's a good punishment for skipping dinner and scaring the hell out of your mother less than a week after your car accident?"

Rebecca Mayhew's voice stirred Jeremiah and Jillian, who both turned away from the dishes in the sink. In my peripheral vision, I could see Joshua wince from all the scrutiny. I gave him a quick, sympathetic smile and then directed my attention to his family.

Though Jeremiah had brown hair instead of black, his dark blues eyes matched Joshua's perfectly. Despite the separation of at least twenty years, the two men could have been brothers; they shared the same high cheekbones and tan skin, the same broad grin. Jeremiah's grin spoke clearly enough: whoever wanted to punish Joshua tonight, Jeremiah wasn't on their side. At least not internally.

Judging from her expression, however, Jillian obviously shared her mother's anger. With both hands, she pushed back her long, black hair and scowled.

She had her mother's angular face. On Jillian, however, the features were sharper, less delicate. Not that Jillian wasn't pretty—she was. But something about the way she held her mouth and tilted her head gave her an arch sort of look, as if she was always crafting some vicious comment.

"Yeah, Josh," she sneered. "So thoughtful of you to join us in time to finish the dishes."

Joshua opened his mouth to protest, but another, older voice cut him off.

"That might be a fitting punishment for him: cleaning this massive kitchen all by himself."

Joshua and I simultaneously spun around toward the speaker. An elderly woman approached us from a dining table tucked into a back corner I'd missed upon my first inspection of the kitchen. The woman had her head down, focusing on a small stack of envelopes in her hands, so I couldn't catch a glimpse of her face.

Still looking at her mail, she sighed heavily and shook her head. Her chin-length hair swung lightly with the movement. Its color—a bright, almost translucent white—seemed to shimmer under the kitchen lights.

Finally, after a few more steps, she looked up at Joshua. Immediately, I knew who had given Joshua and Jeremiah their unusual eyes. Ruth Mayhew's midnight blue–colored eyes looked out from her pale, oval face, which angled slightly at her sharp cheekbones and pointed chin. When she frowned, deep wrinkles creased around her mouth and across her forehead. Instead of making her look elderly and vulnerable, however, the expression made her seem unbreakable.

Halfway across the kitchen, Ruth's strange-colored eyes flickered toward me, and she froze.

"Joshua?" she asked, her tone strained. "Who is that with—?"

She didn't finish the question but instead leaned

forward to peer at the space beside Joshua. The space in which I currently stood.

At that moment I froze, too.

I had the instant, disconcerting notion that Joshua's grandmother was about to ask him who was standing beside him. But that was impossible. Only Joshua and Eli could see me. I'd proved it today in Joshua's classroom. Nonetheless, I itched with the impulse to run; and before I could give it any rational thought, I whispered, "Joshua, maybe I should come by some other—"

The entire sentence hadn't left my mouth when Ruth jerked upright, rigid-straight again. Her eyes riveted on mine. Her right hand, which had previously clutched the mail, dropped to her side, scattering paper in noisy flutters across the kitchen floor. Still facing me, she drew in one sharp breath.

And with that breath, she told me all I needed to know.

Ruth *heard* me. She *saw* me. There was no other explanation for her abrupt behavior. Ruth could hear and see me just as clearly as Joshua could. Realizing this, I couldn't move. I was pretty sure I couldn't even blink.

From the corner of my eye, I shot a regretful look at the dark hallway leading out of the kitchen. If only I'd had the foresight to hide outside, maybe even to crawl underneath Joshua's car, before this woman had seen me.

I glanced at Joshua and saw him blanch. His eyes darted several times between his grandmother and me.

"Grandma," he asked, his voice shaking, "what's wrong?"

Joshua was speaking directly to her, so it stood to reason that Ruth should have looked at her grandson while she answered him. Yet her eyes remained locked onto mine. She held them as she spoke.

"Who is that?" She pronounced the words carefully, enunciating their consonants in a way that made me flinch with each sharp sound. I tried in vain to blend into the cabinetry while Joshua answered her.

"Who is who?" he said, and laughed. But he sounded too jumpy, too obviously aware of her odd behavior. His eyes flickered to mine for the briefest moment before refocusing on Ruth. "Are you sure you're okay, Grandma?"

At the sound of her grandson's nervous laughter, Ruth finally pulled her eyes away from me. She looked up at Joshua with nothing less than a furious glare.

"Don't be condescending to me, Joshua. Tell me what made you think you could bring something from High Bridge into our home?"

"Grandma, I didn't—"

"Don't." Ruth cut him off immediately. Joshua frowned, but she went on, her sharp eyes darting in my direction every few seconds. "Don't say you 'didn't,' because I can obviously see you *did*. I told you to stay away from that bridge—I've told you since you were little. But you go and wreck your car there and then bring *this* into our home? When I've tried so hard to protect you all from things like this?"

Her eyes fell fully upon me as she spoke the last phrase. I couldn't help but shiver and then shrink farther back, toward the hallway.

"Come on, Grandma." Joshua laughed again, although he seemed to have given up on masking the tension in his laugh. "All the stories about the bridge are just . . . stories."

"Yeah, Mom," Joshua's father called from behind us, sounding pretty nervous himself about his mother's behavior. "You know those stories are just made up to scare kids away from an unsafe bridge."

I looked back to see Joshua's father cast his eyes around the kitchen at the rest of his family. Like him, they all stared at Ruth in disbelief. As if they were afraid their matriarch—the family "pit bull," as Joshua had called her—was losing it, taking her little ghost hobby way too far.

Ruth, however, shook her head, her cheeks now blooming a violent, angry red. "I know no such thing, Jeremiah. What I do know is that bridge has a bad history. The kind of history that can change a place. Make it attractive to certain . . . things."

"Grandma, you know I don't believe in—"

Ruth laughed mirthlessly, cutting Joshua off again. "Joshua," she all but whispered, her eyes locked once again onto his. "I'm pretty sure you do believe. At least you believe *now*."

A soft, thoughtless yelp escaped my lips.

I slapped my hand to my mouth. Ruth, however, didn't look at me. Instead, she remained focused on her grandson.

Maybe she hadn't heard me yelp? And maybe I was being hypersensitive, imagining that she saw me, too? Imagining that she referred to me as one of those "certain things" associated with High Bridge?

Maybe. But it didn't seem very likely anymore.

And I didn't want to risk it. In fact, I suddenly felt trapped. The need to run began to burn in my limbs. I threw one more longing glance at Joshua before I crept several paces backward.

Joshua followed my movements from the corner of his eye. "Don't—!" he started to protest, but then clamped his lips down and gave his grandmother a tight smile.

"I'm sorry," I murmured, hovering at the entrance of the hallway. "But I think I'd better get out of here."

He frowned, still staring at his grandmother, who had

yet to drop her eyes from him. I looked back and forth between Ruth and Joshua, gnawing on the corner of my lip. At last my gaze fell on Joshua. I looked down at the hand closest to me and watched him clench and unclench it, like he'd done outside his math classroom today.

Despite my fear, this little gesture made me smile. It emboldened me, if just a tiny bit.

I drew a deep breath and then said, "Meet me at your school tomorrow, okay? At lunch, in the parking lot?"

Joshua gave me just the slightest nod, and my grin widened. The grin shrank, however, when Ruth's eyes darted once more to mine. If I didn't know better, I would have believed that a gaze like that could kill me again.

"Help me get out of here, Joshua," I whispered, as if my hushed tone would somehow make Ruth less aware of me. I spun around and bolted down the hallway before I had the chance to find out.

Once I reached the end of the hallway, I nearly shrieked in frustration. The screen door stared back at me, shut tight against my useless, dead hands. I almost collapsed with gratitude when an arm reached past me and shoved the door open, wide enough for me to pass through it. I crossed onto the deck and spun back around with a wide smile of relief.

"Thanks, Joshua, I really—"

The words died on my lips.

Ruth stared out at me from across the threshold, her hand still clenched to the doorframe, standing only inches away from me.

She was alone in the hallway.

I couldn't seem to pull my eyes away from Ruth's. Watching her, my vision blurred, and I could swear my head actually started to *ache*.

Finally, with an almost nightmarish slowness, I looked away from her. I began taking uncoordinated, fumbling steps across the deck and then down its stairs.

From behind me, I thought I heard something—a soft murmuring, almost like chanting. But I didn't look back at Ruth. Instead, I dashed through the yard and toward the driveway, intent on escape. Before I could flee, however, the sound of Ruth's voice froze me one last time.

When Ruth spoke, she whispered. But this time she did so loud enough for me to hear her, even from across the yard. The very sound of it prickled, icy and cruel at the back of my neck.

"You weren't who I expected," she hissed into the dark, "but whoever you are—leave. And don't come back."

My first impulse was to drop to the ground, curl up into the fetal position, and pray for a nightmare. For a good old disappearing act.

My next impulse was to cry out *Yes, ma'am; of course,*

*ma'am* and promptly obey her orders.

My final impulse was a little less familiar. A little out of my character, as I'd come to know it since death. Following this last impulse, I didn't acknowledge Ruth's edict in any way except to stand as straight as I possibly could and cast my head back.

Then, after this meager act of defiance, I followed at least part of Ruth's instructions and ran, fast, into the blackness of the night.

*Chapter*
ELEVEN

I have no idea how long I wandered after I left Joshua's
house. One hour, four—who knew? All I knew was
that the night had darkened into a sinister black.
Unlike the one in the flash I'd experienced earlier, the
sky above me didn't glow with stars. Instead, a sickly
looking moon provided the only light. It was a ghost
itself, so dull and weak it appeared out of place in the
sky. As if it didn't belong.

*Like me,* I thought bitterly. *I don't belong here, either.*

Well, maybe I belonged *here,* on the desolate stretch of

road upon which I now walked. But certainly not in the place I'd just visited. The place from which I'd just been unceremoniously banned.

Picturing Ruth's sharp eyes and cold voice, I wondered, *Was she right? I wasn't what she "expected" from a ghost. So . . . was I worse? Was I really some dark "thing" from High Bridge, like Eli? Some evil force in Joshua's life, saving him just so I could wreck him?*

I certainly didn't *feel* evil.

But I had to ask myself whether my current feelings even mattered. I knew nothing about myself, nothing about my own nature. The flashes were starting to give me some information, but only slowly and in a piecemeal way. So I'd been homeschooled by a mother I obviously argued with, known how to do differential equations, and had enough nerve to pick out dresses such as the one I would probably wear for eternity. These scant details, however, didn't really tell me anything about myself, whether or not I was a good person.

For all I knew, I spent my life kicking puppies or shoplifting underwear.

Or worse, obviously. Far, far worse.

Maybe something I'd done during life, or even at my death, made me *deserve* the afterlife Eli insisted was waiting for me. Had I been a cruel person? Was my life so terrible, I'd killed myself?

I had no idea.

A sudden wave of frustration washed over me. The flashes were so unrelated, so lacking in meaningful detail, I might never know who I'd been or what I could become. I let out an angry puff of air and began to trudge more forcefully down the road.

I guess I wasn't paying attention to where I walked, because I nearly stumbled over my own feet. Only after I'd steadied myself did I take in my current surroundings, the sight of which angered me further.

In my distraction I'd wandered back to the place I hated most: High Bridge.

I was standing right at its entrance. Its metal girders loomed above me, glinting in the yellow moonlight in a way that reminded me of spiteful winking.

"Oh, isn't this *perfect*!" I shouted.

My voice sounded childish, echoing back at me from the girders. So, in keeping with my petulant mood, I swung my leg back to kick uselessly at a rock on the shoulder of the road.

Before I could complete the kick, a sudden blast of cold air hit my back, running a chill from my neck to my heels. Immediately following, a smooth, familiar voice oozed out from behind me.

"You know, Amelia, you can kick it all you want. But that rock isn't going anywhere."

I closed my eyes, told myself not to shudder—no matter how appropriate it might feel—and then turned on one heel. I fixed a small, derisive smile on my face.

"Eli."

My only word of greeting. Eli's lips curled at one corner in amusement.

"To what do I owe the pleasure, Amelia?"

I frowned. "What do you mean?"

"Clearly," he said, leaning forward and arching his eyebrows, "you wanted something. Otherwise you wouldn't be here."

"And why would you think that?"

"You sought me out. So far I've kept my promise to leave you alone." He gestured with one arm to the metal and pavement around us. "But *you're* the one who returned to the bridge, like I said you would."

I scowled at him. "Trust me, it wasn't intentional."

"Whatever you say, Amelia." He began to turn toward the embankment. Then he looked back at me and, after a moment's consideration, twitched his head toward the river. "Why don't you come with me? We can talk more comfortably down there."

I tried not to laugh. "Uh, no thanks, Eli. I thought I made my feelings pretty clear on the subject of hanging out with you in dark places."

Eli shook his head. "But you do want to talk, don't you?"

"To you? Why would I want to do that?"

"I saw the look on your face before I spoke. You've had a bad night." He stated it like a fact.

"So?"

I sounded defensive, and for good reason. I had no intention of letting Eli know why I'd had a bad night. Eli couldn't know where I'd just been—he couldn't even know about Joshua's existence, as far as I was concerned.

"*So*," Eli said, "maybe you'd like to know why you're frustrated since you woke up from the fog? Why you can't quite figure out where you belong?"

I blinked.

"How did you . . . ?" I began, and then I shook my head. Eli couldn't possibly have known what I'd been thinking about before he arrived. He'd just taken a guess. A very good one.

I shrugged again. "You're right; it would be nice to know some things. But you're delusional if you think I'm going to do whatever you want me to just to get some information."

To my surprise, Eli laughed. "Fair enough, Amelia. How about I give you a . . . what should I call it—a freebie?"

"Meaning?"

"Meaning, I'll give you some details about the afterlife in exchange for nothing but your company for a little while."

I raised one skeptical eyebrow. "What's the catch?"

"No catch . . . for now."

"For now?"

"Well." He sighed. "I'll expect you to think about what I tell you tonight and consider it reason enough to come back to me—for good—later."

"And if I don't?"

"Then we'll deal with that problem when we come to it."

I bit my lip, confused by how suddenly appealing Eli's proposition sounded. I didn't think I could trust him, nor did I really want to. But I also couldn't resist his offer of information, not at this point. I wanted to know who I was, and what happened next. No, I *had* to know. I nodded as decisively as I could, given my lingering reservations.

"Okay, Eli. Lead the way."

Eli looked startled by my sudden agreement. Quickly, though, a pleased smile spread across his face. He rubbed his hands together.

"Excellent."

Without pausing for my response, he spun around and marched down the hill. I took a breath for courage and followed him.

Slowly, carefully, I made my way down the grassy slope. Eli waited for me at the bottom of the embankment, feet planted apart and arms folded over his chest. I stopped several yards from him and mirrored his stance.

"Well?" I asked.

Eli grinned, and ignored my question. "How's the temperature, Amelia?"

"Huh?"

I frowned, hard. Even if I was interested in what Eli had to say, I didn't want to fall for any of his tricks. So I felt extremely foolish—not to mention unnerved—when our surroundings suddenly changed. Without further warning, everything melted into a deep, charcoal gray; and cold air blasted my skin.

Looking around me, I gasped. Again the trees and river had transformed into charcoal and tar. Eli had plunged us back into the place he'd revealed yesterday: the dark afterworld in which I was supposedly doomed to spend eternity, trapped. The passage of a full day had done nothing to improve this place's appearance.

My voice came out timid and wavering when I protested, "I thought you said we were just going to talk?"

"Relax, Amelia," Eli said. "I'm keeping my promise. I just want to keep it where I'm most comfortable."

I peeked above and past him. Neither the black chasm under the bridge nor the weird, moving shapes had appeared yet. I wrapped my arms around myself, trying to block out the chill. "Okay, fine. But do it fast, and let me go. This place gives me the creeps."

"Well," he said, "why don't we start with this place then? Would you like to know where we actually are?"

I nodded hesitantly.

"This *is* part of the afterlife, like I told you."

"That's not really reassuring," I murmured, taking in all the bleak grayness with a roll of my eyes.

Eli shook his head. "It's not as bad as you think, Amelia. Honestly."

Locking his eyes on mine, Eli raised one hand and snapped his fingers. Immediately, the netherworld lightened as if Eli's snap had flipped some kind of supernatural switch.

My mouth gaped.

With the introduction of just a fraction of light, an entire landscape appeared around me. Granted, it was still in various shades of gray. But the scene itself, and not its color, captured my attention.

At first glance the netherworld bore a strong resemblance to the riverbank we'd just left. The vague, charcoal shapes I'd seen yesterday took on more familiar forms: the long prairie grass, enormous trees, and clumps of unruly wildflowers still crowded around us. Each piece of gray plant life, however, differed in slight but significant ways from those in the living world.

Here the tree branches twisted into sinister shapes,

like claws and hooks; the wildflowers and grass snarled around each other, looking as if they were in some kind of angry battle. And, though the plants indicated that it was late summer in this world too, every surface shimmered and glittered with a fine layer of frost.

This netherworld, once illuminated, actually looked like some kind of creepy wonderland. Like a double-exposed negative of the living world: cold, dark, scary. And also unbelievably beautiful.

"Is it always like this here?" I breathed.

"No," Eli answered, his voice low and respectful. "It's always gray, and cold. But I have the ability to lighten or darken the scenery, if I want."

"Are you the ruler of this world or something?"

Eli laughed loudly, breaking the spell this place had cast over me. "Are you asking if I'm a god, Amelia?"

"Not exactly the entity I meant," I muttered, too low for Eli to hear.

"No, I'm not one of the higher powers here," he said. "Although I do work for them."

I pulled my eyes away from the fantastic trees and met Eli's gaze. "Them? Explain."

Eli settled back on his heels. "Well," he said, "I guess I should start with my job description."

I raised my eyebrows, and he sighed.

"I'm the . . . guardian, in a sense, of this afterlife. I've been commissioned to care for it. To grow it."

"Grow it? You mean, with all the plants?"

For some reason Eli's eyes sparkled mischievously. "With those, and . . . other things. Listen," he commanded, and then cupped his hand to his ear.

I obeyed thoughtlessly, clamping my lips tight and focusing on the quiet around me. Initially I couldn't hear anything, except perhaps the weird echo of silence, like the kind you hear when you press your ear to a seashell.

Then, just over the silence, I heard them. Faint at first, but growing in intensity.

Whispers. A chorus of them.

"Who . . . ?" I started, but Eli pressed a finger to his lips, indicating I should stay quiet.

The whispers continued, hushed and insistent. I couldn't be certain, but after a few more seconds, I thought they sounded . . . desperate. Frantic.

Something about them frightened me.

"What are those voices, Eli?" I demanded shakily. "Tell me now."

"I think you already know."

"People?" I whispered.

"Well," he said with a sly grin, "they used to be."

I gulped, feeling strangely dizzy. "What exactly is your job here, Eli? Really."

He sighed as if relieved I'd finally asked an important

question. "I'm not only a guardian, but also a sort of recruiter. I've been chosen to usher certain newly dead souls to this place. Some of those voices you heard are my charges—souls I was ordered to bring over."

"Other ghosts?"

Eli nodded. "I think you saw a few of them yesterday actually."

I thought back to the flitting shapes along my peripheral vision. I looked wildly to either side of Eli, at the empty riverbank. "Where are they now?"

"I told them to stay away for a while so you and I could talk." He jerked his head toward the line of weird trees behind him. "Mostly, they stay in there until I need them."

"Are you . . . their boss or something?"

Eli shrugged, but the gesture looked prideful. Almost self-satisfied. "I recruit them for my masters. In return, my masters give me power over this place, and the recruited souls in it. The souls follow my commands and help me with whatever I need. On big missions they definitely come in handy."

I tried not to shudder, thinking of what a "big mission" might mean to Eli. "And these 'masters,' the ones who gave you this job—are they in those trees too?"

He laughed as if I'd said something ridiculous. "No, of course not, Amelia. This is my realm. Over *there*, however . . ." He trailed off, looking over my shoulder. I followed his gaze to the place where the river moved sluggishly under High Bridge. To the space where the black hole had appeared yesterday.

A few details clicked into place in my mind, and I moaned. "You trap people in this world? On orders from whoever lives in that . . . that hellhole?"

"Only because this is where these souls belong. And that darkness over there isn't hell. It's just one of the places where the higher powers go when they're not giving me my instructions."

Eli sounded sincere. But I shook my head vigorously against his words. No soul deserved to stay in this dark forest, trapped forever, unable to move between worlds like Eli and I obviously could. No matter who, or what, had ordered it.

Thinking about what it might feel like to be trapped inside the dark forest or, God forbid, somewhere in that sightless chasm below the bridge, a thought struck me. A terrifying one.

I raised my eyes to his again, searching their pale blue depths. "What about me, Eli? What about my soul?"

The corner of his lip quirked upward. "Ah, now we get to the real heart of the matter. Isn't that why we came down here in the first place? To talk about your nature?"

"Yes, and . . . ?" I pressed. "What does my nature have

to do with this place?"

He gestured behind him with one arm. "Aren't you wondering why I haven't made you one of those shadows yet? Why I've let you wander, for far longer than I usually allow a soul to remain in the living world?"

I tried in vain to repress a shudder. "Okay, I'll bite. Why?"

"Because you're special, Amelia." He began to take slow, deliberate steps toward me.

"Yeah?" I kept my voice as casual as possible, all the while moving backward, away from him. "How am I special?"

"Thanks to the grace of my masters," he said, still moving forward, "I'm allowed to keep one newly dead soul for myself. As an . . . apprentice. When I saw you, when I watched you, I knew you'd be perfect."

"Why?"

"Because you belong with me, Amelia. You're a kindred spirit."

Eli's words echoed in my brain like repetitions of my earlier fears. So I *was* evil? Everything within me rallied against the suggestion. I didn't believe it. I just didn't.

"No," I insisted, shaking my head again. "No, it's not true. I don't belong here."

"But you do." With just a few, quick strides, Eli closed the distance between us. He leaned over and placed his hands beside my shoulders, hovering above my skin without actually touching me.

"You're fated to help me with my task—I knew it from the first moment I saw you." He shrugged again, but this time the movement looked decidedly less casual. "You *have* to help me, Amelia. Otherwise I'll have no choice but to trap you here and keep you from ever going into the living world again. Unless you're obeying my orders, like the mindless wraiths back there." He jerked his head meaningfully toward the forest again.

Anger and terror bubbled up inside me.

"No!" I shouted into his face. "I can't stay and help you condemn people to this place. I won't."

Without waiting for his reaction—which would undoubtedly be unpleasant—I turned to flee. Of course, I had no idea where to flee since I was directionless in this world. I spun around, searching for some point of orientation, flinging my arms this way and that.

Something brushed my outstretched hand—Eli's fingertips maybe. Whatever made contact with my skin, it plunged me into a brutal cold, shooting what felt like ice water through my veins. The cold came on so fiercely, so violently, my vision began to blur.

I heard Eli call out, "Amelia! Wait!"

Then the dark water of my nightmares enveloped me entirely.

*Chapter*
TWELVE

I bolted upright, gasping.

I couldn't process any rational thought. I could only swallow panicked gulps of air. Soon, though, my instincts reminded me to protect myself from any nearby threat.

Such as Eli, or his "masters."

A quick scan of the area showed no sign of Eli. Still, my heart sank. I now sat in a field of headstones, each throwing a shadow in the bright sunlight. There was no mistaking my location. I was in the graveyard in which I always woke after a nightmare.

I sighed and closed my eyes. This nightmare—my first since meeting Joshua—had been different from the others. This time when I struggled against the river, I'd heard things. Voices, much like the desperate whispers in the dark netherworld. Except that in my nightmare the voices sounded more raucous. Almost frenzied.

I shook my head. Voices or not, this dream had the same effect on me it usually did. I'd lost valuable time while thrashing about in that stupid river. Opening my eyes, I assessed the sunny day—so welcome after all that darkness and ice—and prayed it wasn't too late to keep my promise to meet Joshua. I pushed myself up into a standing position and stretched each hamstring, although I hardly needed to.

"Speed, Amelia," I told myself aloud. "Think speed."

And I began to run, as fast as I possibly could, in the direction of Joshua's school.

I breathed an enormous sigh of relief when I finally came upon the Wilburton High School parking lot, which was still crowded with cars. I wove between the back rows of them to get a better view of the school itself. Outside the low buildings students milled around, waiting for the end of the lunch period, I hoped.

I turned my attention to the cars, searching. A number

of black sedans filled the parking lot, but soon I managed to spot the most familiar one. I walked over to it,
moving as quickly as I could while simultaneously giving
my dress a brief look-over. Once I was relatively certain
I didn't look like a crazy person who'd just woken up in
a graveyard, I stood next to the driver's side window of
Joshua's car and clasped my arms behind me.

Joshua sat in the car with his head resting on his arms,
which he'd laid upon the wheel. After only a few seconds, he looked up. The noon sun lit up his face and, for
a moment, I blinked in surprise.

He looked *terrible*, at least as terrible as someone like
Joshua could look. His hair was a mess, dark circles
ringed his eyes, and he could have used a good shave.
But when those midnight blue eyes caught mine and he
smiled, I couldn't help but sigh happily.

*Wait*, he mouthed, and then leaned over to the passenger side. I heard a metallic pop as the passenger side
door opened, so I circled behind the car and slipped into
it. Joshua pulled the door shut beside me.

Still leaning across me, his mouth dangerously close to
my ear, he murmured, "Hey, Amelia."

"Hey, Joshua," I murmured back, keeping my hands
firmly planted in my lap instead of wrapped around his
neck, where they wanted to be.

Joshua leaned back into his seat and unsuccessfully

tried to stifle a yawn. The attempt made me smile and helped me refocus on what we needed to discuss. Taking in his rumpled appearance, I decided to start with the obvious.

"Um, Joshua? You know your shirt's inside out, right?"

He looked down at his gray T-shirt. "Huh. How about that."

In one swift move Joshua pulled the shirt over his head and flipped it to the correct side. I now had a full view of his chest and abs, and, suddenly, I couldn't remember how to breathe. Which wouldn't have been a problem, obviously, except for the fact that I also started to choke. Joshua watched my entire struggle from the corner of his eye, grinning as he pulled the shirt back over his head.

I tried desperately to compose myself. Finally, I managed to calm down enough and ask, "So, something makes me think we should talk about your night first?"

Joshua laughed and rubbed one hand over his stubbled jaw. "Okay, me first then." He stretched out his legs and then gave me a strange, appraising look. "My night was . . . interesting."

"How so?"

"Well, the Mayhews had a long debate about Ruth's mental health, which is ironic if you consider I'm the only one who knew for sure she wasn't crazy."

I grimaced. "Sorry."

"Don't be," he said, smiling grimly. "It didn't even compare to the ungodly long lecture I got from Ruth after she convinced everyone else of her sanity."

"She lectured you about being late for dinner?" I asked hopefully, foolishly, although I already knew the answer.

Joshua's smile turned gentle, but his expression made it clear what he was about to say. "No, Amelia. She lectured me about you."

I sucked in a sharp breath. *Calm,* I told myself. *Stay calm.*

In my most nonchalant voice, I asked, "Oh? And what did she have to say?"

Joshua laughed bitterly. "What do families usually say? 'Stay away from that one, she's trouble.' Of course, in this case, the 'trouble' is something a little weirder than a girl who smokes or has too many body piercings."

I grimaced again. "To put it mildly, right?" I moved for the door handle, even though I couldn't use it. "If you would just open this for me, I can get out of here and stop screwing up your life. . . ."

"Amelia."

Joshua's tone made me turn back to him. He gave me another gentle smile. "Why don't you listen to my whole story before you go running off?"

Warily, I settled back against my seat. "Okay. I can do that. For now."

He angled his body toward me and, betraying his exhaustion, closed his eyes as he spoke. "For the sake of timing, I'm just going to give you the main points. Point number one you already heard: Ruth thinks High Bridge and the river under it are evil."

"No argument here," I muttered. Joshua popped an eye open, so I added, "I'll tell you about that later."

He nodded, shutting his eyes again. "According to Ruth, after my dad was born she basically insisted the family move to this area for the sole purpose of guarding the river . . . keeping people safe from whatever controls it. Supposedly, lots of people have done the same thing, including her friends and their families. Because the area's so 'supernaturally charged'—Ruth's words, I swear."

Joshua snorted and shook his head. After another long pause he went on. "That's point number two, and the real reason Ruth's friends have always acted so spooky: they really are a group of—I don't know—ghost hunters. Their whole mission is to keep on the lookout for 'unclaimed' spirits and banish them. Exorcize them. They've been hunting a specific unclaimed ghost for years. Some guy, Ruth said. But when *you* showed up at the house . . . well, you can just imagine Ruth's frenzy, right?"

I leaned back in my seat, shocked.

Were "claimed" spirits actually the recruited souls Eli had confined to the supernatural world? Would that then make Eli an "unclaimed" spirit, one that could walk between worlds?

Eli *had* to be the ghost they've been hunting. So . . . did that mean they would start hunting me too?

Was I also an unclaimed spirit?

Shaking my head with a weak laugh, I asked, "Doesn't it feel good to know your grandma isn't actually crazy?"

The corner of Joshua's mouth lifted, but not very high. "Not really, Amelia. Not when we get to point number three. Apparently, the Witches of Wilburton want me to join their little coven."

"What?" I gasped.

"Ruth says it's my heritage. My destiny, whatever that means. I come from a long line of 'Seers,' and there's nothing I can do about it."

"Seers?"

"Yeah. People who can see the supernatural. Unclaimed ghosts, mainly. Ruth says I've probably always been able to sense them without really knowing what I was sensing. That's why she told me those ghost stories when I was a kid—as some sort of training. The only way to see ghosts outright, though, is to go through some sort of 'triggering event.' Something that forces you into an awareness of the spirit world."

"Like meeting a dead girl right after your heart stops?"

"*Exactly* like meeting a dead girl right after your heart stops." He sighed and rubbed his forehead. "Ruth says the only reason I'm even drawn to you is . . . I don't know . . . my genetic predisposition to exorcise you. Her version of a Seer is someone who *does* something with their 'gift,' not just enjoys its benefits like I've been doing. In other words, Seers use the gift of sight *against* ghosts. Apparently, this is what I'm supposed to do when it comes to you."

A heavy silence fell over the car. Inexplicably, my eyes glued themselves onto the dashboard. After a few seconds of searching for invisible patterns in the leather dash, I stirred. When I finally looked back at Joshua, his eyes were still closed, his body still motionless.

"So," I whispered, "does this mean you don't want my help in Calculus anymore?"

Joshua's eyes shot open and locked onto mine. I felt a little dizzy staring into all that dark blue, even when he didn't laugh at my lame joke.

"That's point number four," he said. "You see, my grandmother makes a pretty hard sell about me not hanging out with you."

Although he kept his voice soft, I flinched. I didn't want to hear what was coming; I really didn't.

Joshua surprised me, however, by smiling as he went

on. "But I've got to tell you, Amelia, I really don't want to add a coven to my list of extracurriculars."

I parsed through his words slowly and felt myself start to smile. "And here I thought you were such a joiner."

Joshua merely laughed, but I wanted to push the issue further. "Just so we're clear: you're not going to become a Seer and hunt me down for exorcism?"

"I don't think I can stop being a Seer," he said. "It's just part of who I am now, I guess. But as for all the stuff about the banishment of ghosts . . . thanks but no thanks."

The little ache in my chest unfurled for the first time in hours. Before I got too far ahead of myself, however, I had to be sure of one more thing.

"Just so we're, you know, even *clearer*," I pressed. "You're not going to embrace your heritage because . . . ?"

Joshua grinned, wry and sweet like the first time he smiled at me on High Bridge. "Because I can't hunt you and be with you at the same time, can I?"

"'Be' with me?" I whispered.

Joshua didn't answer. Instead, he held out his hand.

I stared at his outstretched arm for a moment, unsure of what to do. What a scary, thrilling idea—holding his hand, touching him for more than a few brief seconds. Shaking a bit, I tentatively stretched out my hand and let it fold into his.

Once again pulsing fire shot through my veins. Joshua and I responded as we had the first time we touched: gasping, smiling, reactively trying to recoil from the shock of it. But we both fought the impulse to jerk away and instead held on to each other's hand tightly.

Initially his hand cupped mine, holding it in a formal, almost businesslike way. Then, very slowly, he rotated our hands upward until they were perpendicular, palm to palm. With the slightest turn of his wrist, Joshua wove his fingers between mine and clasped my hand. I let my fingers glide down to clasp back.

Once our hands intertwined, the current over my skin began to change itself subtly. Now, instead of flaming out from my hand and into the rest of my body, the slow burn engulfed me everywhere *but* the hand I'd interlocked with his. That hand was covered with strange little stabs all over the side of my palm that touched Joshua's—like the pins-and-needles feel of a limb after it's been held in one position for too long. Like my hand was waking up.

The analogy fit even better when the stabbing sensation faded and was replaced by something else entirely.

Suddenly, I felt him. Not the numb pressure, not even the thrilling current, but *him*. I felt the warmth of his hand and the texture of his skin pressed to mine. I felt him, just as I had in the river, when he was temporarily made of the same otherwordly matter as me.

Joshua must have sensed this change too, because his eyes flitted from our hands to my face.

"Do you feel that?"

He sounded awed, and uncertain. I nodded, my eyes locked onto his. When I spoke, it was haltingly.

"Joshua, I . . . I told you I hadn't felt anything since I died. Not like this. The first time I felt something was when you were in the river. And since we met, I've started to feel little things, little sensations. But those sensations disappeared, fast. This isn't . . . this doesn't seem to be going away."

I lifted our woven hands to emphasize my point. Doing so, I could feel the weight of his arm and the rough skin of his palm as it shifted against mine.

Keeping his hand firmly wrapped in mine, Joshua leaned closer to me.

"Then maybe I'm making the right decision after all," he murmured.

Impulsively, acting as one might during an involuntary reaction, I arched my body toward him, curving myself until our faces were only inches apart. Our closeness sent a different set of tingles through me, tingles I was certain weren't entirely inspired by the supernatural. More like the most natural thing in the world: simple, human attraction.

Despite our proximity, or perhaps because of it, Joshua's expression became serious, his voice fervent.

"I could get used to this," he whispered, nodding toward our clasped hands.

"What, the high voltage or touching me in general?"

"Both." With his free hand, he gestured back and forth in what little space was left between us. "Whatever is happening, it means something. Something more than just us being dead at the same time, in the same place. Something more than you being a ghost and me being a Seer. Don't you think so?"

My brain buzzed so loudly, I almost couldn't answer. "I think . . . maybe."

He grinned, moving in so close that our lips would touch with just the slightest twitch from either of us.

"Maybe what?" he prompted.

"Maybe yes?" I gasped, imagining the feel of his lips on mine. How hot would they burn me? How quickly would I feel his real lips beneath the fire? I tried to steady my breath and prepare myself for the moment I wanted so much.

Of course, I wasn't exactly prepared for that moment to be interrupted by a sharp, rapping knock on Joshua's car window.

*Chapter*
THIRTEEN

At the sound of the knock on the window, we froze, our lips only a breath apart.

"Who is it?" Joshua asked me through clenched teeth. Without moving my head, I strained to peek around him.

"A girl," I whispered.

Joshua pulled his hand from mine, giving my fingers a gentle squeeze before turning to face our intruder. He rolled down the driver's side window and then laughed.

"What can I do for you, sister of mine?" he asked the intruder.

"You could stop embarrassing me, for one," the girl snarled.

Jillian, of course. I leaned to the right to get a better look at her, but I could only see narrow hips with tiny hands clenched angrily to them.

"Oh my God, Jillian," Joshua gasped in mock horror. "I'm so sorry. You know your popularity is the most important thing in my life."

"Cut the crap, Josh," Jillian snapped. "It's bad enough that you showed up at school looking like a hobo, but now you have to spend lunch talking to yourself in your car?"

"I was practicing for Debate."

She snorted in derision. "You're not even in Debate. And anyway, you haven't eaten lunch by yourself since . . . ever. So people are talking."

"And I care because . . . ?"

Jillian's tiny hands flew off her hips and folded together in a gesture of prayer. "Because your little sister really, really wants to be Homecoming Queen her senior year, and she can't do that if you don't leave her some coattails to ride on."

Joshua groaned and sank back into his seat. Undeterred by the groan, Jillian ducked down to pop her head in through the open window. She still wore that perpetually wry look even when she forced her lips into a begging pout.

Lucky for her, her pleas worked on Joshua. Seeing her attempt at contrition, he barked out a genuine laugh. Jillian laughed too, and her entire face changed. The sharp edges softened, and her hazel eyes sparkled. She was beautiful when she laughed.

"Fine," Joshua conceded. "I'll socialize. But just because your entire future depends on it."

Jillian snorted again but must have thought better than to continue fighting. She straightened, propped her hands upon her hips once more, and waited while Joshua rolled up his window.

Once the window had closed, Joshua turned back to me. "Coming to class?" he whispered.

I hesitated, just for a moment, and then whispered back, "Well, someone has to make sure you don't fail Calculus."

Joshua opened his door and got out of the car, shoving past Jillian and circling to the passenger side. With one quick glance at his sister, possibly to see how closely she watched him, Joshua pulled open my door and ducked down to grab his book bag from the floor. I pushed myself up and squeezed through the narrow opening between his body and the doorjamb, careful not to brush against him.

Apparently, he didn't feel the need to be as careful with me as I was being with him. When I passed him, he ran his fingertips softly down the length of my calf. An instant wave of heat shot across the back of my leg.

"Hey!" I cried. I heard Joshua snicker as he shut the door behind me. I started to reprimand him—at least, halfheartedly, anyway—when Jillian interrupted us again.

"Josh, what was that noise?"

Joshua froze, one hand still grasping the door handle. Slowly, cautiously, I spun around on one heel until I could see Jillian's face over the top of the car. She looked serious now, with a confused frown dragging at the corners of her mouth.

"Are you talking about my laugh?" Joshua asked her.

"No, it sounded higher. Like a girl's voice."

Joshua and I both balked, but he recovered faster. "Maybe you heard someone calling you, from the back lawn?" he suggested.

She shook her head, a stubborn line forming between her eyebrows. "No, Josh, it was right here. By the car."

"Okay, okay." Joshua held up his hands and gave a nervous, deflecting sort of laugh. "But you know they don't give Homecoming crowns to girls who hear voices, right?"

Jillian's frown softened then. She looked as if the idea of appearing crazy was more frightening than some disembodied voice. She shook her head again, perhaps to shake away whatever she thought she'd heard, and smiled. "You never know—maybe psychosis will be the hot new thing in two years."

"Let's hope so, for your sake."

Jillian rolled her eyes and jerked a thumb toward the school. "Socializing, Josh. Pronto."

Joshua gave her a dismissive wave, but Jillian seemed placated enough to turn and walk back to the school yard. Once she had moved out of earshot, I looked up at Joshua.

"'A girl's voice'?" I whispered. "Do you think she heard me?"

Joshua's eyebrows drew together in thought. After a few more seconds of watching his sister's retreat, he looked at me from the corner of his eye and mouthed, *Seer?*

"Maybe," I mused, also following Jillian's figure as she strode onto the back lawn and into a pack of young girls. Before immersing herself in the pack, Jillian tossed a last glance over her shoulder at her brother. Her expression was one of annoyance, but she also looked puzzled—as if she wasn't really sure what she'd just heard.

"Maybe, maybe not," Joshua whispered, and then pulled

his bag farther onto his shoulder. "Ready for class?"

I nodded and then followed closely behind him through the parking lot, gnawing at my bottom lip. I couldn't shake the image of Jillian's confused, contemplative look. What exactly would it mean if I had another spiritually aware human to contend with? I loved Joshua's awareness, but I didn't really need Ruth Junior on my hands too—not right now.

I was so lost in thought that I almost missed the sound of rushing air beside me. I only had time to cry out "Joshua!" before something large and grunting hit him in the back.

It took me a second to realize the charging object was the burly, red-headed boy from Joshua's Calculus class, the one who'd told him he should have skipped yesterday. Now I could see that the boy hadn't actually hit Joshua; he'd merely wrapped one thick arm around Joshua's neck and pulled him into a playful headlock.

"Mayhew, dude, I knew you were a genius, but *damn.* Yesterday's performance in Wolters's class was epic."

Joshua laughed, but it came out sounding more like a strangled cough. Turning a little pink, Joshua began tapping on the boy's arm.

"O'Reilly, man, loosen up your kung fu grip."

"Oh." With surprising speed, the boy—O'Reilly—let go of Joshua and gave him a few rough pats on the back. "Sorry, dude."

"No problem," Joshua choked hoarsely.

"So," O'Reilly said as he picked up the bag he'd knocked off of Joshua's shoulder. "You still stuck in the library for seventh period?"

"Yeah, the doctor said I can't do strength training until probably around Christmas. Because of the whole heart thing, you know?"

"Dude, 'cause you, like, died, right?"

O'Reilly's words might have been offensive if they weren't so guileless. When O'Reilly handed Joshua the bag, his brown eyes were wide with nothing but concern for his friend. I liked him immediately.

"Yup. Because I died." Joshua laughed and gave me a sly glance before continuing. "But don't worry—I'll be in condition for baseball season."

"You'd better be, dude. I need my center fielder. If you don't show, I'll probably throw you back in the river myself."

"Yeah, with one guy dead and one guy out for homicide, we'll *really* be sure to win the regional championship."

The soft, unfamiliar voice surprised me, and I looked around the hulking form of O'Reilly for its source. Standing there behind O'Reilly was the other boy I'd noticed yesterday in Ms. Wolters's class.

This second boy was about Joshua's height and build,

but he had shaggy, sandy-colored hair and dark brown eyes. When O'Reilly leaned over to give him a light-hearted punch on the shoulder, he merely smiled slightly and curved his shoulders forward in a protective sort of way. The movement made him look shy, and I instantly warmed to him too.

Joshua turned to the boy, holding up one hand for him to clasp. "Scott, man, what's up?"

Scott smiled more brightly. "Not much, Mayhew. How you feeling today?"

"Great. Better than ever." I couldn't be sure, but I thought I saw Joshua's free hand twitch toward me.

"Sweet," Scott said, nodding.

As if Scott's appraisal of Joshua's health was some secret code, the boys begin to move collectively across the lawn without further commentary. I followed after them, a little mystified by their exchange.

We'd nearly made it to the door to Ms. Wolters's classroom when a series of giggles erupted behind us. Immediately, O'Reilly and Scott skidded to a stop and spun around. Joshua, however, sighed heavily before turning in the same direction.

I turned, too, and saw a group of teenage girls crowded together in a mass of low-cut tops and cheerleader skirts. In its center stood Jillian, surrounded by what was apparently her entourage. Unlike her friends, she looked bored and irritated. I got the sudden impression they'd forced her to come over here.

"Ladies." O'Reilly greeted them with a suggestive raise of his eyebrows. Unfortunately, the flock ignored him entirely and focused their attention on one thing, and one thing only: the handsome, dark-haired boy standing beside me.

"Not ditching today, Josh?" one of the girls called out from the back. In unison, the flock began fluttering eyelashes and flipping hair.

Joshua cocked his head to one side and smirked. "Not today. I've decided to grace everyone with my presence."

Jillian snorted and, true to form, rolled her eyes. But most of her friends obviously didn't share her derision; all of them giggled as if Joshua had made the most hilarious joke they'd ever heard. A few girls even began to flip their hair more frantically, like showy birds in some weird mating ritual.

"Oh, you've *got* to be kidding me," I grumbled under my breath.

Oblivious to both my and Jillian's irritation, one girl disentangled herself from the pack. Once free, the girl drew herself up to her full height, which was still several inches below mine, and flashed Joshua a brilliant smile.

"Josh," she purred, her voice throaty and deeper than I'd expected. Like her friends, she flipped back a strand of her honey blond hair. On her, though, the gesture seemed decidedly less childish, and her pale blue eyes had a calculating glint in them. "You can tell me—is Jillian being mean to you again?"

"Well, she's trying."

To my eternal relief, Joshua directed his answer at Jillian and not her pretty friend. The girl, however, wasn't deterred. She slunk forward, passing her friends without a backward glance.

"You just let me know if you need protection from mean old Jillian." Her words dripped with innuendo, aided in no small part by the suggestive way she leaned toward Joshua.

When he squirmed away from her, I felt the strangest mix of emotions. First, I wanted to jump into Joshua's arms and give him a series of grateful kisses—rewards for his apparent disinterest in her. Next, I wished I was substantial enough to tackle this stranger and pull out her pretty hair.

I shook my head, shocked at myself. Who *was* I to think such terrible things? The impulse unnerved me and made me think back to my fears about my nature. The nature Eli so strongly insisted would condemn me.

Thankfully, Joshua shook his head, too, in response to the girl's offer. "I appreciate it, Kaylen," he said. "But I'll stick with my regular bodyguards."

He nodded to O'Reilly and then to Scott. The boys, however, didn't look as if they wanted to pull bodyguard duty. They looked as if they would let this girl protect them, any day, in any way.

Kaylen merely shrugged. "Suit yourself," she said with a smile, not moving an inch away from Joshua.

Jillian sighed and rolled her eyes again, her irritation now barely concealed. "Let's *go*, Kaylen."

Finally—a few infatuated sighs and surreptitious second glances later—the crowd wandered off. Kaylen, of course, looked the most unwilling of all. She continued looking back at the boys as did Jillian, although I could swear Jillian's eyes kept drifting to the spot in which I was standing. Though I felt a little foolish doing it, I wriggled behind O'Reilly and out of sight until Jillian rounded a corner.

Once the girls were gone, O'Reilly and Scott released big, gusting breaths they had apparently been holding during Kaylen's performance.

"Dude, Kaylen Patton is smokin' hot." O'Reilly's proclamation sounded worshipful.

Hesitantly, I turned to see whether Joshua also intended to chime in with his own awe and reverence. Without taking his gaze from mine, Joshua shrugged.

"I've seen better, boys. Much better."

Like an idiot, I giggled and had to grab a fold of

my dress to keep my hand from reaching up to flip my hair.

I sat on the edge of Joshua's desk, trying not to distract him from a particularly dull lecture about integers. Soon enough, though, Ms. Wolters turned the class over to free study.

Almost immediately after the room quieted, Joshua slid a piece of lined paper across his desk toward me. On it he'd written in thick, capable-looking script: *I have a brilliant plan. Want to hear it?*

I laughed, but then instinctively slapped my hand over my mouth to muffle the sound. Without looking at me, Joshua grinned and wrote in the margin of the paper: *You do realize no one else can hear you, right?*

"Don't be so sure," I whispered, picturing Jillian's expression at lunch. Then I shook my head at my own ridiculousness and, louder, said, "Okay, I give in. What's your brilliant plan?"

Joshua tore another page out of his notebook and began to scribble furiously. Once finished, he pushed the paper over to me and then pretended to return to his Calculus book, watching me from the corner of his eye while I read.

*Okay,* his note began, *my plan sort of fits into a theory I came up with last night. We know you died in the river, and you're still hanging around here. So, maybe you're from here. You said you remembered these buildings, right? Maybe you even went here, before or after you were homeschooled. This is what I'm thinking: my study hall is in the library, where the old yearbooks are. We can go through all of them, starting with the most recent, and see if we can find your picture.*

Upon reading the last few words, I had the strangest sensation of the floor dropping out from under me.

"Aren't you supposed to, I don't know, study, in study hall?"

Joshua stared fully at me for a moment and then wrote again.

*Bad idea?*

I thought about that for a while. What was it about his suggestion that frightened me so much? After all, it might lead to some shred of information about my life. It might provide answers to so many of the questions that had plagued me the last few days, about who I had been, who I might become. Something that could combat what both Eli and Ruth had implied about me.

But therein lay the problem, too. Because once I knew this information, once I pieced together the missing parts of my identity, I would become *real*. I would be a real person, with a real story. A story that had ended.

Maybe that was the entire reason I'd never tried to find my headstone in the graveyard. Because, with such information, I would finally know—not just intuit, but truly know—I was dead.

And so would Joshua. This was a milestone for which I wasn't completely sure we were ready.

"Joshua," I started, my voice soft, "do you really believe . . . no, do you really *know* I'm dead? That I'm not alive? And I never will be again?"

As he looked up at me, all the playfulness, the relaxed confidence, left his face. His expression softened and became one that was simultaneously sad and sweet. Very slowly, he nodded.

I continued to stare at him. I really had no idea how to move forward from here. With my teeth clenched against the soft skin of my lip, I twisted my mouth to one side in frustration. In return Joshua gave me a small, close-lipped smile.

I wasn't imagining the hope I saw in that smile. In it I could almost read his thoughts: yes, he knew I was dead; but he still hoped that this deficiency of mine wouldn't be a problem. Or maybe he thought he could find some kind of solution for me. For us.

The incapacitating ache unfurled itself in my chest again. It told me, in the most basic if silent terms, what I knew I would do now. What I knew I would always do, whenever Joshua suggested something scary or unknown.

I sighed heavily. "Okay. We'll go to the library. We'll try to find my picture."

It was now Joshua's turn to frown. *You sure?* he mouthed.

I started to answer, *No, I'm not sure I want to know who I am.* Then I thought better of telling him the whole truth and instead chose to tell him only part of it.

"If you're with me, I'm sure I'll be okay."

*Chapter*
FOURTEEN

After Ms. Wolters's class ended and other students made their way to their next classrooms, Joshua and I strolled across the empty back lawn of the school.

Every few seconds, Joshua would brush his hand against mine, sending sparks up, then down, then back up my arm. Despite the thrill of his touch, I moved with an intentional slowness toward the main building, knowing that through its door lay the library.

"You know," Joshua said, interrupting my thoughts,

"we don't have to do this if you don't want to."

He kept his expression perfectly even, perfectly casual. I knew better, though.

I'd only known Joshua for three days. Yet I knew him well enough to hear the false note in his words. I could see the thoughts dancing in his eyes: unlike me, he *wanted* to go to the library. He wanted the excitement of discovering something new about me, of piecing my past together.

And he was right; I knew it.

Last night, after talking with Eli, I knew that my "nature"—the kind of person I was, both before and after I died—played a crucial role in how I would spend my afterlife. So I needed to know everything I could about myself before I had to face Eli or Ruth again. In fact, if I was completely honest with myself, I knew how essential today's mission was.

Of course, that didn't mean I had to share Joshua's enthusiasm. As he walked beside me, I could see him bouncing ever so slightly, jittery from excitement about our task. The brightness in his eyes and the happy swing of his arms contrasted starkly with my own appearance, which probably had a funereal sort of air.

Whatever my mood, it was hard not to be a little flattered by Joshua's behavior. I stifled a sigh before plastering a cheerful smile on my face.

"No, Joshua, I'm ready. Let's go."

He must have been too excited to catch on to the undercurrent of my words, because he looked completely satisfied by my terrible lie. His entire face lit up as he skidded to a stop and leaned close to me.

"Really? Because I had another idea. You know, if the whole yearbook thing works out."

"Oh, and what's that?"

"Well, say we find your picture. That'll mean we've also found your last name. All we have to do is find it in the phone book and then, presto, we've found your family. It's not like Wilburton's that big of a town. If you've got an uncommon last name, chances are pretty good the people who share it are related to you, right?"

When he finished his excited little rant, I gulped. His idea put another wrinkle in this afternoon's plans—a new level of anticipation and fear.

"Let's . . . uh . . . let's take this one step at a time, okay?" I laughed shakily.

"Yeah. Yeah, you're definitely right. One step at a time."

Once again, he couldn't fool me. Though he sounded serious and he frowned as he nodded, his eyes sparkled with his new idea. I didn't even try to hide my sigh this time as he hurried toward the back door.

We entered the school and strode through its

halls—each of them itching at me with familiarity, just as the buildings themselves had done previously—before we reached two double doors. Through their glass panes I could make out rows and rows of tall bookshelves. I grabbed the fabric of my skirt and began twisting it wildly.

With one hand pressed against a door, Joshua looked down at me. Though he seemed a little less eager now, his expression was still resolved. Whether I liked it or not, he was going into that room.

"Ready?" he asked.

*No.*

"Sure," I squeaked aloud.

He nodded and pushed open one of the doors. I tried to clear my throat of the stupid squeak, steeled myself a bit, and then followed him into the library.

A long reception desk guarded the entrance. Its counter was piled high with returned books, and its sides were taped up with a cluster of inspirational posters. One proclaimed YOU CAN DO IT!, so I gave that poster a spiteful glare.

Joshua walked purposefully toward the back of the library, and I followed behind him as he wove through the rows of shelves. Finally, Joshua stopped between the last row of bookcases and the farthest wall of the library.

We were in the reference section, judging by all

the outdated dictionaries and encyclopedias. Joshua bypassed these in favor of a few shelves near the floor. He crouched down and began running his index finger along a row of thin books, each covered in black or purple. I shuddered.

Yearbooks.

After only a few moments, Joshua apparently found the group of books he was seeking. He began pulling out handfuls, reading their spines before putting them back or tucking them into the crook of his arm. When he eventually stood, he held about ten Wilburton High School yearbooks. I leaned to one side in order to stare at their spines. Printed there in varying shades of metallic ink were dates, all ranging from the 1990s to the mid–2000s. I leaned back up and stared at Joshua, terrified.

Joshua, however, was all business as he carried the stack of yearbooks over to a desk. He separated the books into two piles on the desktop, drew out one chair for me, and sat down in his own. I slipped into my chair and folded my hands in my lap, unsure of what to do next.

Joshua pushed one of the stacks closer to me and then pulled the other toward him. He opened the yearbook on top of his stack and flipped through its pages until he found the first one with student pictures. Placing a finger on the page, he began to scan the photos, comparing each face to the corresponding name printed near the margins.

After he'd done so for a few minutes, I cleared my throat. He glanced up at me, still frowning in concentration. Then he frowned harder and tilted his head.

"Why aren't you looking through your books?" he whispered. I answered in my regular voice, although the words themselves came out soaked in embarrassment.

"Because I can't open the books, Joshua."

"Huh?"

I stared down at my lap and began to scratch at my dress with one fingernail. "I told you—you're the only thing in the living world I can feel or affect. I can't open doors, remember? So why would I be able to open a book?"

I just shrugged, but Joshua tucked a finger under my chin and lifted my head, holding it up until I met his gaze. When I looked, he was still frowning.

"Oh." Joshua now sounded embarrassed, too. "I guess I wasn't thinking. Sorry."

I shrugged again, this time smiling wanly. "No big deal."

He shook his head, not fooled, but returned the yearbook without another comment. He scooted the book closer to me on the desktop and leaned over as he flipped the pages, clearly intending for me to search with him. I chuckled a little to myself. Obviously, no death-related disability could get me out of going through these yearbooks with him.

We sat there, flipping through page after page in book after book, to no avail. We chose the books in no particular order, jumping from the 2000s to the 1990s and back again. I made no effort to point out the inefficiency of this process to Joshua, since each page-flip made my stomach drop in anticipation.

At one point Joshua looked down at his watch impatiently. It was almost 2:40, only fifteen minutes until the end of school. As he read his watch, I could see one emotion all over his face: frustration at the apparent failure of his brilliant plan. He grabbed one of the few books left on the stack, handling it with less care than the others and flopping it open to the first page.

That's when it happened.

The first page was as innocuous as those of the other yearbooks. It boasted a picture of a cartoon man in a hardhat (a Digger, apparently the school's mascot), and the dates 1998 to 1999. Nothing out of the ordinary.

The second page, however, was much different. This second page contained a large, full-color photograph of a girl. Underneath the picture was a caption, which read:

*In Loving Memory of Amelia Elizabeth Ashley*
*April 30, 1981—April 30, 1999*

I stopped breathing. Then I began to choke.

I stood up suddenly, forcefully. The chair in which I'd been sitting flew back across the tiles with a loud screech before it slammed against the library wall.

My head swung around toward the sound. I stared at the chair, openmouthed. It seemed ordinary enough—a red plastic seat atop thin metal legs. Just a plain old chair. And the first object in the living world, other than Joshua, I'd been able to move since my death.

The thought of my death sent my head flying back around to the photograph in the yearbook. To the girl in it, and the name under it.

The chair would have to wait.

This picture scared the hell out of me. I wanted nothing more in this world than to turn away from it. But I was transfixed.

The girl in the picture stared up with the tiniest smile on her lips. The smile curved up just a bit at the corners; it was pleasant but wary, as though the girl had heard something funny but wasn't sure if it was okay to laugh. Her eyes—a bright, woodsy green that matched her dress—sparkled with the laugh. Her wavy brown hair fell past her shoulders and framed her thin, oval face. A pink flush couldn't quite cover the tiny freckles sprinkled across her cheeks and the bridge of her nose.

She looked timid and sweet, but also vibrant. And very alive.

A drop of liquid fell from my chin and hit the page, darkening into a round little spot on the girl's neck. I wiped at my cheek, reflexively knowing the droplet was a tear—my tear.

"That's me in the picture, isn't it?"

I couldn't even look at Joshua, couldn't pull my eyes away from the picture as I spoke. I whispered, as if a loud noise might break the spell that had fallen over us. Nothing but silence answered me. Then—

"Told you you're beautiful."

I turned toward the soft sound of his voice. Actually, only my head moved, since my body appeared to be anchored to the desk. I didn't realize until now that I'd gripped the edge of the desk with both hands, knuckles clenched to white above the wood grain. Under my fingertips, I could feel the slick surface of the wood breaking through the numbness. This sudden, physical sensation didn't surprise me in the least; actually, I was kind of shocked I hadn't splintered the desk with the force of my grip.

I wasn't the only one in shock, either. Joshua stared back at me; belief, disbelief, and a multitude of other emotions played across his face. But no matter how disparate his changing facial expressions might be, each of them told me the same thing.

He knew. Beyond any doubt, beyond any wish, beyond any hope. He knew I was Amelia Elizabeth Ashley. And I was dead.

I didn't say anything. I couldn't.

Joshua slowly rose from his chair. He held out his hands in front of him in a gesture of surrender. The action reminded me of the way he'd approached me three days ago, on High Bridge Road. Like he expected me to run away at any second.

Still moving with absolute care, Joshua placed his hands on either side of my face but didn't touch me. He looked directly into my eyes and raised his eyebrows. Warning me of his next move, or maybe asking permission for it.

Though I didn't respond, he must have sensed some kind of assent on my part. He lowered both of his hands to my cheeks, gently cupping my face. I held perfectly still, even when it felt as if his hands had burned prints onto my skin. Joshua leaned forward and, very softly, pressed his lips to my forehead, just above my eyebrow.

The kiss sent a jolt through my entire body. The sensation was more intense than any I'd felt until now—a pure shock wave rushing along my spine and down each of my limbs. I gasped from the strength of it, dragging in a near-shriek of air.

Reacting to the sound, Joshua tried to pull away to see if I was okay; but I clamped my hands down on his, holding them to my cheeks. I closed my eyes and tried to steady my ragged breath. I shook my head *No,* willing him not to move.

He complied, standing close to me and cupping one side of my face in his left hand while stroking my other cheek with the fingertips of his right hand. Eventually, my breathing began to even itself, coming out in a slightly less alarming way than its previous pant. After a few seconds I released his hands and nodded to let him know I was better. Far from okay. But better.

Joshua ran his fingers down my cheek once more and then dropped his hands. I felt him move away from me, though I didn't open my eyes. I could hear him rustling around somewhere a few feet behind me. Slowly, I opened one eye, then the other. I turned my head to peek at my picture, which stared up innocently from the desktop.

I was still staring at the picture when Joshua walked back around me and placed something on the table next to my picture. It was a phone book.

"Trying to find the Ashleys?" My voice broke and cracked, as if it had been hours since I'd last used it instead of minutes.

"Only if you want to," Joshua whispered.

"Open it," I said, not taking my eyes from the desk.

Joshua leaned around me and bent over the phone book. He flipped through each of the vellum-thin pages until he reached one specific page. He traced his index finger down the list of *A* names and then stopped, leaving his finger in the middle of the page. I leaned over him and stared at the spot where he pointed. Above his finger, one line held my attention.

Accompanying a phone number and an address was a singular name. A very familiar name.

*Ashley, E.*

I stared at that line for an eternity. I stared at it when the bell rang, signifying the end of the school day. I stared at it while the other students packed up their things and left Joshua and me frozen in the back row of the library.

Finally, I stirred.

"E. Ashley—that's probably my mom, Elizabeth. I don't know why my dad's initial isn't there. His name is Todd. Todd Ashley."

My voice came out flat, unemotional. Nonetheless, I began to shake a little.

The image of that printed name and its missing companion floated around in my head. Then, mixing in with the names were flashes of other, blurrier images. The faces associated with those names. The faces of my family.

Forgotten faces. Impossibly, irrevocably forgotten. And yet, like my flashes of memory, here they were—regaining shape and form in my mind.

I wrapped my arms around my frame, hugging myself tightly. Joshua moved closer, almost touching me but not quite. We stayed like that for a while—ten minutes could have been ten hours for all I knew—until, miraculously, I felt . . . lighter.

In that lightness was the strangest, most inexplicable flood of relief.

I don't know how it was possible, but Joshua seemed to sense the change in me. This time, he was the one to break the silence.

"So, Amelia Elizabeth Ashley," he said quietly. Carefully. "Do you want to see your family again . . . today?"

My whispered response shocked me, mostly because it was true.

"Yes. I do."

*Chapter*
# FIFTEEN

Joshua guessed it would take us at least twenty minutes to drive from the school to the first address he'd written down on a scrap of notebook paper. He pulled out a tiny phone. (I'd seen cell phones while alive, I was sure, but none of them could fit in the palm of your hand like this one.) From this practically invisible device, he called his mother to let her know he'd be home late. With that responsibility handled, Joshua fell quiet as he drove, casting the occasional, worried glance in my direction. I'm sure he could tell I was too lost in my own thoughts to carry on a conversation.

But, to be fair, the things in my head weren't exactly thoughts. They were remembered images and sounds, accompaniments to the hazy, long-buried memories of my family. People who had all but vanished from my mind, until the past hour. People whom I would see, for the first time in more than a decade, in just a few minutes.

First, and most disconcertingly, I saw my father's face. A strange haze clouded most of the memory, obscuring the setting and the other people in the scene. But there, clear and unmistakable in the center of the image, was my father. His green eyes crinkled at the corners as he ran one hand through his thinning blond hair. Then, in a blur, the image cut over to a woman. My mother. She was sitting on a threadbare recliner, the one in our living room maybe, and looking up at my father. No, not at my father. At the small, amber-colored drink in his hand. Dad liked to drink at Christmas, and my mother didn't approve.

Soon these remembered images blurred with the scenery flying outside the car windows. The effect started to make me dizzy and, in turn, nauseated. This was an odd feeling, considering ghosts couldn't get sick. I leaned over slightly, placing my elbows on my knees and rubbing my temples with my fingertips.

"Amelia? You okay?"

Without taking my head from my hands, I peeked at Joshua from between my fingers. While trying to watch the road, he was also sneaking as many worried, sidelong glances at me as he could without driving into a ditch.

I sighed and leaned back against the seat.

"No, I'm not okay," I answered with a wan smile. "I just keep . . . remembering things. People, actually. My family. So, naturally, I'm terrified."

"Yeah, me too, kind of."

I frowned. This afternoon Joshua had been absolutely confident—confident that, in discovering my name and my family, we'd made the right choice. Now his confidence seemed shaken.

"Why should you be scared, Joshua?"

"Well, I guess I'm mostly nervous," he said. "For you."

I nodded, laughing quietly. "Would you be mad if I said I'm glad to hear it?"

Joshua laughed too. "Not at all. We're kind of in this together, right?"

"I guess so," I said with a faint smile.

"So," Joshua went on, "do you want to talk, to distract ourselves? We can still talk about the serious stuff, if you want."

I thought about his suggestion. Actually, a distraction from my memories sounded nice. Even if we had to talk about the memories themselves. At least then I wouldn't be alone with them in my own head.

"Yeah," I said. "That sounds like a good idea."

Joshua nodded. He gave me a quick, worried glance, the kind he gave when he wanted to ask something tough but wasn't sure if the question would offend me.

"Something on your mind, Mr. Mayhew?" I forced the playful note into my voice, pressing it past my tension and nerves.

"Well, I was just thinking it kind of sucks."

"What sucks?" I asked with a smile.

"That you died on your birthday."

My smile faded. "Oh. That."

Joshua didn't respond with anything but a raised eyebrow. I could tell from his expression that he wasn't trying to push me for more answers. He just didn't know what to say next.

"Apparently," I said, not waiting for Joshua to find his response.

"Apparently?"

"Apparently I died on my birthday. I don't actually remember my death."

"But you're starting to remember other stuff? Like your family?"

"Yeah, sort of. But not my death. Well, nothing except the actual dying part. I can't remember why, or how, I was in the water when I drowned." I shuddered a little and went on. "Maybe that's just part of being a ghost. Not remembering most of the death stuff."

"Do you even want to know about the rest of it?"

"You know, I'm not sure. Let's see. . . ." I searched for the most apt analogy but could only find a weak one. "The closest thing I can compare it to is being in a car accident, or breaking your leg or something, and not wanting to look because it will make you sick, but really wanting to at the same time."

Joshua fell silent for a moment. He frowned heavily, just before shooting me a wary look.

"Do you think the problem is psychological maybe?" he asked. "Instead of supernatural?"

"Huh?" I frowned too, and tilted my head to one side.

"Well, maybe you're subconsciously blocking those memories. I mean, if other memories are coming back to you but not those."

I twisted my mouth, pondering this suggestion. After a few seconds I nodded. "It's possible, yeah."

He glanced at me again, worry still in his eyes. When he spoke, he did so with hesitation. "So did you . . . um . . . kill yourself, you think?"

I lowered my head. *Of course he'd have to ask this question.*

Aloud I said, "You know, I kind of always thought I did. My death seemed pretty depressing, so it wasn't too big a stretch to think my life must have been too. But lately, since I met you, I'm not so sure. I know I fell off the bridge. Now I'm just not sure I jumped."

Joshua surprised me by taking my hand from my lap and lacing his fingers through mine. "Maybe you didn't. In fact . . . I'd bet you didn't. That's just not like you. Not at all."

My head flew up, and I gave him a small but widening smile. The ache in my chest radiated outward in deliciously warm arcs, mimicking the heat I now felt in my hand.

So maybe Joshua was wrong. So what? Maybe I had killed myself, maybe I hadn't. Likely, we would never know. But Joshua didn't believe I had. He believed I was better than that, in life and now. His belief touched something inside me, something that insisted that maybe, just maybe, I hadn't done anything to deserve this death.

Before I could tell Joshua as much, he suddenly glanced out my window and frowned. He slowed down before turning the car onto a side road.

Realizing what was happening, I stared at Joshua with a renewed sense of terror. I refused to look outside the car for even a second and kept my eyes locked on his grim expression. For the briefest moment I willed myself to go back into the fog. Just for some peace, some quiet preparation for what was about to follow. Joshua's voice, however, forced me to focus.

"We're here."

To my surprise, his eyes mirrored my own panic. I gulped, clenching his hand even harder. He squeezed back to let me know that he didn't mind if we sat like this for the entire afternoon, staring at each other instead of at the house behind us.

But we couldn't stay like this forever.

With painful, near-creaking slowness, I let go of Joshua's hand and turned in my seat until I faced out the passenger side window.

Across a postage-stamp lawn was a tiny clapboard house, no more than a thousand square feet in size and no less than fifty years old. The exterior's white paint had started to peel a long time ago, and the roof sagged under the remembered weight of a half century of snow. Behind the building, overgrown grass spread out until it met the thick woods that bordered the backyard.

This was my parents' house. My house.

Two ruts cut parallel paths in the dirt next to the house. It was a not-quite driveway, which was now free of cars.

"They aren't home."

The words tumbled out of my mouth before I had time to think about their meaning.

I blinked, shocked at the ease of that statement. I

hadn't seen this ramshackle little house in many years, much less seen my parents' cars parked outside of it. Yet I suddenly remembered exactly what this house looked like when it was empty.

Joshua's voice nearly made me jump in my seat.

"Do you want to go see it?"

I nodded without looking at him. I didn't even tear my eyes away from the house when Joshua got out of the car, opened my door, and helped me out onto the grass. Dazed, I walked hand in hand with him across the front lawn. It wasn't until he took one step onto the front porch that I yanked on his hand, jerking him to a stop.

"What are you going to say?" I asked. "If someone's actually here?"

"I was just thinking about that. What do you think? Vacuum salesman?"

"You don't have any vacuums!" I hissed.

"Fund-raising for the baseball team?"

"Better. Kind of."

Somewhat prepared, we walked up to the front door. As Joshua let go of my hand, he turned to me and gave me his most reassuring smile, which, unfortunately, twitched with almost as much fear as I felt. Then he raised his right hand and rapped on the door.

The door immediately swung open under Joshua's touch. We both gasped and stepped backward.

On the other side of the door, a dark, shotgun-style hallway led to the back of the house. It took us a few seconds to realize that the hallway was empty and that no one had opened the door from the inside. The door must have already been ajar. Joshua's knocking had merely pushed it open.

I had the briefest flash—an image of that door swinging open beneath a woman's hand.

"My mom always did that," I whispered, nodding. "She'd forget to close the door when she went out somewhere."

"What should we do?" Joshua whispered back.

"Let's go in."

I pushed past him, squeezing myself between the doorjamb and the door until it was too late for either Joshua or me to argue with this plan. After he closed the door behind us, I let my eyes adjust to the dimness inside.

We were standing in the only hallway, off of which were several rooms. To my immediate right was a living room, crammed with secondhand furniture and an old TV. The entrance to another room was just visible in the back, to the right. Across from it I could see a tiny kitchen, next to what appeared to be an even tinier bathroom. I turned slightly to my left and stared at the door beside me, which was shut tight against the hallway.

However cool I was trying to play it, I had to stifle a

gasp of shock at the flood of familiarity in this house: the sound of the creaking hardwood floors under Joshua's feet; the *tap-tap-tap* of the leaky kitchen faucet in the back of the house; the sight of the faded, pink paper *A* taped in the middle of the closed door to my left.

I couldn't help it. A whimper escaped my mouth just as I clutched my hand to my heart. The ache that now gripped my chest was new, and not even a fraction as pleasant as the one I felt with Joshua. This ache was terrible. It tightened against my lungs until I could hear myself begin to hyperventilate.

In an instant Joshua had wrapped his hands around my waist and pulled me to his chest. It was the closest we'd ever been, but I couldn't seem to spare a fraction of my concentration to enjoy that fact.

"We can leave," Joshua murmured into my hair. "We can leave right now."

I shook my head.

"No." The word was low and rough. "I can't leave yet."

I could feel Joshua nodding as he pulled me even closer. We stayed that way until I stopped gasping. Once my breath had steadied, Joshua released me. He looked me up and down, saving his longest look for my face.

"You know," I said with a shaky laugh, "I think I might have been an asthmatic when I was alive. With all the gasping and stuff."

Joshua just shook his head at my failed attempt at levity. "Do you really want to stay?"

I pressed my lips together into a tense line and nodded.

"Well . . . what do you want to see first then?" he asked.

I thought about that for a moment and then flicked my head at the door to my left.

"Could we go into my old bedroom?"

"O-kay."

Like he always did when approaching something with caution, Joshua drew out his long *O*. He still sounded worried, still sounded as if he wasn't sure I was ready for all of this. I kept my expression impassive and tried to look ready for anything. Seeing this (but obviously not believing it entirely), Joshua reached across me to turn the handle of my old bedroom door.

The door opened, and when it did, it released something I hadn't anticipated.

A slight gust of warm air brushed my skin. I could *feel* it—feel its movement and its warmth. I could smell the air, stale from being trapped in the room for God knows how long, but with a faint hint of old perfume. It smelled vaguely of fruit . . . maybe peaches, or nectarines.

As quickly as the sensations had come, they were gone again, leaving me numb. But the sensations had come, that was the point. I closed my eyes briefly and savored the thought.

When I opened my eyes, I was surprised to find that I'd already crossed the threshold. I turned back to see Joshua hovering uncertainly in the doorframe. I smiled at him and gestured him into the room with one hand.

The room was tiny, with barely enough space for both Joshua and me to stand in it. Shoved against one wall was an old dresser and shoved against another was a twin-sized bed, which overflowed with purple and green pillows. Above the bed, a handful of gold paper stars hung from the ceiling by threads. They matched the curtains, which someone had closed against the light, rendering useless the small telescope propped against the window.

Even in the gloom I could see the only collection of items I'd ever owned: my books. Stacks of books, rising from the ground to almost waist height and running along every free inch of the tiny room. I'd found these books in used bookstores, thrift store bins, library sales. Each book had been read, reread, and then lovingly placed on top of a stack.

I pressed my hand to my heart again. This time I didn't feel the need to gasp or sob. I felt . . . sad, yes. Deeply, deeply sad. But also glad to see all of this again. To know I had existed. That I still existed, at least in some form.

I smiled slightly and turned to Joshua. I flicked my head back to the hallway, indicating that it was time to leave the room. He picked up on my cue and turned around quickly—ready, I think, to be away from these images. *I know the feeling,* I thought as I moved to follow him.

Before I left the room, though, I peeked back over my shoulder. Just to memorize the tiny space one last time.

That's when I noticed the thick layer of dust over everything. A transparent brown film covered the gold stars, the dresser, the books. I paused, frowning at the dust.

Though my parents hadn't changed a thing in this room, they certainly hadn't entered it in a long time, either.

For some reason that saddened me even more. Not because my mother didn't trudge each day into some room-sized shrine to me, dust rag in hand. But because my parents had kept the room this way *and* sealed it up, as though it were some tomb, filled with things too painful to come near.

Which it likely was.

I shook my head, stepping out of the room and into the hallway without another backward glance.

"Close it, please," I asked Joshua, my voice hoarse. He did so without a word, pulling the door shut behind me and sealing the tomb once again. I shuddered at the sound.

Joshua came and stood beside me. I looked up at him grimly, too spent to even attempt a smile.

"Was that hard?" he asked.

I just nodded.

"If it makes you feel any better, I think you have almost as many books as I do."

"Had," I said. "I *had* almost as many books as you do."

He frowned. "Amelia, you can have all my books."

"Which would be awesome, if I could ever turn the pages."

Joshua ducked his head, and I felt instantly ashamed of myself.

I ducked down too, met his eyes, and gave him a slight smile. "But you know, Joshua, no matter how I feel right now, that's still very good to know."

"Hope so," he said with a timid, answering smile.

I took a huge breath, drawing my shoulders up and then letting them fall back into place. I felt raw, and oddly bruised. Yet there were still more things I wanted to see.

"Mind if we check out the living room real quick? I think . . . my mom used to keep a bunch of pictures in there."

"Not at all." Joshua swept his arm toward the living room, so I crossed in front of him and into the room. I scanned the walls until I found it: the little shelf my mother had nailed to the far wall in place of a mantel.

Joshua and I wove our way through a maze of chairs and ottomans until we stood directly in front of the shelf. It was still cluttered with the same pictures, each framed in cheap plastic or wood. A few new items also decorated this area, most noticeably the two large photos now hanging above the shelf.

I recognized the photo on the left immediately. It was my senior picture, the very one Joshua and I had found in the yearbook this afternoon. My living face stared out at us, surrounded by an expensive-looking wooden frame. To my horror, someone had draped wide black ribbons around the perimeter of the frame. The ribbon on the left side had been printed with my name in silver, metallic ink; the ribbon on the right proclaimed the dates of my birth and death. The otherwise pretty picture was thus transformed into the kind of macabre memento you might leave on someone's grave.

The embarrassing display, however, wasn't the thing that horrified me most. Instead, it was the other picture hanging over the shelf, the one directly to the right of mine.

The photo itself didn't scare me. Under any other circumstances, it would have made me smile. The photo was of my father, taken around the time he and my mother had married. Back then my father still had a thick mop of hair. His tan skin was less lined than I remembered, but his green eyes still creased at the corners as a result of his huge grin.

Yet, despite the happy tone of my father's photo, I began to shiver uncontrollably.

Because, like my senior portrait beside it, my father's photo was draped in black ribbons.

The ribbon to the left of my father's picture bore the name Todd Allen Ashley. It glinted out at me in the same embossed silver that surrounded my own portrait. I couldn't quite read the ribbon on the right, nor did I want to. No matter what the dates printed on the ribbon read, I knew what they symbolized: a birth date . . . and a death date.

At first the individual pieces of what I saw didn't make sense. But the longer I stared at the photo, the more the details came into horrifying clarity. The moment they all clicked into place, the bottom dropped out from my world.

But I wasn't scared. I wanted it. I wanted darkness, nothingness. I wanted a nightmare right now. I wanted to let the river suck me down, to make me drown or trap me in Eli's horrible netherworld.

I wanted anything but this.

No matter what I wanted, I didn't fall into darkness. I stood motionless in the cramped living room in which my mother probably sat alone, night after night. No daughter to fight with, no husband to talk to.

Because I was dead.

And my father was dead.

I placed my hand over my mouth to stifle a sob. Joshua reached for me, but I pulled away and shook my head.

As if he had just read my thoughts, Joshua whispered, "It's not your fault, Amelia."

"It is. I know it is."

"How?" he urged.

"Look at this place!" I gestured around me, to the ramshackle contents of the room and the entombed bedroom just outside of it. "It all fell apart when I died. It's all fallen apart."

"I know, and it's horrible." Joshua's voice was softer, but still insistent. "Terrible. And I'm sorry, Amelia. But—sometimes it happens. And the important part is, you didn't make it happen."

It didn't seem to matter what Joshua said—I couldn't stop shaking. "I wasn't there, Joshua. I wasn't there when . . . when . . ."

I choked on the thought. Joshua rushed over, reaching out for me; but I forced the words out of my mouth before he could touch me. In fact, I nearly spat the words at the floor.

"I wasn't there when my dad died. Now my mom's all alone, and my dad could be *anywhere*. He could be lost, like I was. Or he could be . . . someplace worse." I shuddered, thinking about Eli's dark world and the poor, trapped souls there. "And I can't do a damn thing about it."

My eyes prickled. I wasn't surprised when one tear managed to course its way down my cheek. But I was stunned when an entire flood of tears followed.

I looked up at Joshua, my mouth open, my face probably the picture of miserable shock. I wiped furiously at my cheeks and stared down at my hands, which were quickly becoming soaked.

"I . . . I've never cried," I stuttered, staring back up at him. "Not like this."

He grabbed my arms and practically yanked me to him.

"Whatever you do, Amelia, it's all right with me." His voice was rough, deepened by emotion.

I was shocked yet again by what the sound of his voice did to my body, no matter how desolate my mind might be. Suddenly, my arms were wrapped fiercely around Joshua's neck. Just as fiercely, he wrapped his arms around my waist and pulled me to him faster than I could pull myself. Now there was no space between us. We were curved against each other;

and when he shifted closer, I thought I might actually stop breathing.

I could feel it all: the pressure of his arms around me, the grip of his fingers at my waist, the warmth of his breath on my skin. Everything I knew about myself and my relationship to the living world told me this was impossible. But that didn't matter right now. What mattered was that I felt alive. I felt *everything*.

Joshua stared down at me, and I could feel the heat of his midnight blue eyes on every inch of my body. When I curled my fingers in the hair at the nape of his neck, he moaned. Once the sound escaped his lips, we didn't even give it a second thought. We leaned into each other and pressed our lips together.

The kiss crashed over me, wave upon wave of fire. The ache exploded across my chest like an atom bomb, incinerating everything in its path. I let it burn me; I let it consume me.

As Joshua parted his lips and moved them against mine, I felt his lips—felt the soft, warm skin of them.

At that moment I *was* the atom bomb. I was the orange, brightly glowing ball of fire. The exact spot where a lit match touches a pool of kerosene.

Then I was cold. Terribly cold.

I opened my eyes and gasped. I began choking and clutching around me, futilely trying to find something to anchor me. Something to help me claw my way out of here.

Because I was suddenly in the black water of the river. And I was drowning again.

*Chapter*
SIXTEEN

hen the oppressive black water finally vanished, I woke up, coughing and sputtering
in the morning sunlight. I found myself
on my knees, leaning over on all fours and clutching the earth as if it were a life preserver. Which, in
essence, it was.

For the longest time I stayed in that position, bent over
and staring at the ground. My hair hung in thick curtains
on either side of my face, blocking my view of everything
but the dry grass and patches of red dirt beneath me.

Then I turned my head only a fraction of an inch to the right. Through my hair I could just make out my surroundings.

The field. The trees. The headstones.

I sat back on my bare heels and wrapped my arms around my chest. Only after providing myself that feeble protection did I shake my hair back so I could see the scene more fully.

I'd had another nightmare, one far worse than any of the others.

It began normally enough: the flailing, the coughing, the general sense of desperation. Soon, though, after I'd quieted from the initial shock of the water, I could hear the strange voices again, the raucous ones that reminded me so much of Eli's netherworld. But this time, in addition to the voices, I heard laughter. Angry, violent laughter, coming from what sounded like a party.

When I looked up to find its source, I saw them: a crowd of figures, standing high above me on High Bridge. Watching me struggle. Before I could make out their faces, I plunged once and finally under the water. Only then did I wake in this graveyard.

Who were the people on the bridge? And why were they watching me with such obvious joy?

These were questions I really couldn't answer. And, of course, they brought up even more questions concerning *why* I could see them in the first place. Maybe I heard and saw them because I'd become more aware lately? Or perhaps it was like Joshua said: I'd repressed most of my memories about my death and now they were returning in vague but painful detail.

*Thanks, nightmares,* I thought wryly, *for being so consistently fun.*

This consistency, of course, led to another thought. A pattern seemed to have emerged in my nightmares, particularly with the way they began. Something to do with my emotional state maybe. After all, the last one began when Eli upset me the night he told me I had no choice but to join him in the darkness. Then this nightmare started with the touch of Joshua's lips.

*No,* I thought with a shake of my head. Not at the moment he first kissed me. But instead, at the moment I'd thought I might explode—from misery at the loss of my father and my mother's forced isolation; from desire, sparked by the feel of Joshua's lips against mine.

At the thought of Joshua's lips, I pushed against the grass and jumped up. I could think about the nightmares later; right now I had more important problems to solve. Such as the fact that a day had passed since our kiss, probably leaving Joshua with more than a few questions about my whereabouts. Without another glance at this terrible place, I broke into a sprint.

Possibly a half hour later—I wasn't sure—I skidded to a stop in the Wilburton High School parking lot. I panted, not from the effort of the run, but from fear that I'd arrived too late to find him.

Luckily, one glance at the back lawn of the school let me know I wasn't too late. All across the lawn, students gathered in little clusters over their lunches, laughing and basking in the sun. I hurried past them, studying each of their faces as I walked.

Not seeing the one face I wanted, I had no choice but to wait outside the cafeteria door, tapping my foot and fidgeting until someone finally pushed the door open. I took one cursory glance at the students coming out of it and, dismissing them, circled around to squeeze inside before the door slammed shut. Once inside the cafeteria, I scanned the room impatiently and then began to walk forward.

I was searching the tables so intently, I didn't see him until I'd almost smacked right into his chest. We both skidded to a stop before impact, less than an inch from each other.

A brief wave of real scent—sweet, musky, warm—washed over me and then disappeared. I raised my head, ever so slowly, until I met his gaze.

I'd found Joshua.

I felt a swell of joy. Joshua, however, appeared as though

he didn't share my feelings. In fact, he looked down at me with no expression at all, his dark eyes unreadable.

"Joshua—," I began, but another voice interrupted mine.

"Mayhew, dude, what's the holdup?"

"Nothing," Joshua shot back without looking at O'Reilly.

"You're blocking the door, handsome," a girl—Kaylen, I think—called from the crowd behind Joshua.

But Joshua still didn't move. He stared down at me in that frozen, immobile way. Eventually he stirred, keeping his gaze locked onto mine but turning slightly backward.

"Just remembered," he told his friends, "I forgot something in my car."

"Then could you, like, go get it?" Jillian whined. "Because 'Joshua Mayhew' isn't a tardy excuse for the rest of us."

"It isn't an excuse for me, either. Just ask Ms. Wolters." He turned fully to the crowd behind him and gave them his normal, broad grin. But when he turned back to me, the grin faded and his eyes finally flashed with real emotion. He shrugged and pushed past me, exiting the cafeteria.

I felt cold all over. Colder, even, than when the chilly air in the netherworld cut me to the bone. I easily recognized the emotion that had flashed in Joshua's eyes, although I'd never seen it there before.

It was fury. Joshua was furious.

Trembling, I found an empty space between some of the students who were filing through the door and followed them. Once outside, my head swiveled around to find Joshua. I spotted him, already several paces away from his friends and striding quickly toward the school parking lot.

Finally, I was able to break through the crowd, and I hurried to catch up with Joshua. One look at the rigid muscles in his neck, however, made me hesitate. I stalled several feet behind him, with one foot on the curb and the other wavering just above the asphalt.

Joshua reached his car, opened the passenger side door, and made a show of digging around on the floorboard for his imaginary forgotten item. Standing upright, he gave me a sidelong glance and jerked his head toward the open door. Both gestures gave off a decidedly angry air.

As my foot dropped to the asphalt, I gulped. I trudged past him and then crawled into the car. Joshua slammed my door shut and, once he was in the car, jerked his own door shut as well. I winced at the sound.

Joshua didn't look at me. He just sat there, hands gripped to the steering wheel and eyes glued to the dashboard. A thick silence fell over us. It seemed to squeeze out all the air in the car and, in the process, smother me. I would have preferred any amount of door slamming to this.

"I had a nightmare—," I began lamely.

"Is that why you disappeared into thin air?" He spat out the interruption without taking his eyes off the dashboard.

"I did what?" I asked.

"You disappeared. Right after I kissed you. Or you kissed me. Whatever. We were kissing, but when I opened my eyes, you were gone."

"Joshua, I—I had no idea it happened like that," I sputtered. "That I just disappeared. All I know is that I was kissing you and then I had a nightmare. I woke up less than an hour ago, and I ran straight here."

He finally turned toward me, scowling. "What do mean, 'nightmare'? You had a bad dream or something?"

"Not exactly." I held his gaze while I explained. "Every time I have a nightmare, I don't really sleep. I just go unconscious and—apparently—disappear from wherever I am before the nightmare starts. It's like I black out, and then suddenly I'm drowning again. I call them nightmares because eventually I wake up."

Joshua remained silent for a long time. When he finally

spoke, his words still rang with disbelief. But I heard another chord in his voice, too—that of hurt.

"But you just woke up an *hour* ago?" he asked. "It's been almost a full day since you disappeared. How is that even possible?"

I struggled to breathe normally. Calmly. "Like I said, sometimes I just go unconscious. After that I wake up somewhere else, and apparently some *time* else."

"So . . . you really didn't just run away from me?"

Now the wounded tone in his voice was perfectly clear. I realized then that all his anger probably hid a simple truth: my sudden disappearance had hurt him. A lot.

Still, I threw my hands up in the air in exasperation at his stubborn refusal to believe me. "Why would I want to run away from you, Joshua?"

"Because I kissed you."

"I kissed you back," I pointed out, and then added, "and I *wanted* to."

Joshua frowned, but when he spoke, his voice was significantly softer. "Are you sure, Amelia?"

I nodded vigorously. "Yes! Yes, to a million degrees! It's just . . . well, I got really upset about my parents, and I guess I sort of lost it. After all, I'm a *ghost*. You know that."

"Actually," he started hesitantly, "I kind of thought that had something to do with it. Like you were afraid I was going to exorcise you."

I blinked. "W-what? Were you thinking of doing that?"

"No!" He shook his head, looking surprised. "No way. I just thought maybe you'd be worried about it."

"Well, *now* I am," I gasped.

"Don't be," he said, suddenly intent. "I wouldn't do that, no matter what. No one could make me."

I blew out one frustrated puff of air. "Well, we've certainly got our problems, haven't we?"

Joshua gave a bitter little laugh. "Yeah, the list isn't a short one."

"The nightmares are on there," I pointed out. "So is the fact that you're technically supposed to exorcise me."

*And let's not forget about Eli,* I added in my head. *Or my inability to help my mother and save my father from darkness. Or how about what happens when you age and I don't, or when your grandmother finally decides enough is enough as far as I'm concerned . . . ?*

For now I kept those thoughts strictly internal. Aloud, I simply added, "I wish I could come back to life and make this easier on us. I really do."

Joshua seemed to be thinking along the same lines. He frowned heavily and then dragged his hand through his hair toward the back of his neck.

"This is going to be complicated, isn't it?" he asked.

I nodded. "Seems like it, yeah. You know, I have no idea how this works. The nightmares, the whole 'you and me, Seer and ghost' thing. I just don't know any of the . . . rules. . . ."

The last word trailed out of my mouth, falling like a feather from my lips. It drifted away under the weight of something greater, something that had just occurred to me.

Two people—well, one person and one spirit—knew the rules and could help me. Could help *us*.

As I formed my plan, my eyes became transfixed on an invisible point outside the car. I started to speak in a businesslike clip to distract myself from the dark turn our conversation had taken.

"Here's the deal, Joshua: I think I know someone who might explain what's happening. Someone who could actually help us understand how I . . . *work*, I guess. But I've got to go somewhere this afternoon to see if my idea is even possible. So can you meet me there after school? And can you trust me to be there?"

"I think I can."

"Good," I repeated. I bit my bottom lip and nodded emphatically. "Now, could you tell me where your grandmother is right now?"

It didn't take long to walk to the largest church in town, nor did it take long for someone to push open one of the doors and unknowingly let me inside. As Joshua had said, the church swarmed with people preparing for tonight's midweek service.

Finding Ruth within the church also proved easy enough: she was the one at the front of the chapel commanding a small troop of women in an imperious tone. Each time she shook her head—probably to reject some lower-ranking person's suggestion—she reminded me of Jillian, and I had to stifle a smile.

Any hint of the smile disappeared the moment Ruth turned around and caught sight of me. Upon meeting my gaze, she froze in mid order and let out a strangled noise of protest. Then, without breaking our eye contact or finishing her sentence, Ruth pushed past her minions and marched down the center aisle of the church.

She only released me from her icy glare when she stormed past and hissed, "Outside. Now."

I followed Ruth outside the double doors of the chapel to the bottom of the church steps, where she waited with her back to me.

"Ruth . . . I mean, Ms. Mayhew," I started, keeping my voice steady. Self-assured. "I know you don't want to talk to me, but—"

"You shouldn't be near such a sacred place," Ruth interrupted, spinning around to face me. She didn't meet my eyes but instead glared up at the church as if it, and not some teenage ghost, had addressed her. "You aren't worthy to be here, much less to exist."

Suddenly, I wasn't cowed, or even respectful. I was angry. So angry, in fact, I forgot what I'd undoubtedly been taught about respecting my elders.

"Well, it's not like I turned into a pillar of salt when I walked through the doors," I snapped. "So obviously, *someone* divine is okay with my existence."

Ruth shook her head stubbornly. "If you're dead and still walking this earth, you're an abomination."

I tried, unsuccessfully, not to shout. "Abomination? How dare you! You don't know anything about me."

"I know enough," she said. "I know if you're still wandering around, chances are good you came from that bridge."

She had me there. I could only sputter, "Yeah . . . but . . ."

"But nothing. Even if you *aren't* evil at this point, you're—at best—an empty vessel that evil will eventually fill, and use. You're unclaimed, but you won't be for long. I'm sure *he* wants you . . . the boy who haunts that place. The one we've been hunting for years. So now that you're here too, our work just got more complicated."

The memory of Eli's warnings about my nature— and my future—flashed unbidden into my mind. Then something else struck me. As I'd suspected when Joshua first described the Seers, Ruth and her friends knew about Eli, at least vaguely. They'd been hunting him for years, apparently without success.

"How do you know all these things about ghosts, and about High Bridge?" I asked.

"Because I've been studying the supernatural most of my life and watching that bridge for decades. I know what happens to the very few souls who don't move on to an afterlife. And I know what happens to the ones who haunt High Bridge: they become slaves to it, just like that boy we've been trying to catch."

"But I'm not haunting High Bridge," I protested weakly.

Ruth finally met my gaze and gave me a cold smile. "You're haunting my grandson. That's enough for me."

So this must have been what she meant that night at the Mayhews' house when she'd said I wasn't what she'd expected: although dead and freely roaming, I wasn't the "boy" she'd been trying to catch. Even so, Ruth obviously intended to treat me in the same manner as Eli. As if I were some evil, rogue spirit.

I held my head as high as it would go, considering how much I'd started to tremble. "Joshua likes me too, you know. I'm not haunting him against his will."

"That doesn't matter. He'll understand his role as a

Seer soon enough, and then he'll make the right choice."

Ruth nodded, as if to emphasize the inevitability of this conclusion. But something about her words made me pause. I tilted my head to one side.

"Just so I understand all the rules: Seers get a choice to participate in this battle?"

She waved her hand dismissively. "That question doesn't really matter since *every* Seer has participated after they've had their triggering event."

"Until now," I pointed out.

Ruth blinked, obviously surprised. She recovered fast, though, and shook her head. "Joshua hasn't made his choice yet. He wouldn't have, without consulting me first."

"Don't be so sure," I answered, speaking softly but with a certainty even Ruth couldn't doubt. However angry Joshua had been (and might still be) with me, I believed him when he promised he wouldn't use his gift against me. Ruth looked as if she believed it too, now.

She stared at a point past me, not really looking at anything in particular. Thinking. Then, more to herself than to me, she began to murmur.

"I was biding my time with Joshua. Waiting for the right moment to tell him about his heritage. But maybe that was a mistake. . . ."

She trailed off, and I took advantage of her distraction

to push the issue further.

"If Joshua made a choice you didn't think he could make, then doesn't it make sense that I could do the same thing? That I could choose not to be evil?"

Pursing her lips into a thin, prideful line, Ruth drew herself up to her full height. "Joshua can deny his nature all he wants, but eventually he'll come back to it. He has to."

I raised one eyebrow. "Are you saying *neither* of us has free will?"

Ruth narrowed her eyes; and, for all their beauty, they suddenly appeared predatory.

"Joshua is free to make his mistakes," she said, "for now. But I wouldn't want you to think, for even a second, that we're going to give you the same opportunity of choice."

I felt an ominous little shiver crawl up my spine. "What exactly are you saying?" I whispered.

"I'm saying you'd better get moving to one place or another, because your days in the living world are numbered. We have plans for you, and they don't involve dating my grandson."

The ominous shiver broke free of my spine and turned into an allover tremble, one that threatened to make my teeth clack together. I fought to wear a cold, calm expression and to keep my arms at my sides instead of wrapped protectively around me. Before I could show Ruth how much she terrified me, I had to get out of here.

"Well, thanks for the heads-up," I mumbled, practically leaping down the last few steps.

I moved away from Ruth as quickly as I could, seeking out the shortest path through the church parking lot to the woods surrounding it. I hadn't made it more than a few feet toward the trees when Ruth called out after me.

"We're coming for you in two days, when the moon is waning and our banishing spells are their strongest. So be ready."

Without warning, a stabbing sensation shot through my head. Involuntarily, I hunched my shoulders and bent my neck against the pain. I whipped my head from side to side, uselessly trying to shake off the pain.

Then, like some awful companion to the ache at my temples, a blur of images filled my mind. The images moved at such a dizzying speed across my vision, I couldn't make out their details. They flashed, relentless and brutal in my head, until I felt an actual wave of nausea rise up within me.

The force of the sensation was so disorienting that I stumbled, tripping over my own feet and falling to my hands and knees on the ground. My hands slapped hard against the graveled parking lot, and, suddenly, I could feel the sharp bite of the gravel. It cut into the skin of my palms and knees, breaking through my ghostly numbness at the worst possible time.

At that moment the pain dissipated—so quickly that I almost wondered whether I'd experienced it at all. Still bent over, I shook my head in confusion. I barely had time to ask myself what could have caused the pain before I heard a soft, feminine laugh behind me.

At that moment I knew exactly who had hurt me.

Pushing myself up from the gravel I could no longer feel, I didn't acknowledge Ruth's earlier warnings, or the cruel headache. At least not outwardly. Instead, I sprinted for the woods, waiting until I crossed into them before I broke into violent shudders of fear.

*Chapter*
SEVENTEEN

Long after Ruth disappeared back into the church, I paced among the trees just along the edge of the parking lot. Ruth could probably still see me from a church window if she wanted to, but I wasn't really thinking rationally enough to care.

In fact, for a while I couldn't think at all. I could only feel the phantom clench of terror in my stomach, could only hear my wild gulps for breath. Eventually, though, I calmed down enough to try and make my brain function again.

Once freed from blind terror, however, I couldn't help but imagine all the alternate futures I had in store: exorcism—and obviously, a painful one—at the hands of the ladies of Wilburton Baptist Church; entrapment in the dark netherworld forest, courtesy of a dead guy in skintight pants; or employment as some sort of grim reaper for the dead guy and his evil masters.

And, of course, the worst aspect of each possible future: no Joshua in a single one of them.

"I'm doomed," I said aloud with a hysterical giggle.

"And why exactly are you doomed?"

At the unexpected voice, I spun around, my hands in defensive claws. A quick scan of black hair and midnight blue eyes, however, made all my anger, if not my fear, evaporate.

"Joshua, I'm so sorry." My arms dropped to my sides in defeat. "I thought it would help, but I just ended up making things a million times worse."

"It's okay, Amelia. It's going to be okay." He kept his voice low, soothing.

"How?" I asked, the hysterical edge creeping back into my voice. "How's it going to be okay? How do you know I'm not evil and need to be destroyed? *I* don't even know, and I'm me!"

"Because I just do, that's all."

Joshua stood with one foot on the asphalt of the

parking lot, one on the edge of the grass that led into the woods. With his arms crossed casually over his chest, he didn't look the least bit concerned. When he gave me a reassuring smile, the ache in my chest stirred slightly. But I had to ignore it, for now.

"You have no idea how much that means to me, Joshua, honestly. But even with what we found out about my home and my family, I still know so little about myself—too little to know where I belong or what I deserve."

"What do mean, 'deserve'?"

I dropped my head into my hands. "Basically, your grandmother just told me I deserve to go to . . . hell, I guess; and if I didn't, she and her friends would send me there. In two days."

"Wait—what?"

I sighed, still not looking up at Joshua. "Ruth and her little coven are going to exorcise me in two days."

"No, they aren't," Joshua growled.

My head shot up from my hands. Before I could ask him how he intended to stop them, Joshua lurched forward and closed the space between us. He leaned over me, locking my gaze with those strange-colored, beautiful eyes of his.

"Come with me," he murmured. "Now."

I tried to focus, tried to ignore the intensity of his stare. "Where? Why?"

"To my house. We're going to try and figure out a few things about you."

"But Ruth said—"

"Screw what Ruth said," he interjected. "I live in that house too, and I say you're always welcome. More than welcome, actually."

"Oh."

A number of emotions warred inside me: fear, anger, uncertainty. But now, a jittery kind of happiness warred right beside them. Joshua just had that effect on me.

"So," he said, holding out his hand. "Want to come home with me?"

I smiled and stretched out my hand to his.

During our car ride, I described my conversation with Ruth in greater detail. I finished the story just as we pulled into Joshua's driveway and he killed the engine. Joshua stared silently out at the Mayhews' garden.

Then, frowning, he rested one arm on the steering wheel and turned toward me. "I think I need to apologize for my grandma being such a—"

"Concerned relative?" I offered before Joshua could say something he'd regret.

Joshua just grinned, easily seeing through my effort at diplomacy.

"Concerned." He laughed. "Right." He leaned over

me to open my door and then leaned back, lingering for a moment near me.

"Promise me something?" Joshua asked, still very close to me. I simply nodded, too befuddled by his proximity to say anything even remotely clever.

"Promise we're just going to enjoy tonight? And not worry about Ruth?"

I grimaced. "She's going to make that pretty hard on us, isn't she?"

Joshua shook his head. "She'll be at the church almost all night. After we make it past the rest of my family, it's just you and me."

I felt a slight flush at the thought. I didn't waste more than a second wondering how a dead girl could feel so warm. How could I care, honestly, when anticipating an entire night with him?

"Let's go," I managed to say. Joshua nodded; and quickly we were both out of the car, walking through the garden toward the porch. Crossing the upper deck, Joshua came to the back door first and opened it for me.

As I passed through the open doorway, he pressed his hand against the small of my back to guide me forward. The mere pressure of his hand played havoc with the speed of my breath, but I only had a few more steps to enjoy the sensation. Within seconds we had stepped into the Mayhew kitchen.

Like the last time I saw it, the kitchen bustled with activity. To my immense relief, Ruth hadn't joined her family for dinner, as Joshua had predicted.

To our left, Joshua's father and Jillian stood over a half-constructed salad, laughing. To our right, Joshua's mother hunched over a pot, pouring what looked like an enormous amount of pasta into a serving bowl. She set down the pot and absentmindedly ran a hand through her hair, a gesture I recognized well from her son. Then she crossed over to the kitchen island and began to sort through a small stack of dishes, arranging them for the dinner table.

"Just three plates tonight, Mom," Joshua said by way of announcing himself.

"Oh?" She sounded curious but not offended by her son's request. "Not joining us?"

"Loads of homework." Joshua shrugged, and gave me a covert wink.

"I'm not the only one who has to do the dishes after dinner, am I?" Jillian whined, looking first to her distracted mother, then to her father's back. When both of her parents ignored her pleas, Jillian gave Joshua a small sneer and turned back to the salad, picking angrily at a few protruding leaves.

Joshua ignored his sister and crossed the kitchen to swat his father playfully on the arm.

"You know," Joshua said in a light tone, "they've invented this magical thing called a dishwasher. I hear it's life changing."

His father chuckled. "Yeah. Her name's Jillian."

"Not funny," Jillian protested, still facing the salad. With the palm of her hand, she shoved the bowl away from her. She spun back around toward her family, opening her mouth in what would inevitably be some petulant comment.

She closed it with an audible pop, however, when her gaze landed on the space where I was standing—on the space that should have appeared empty to her.

Like yesterday, her gaze didn't fall on me. Not exactly. But she still stared in my direction and looked as if she were trying, with difficulty, to peer through a heavy screen of smoke. Still without the benefit of her grandmother's powerful sight, Jillian's gaze didn't pierce me . . . couldn't harm me. Yet it made me nervous, and caused me to cast my eyes around the kitchen in the fear Ruth would burst into the room at any moment.

As Joshua had promised, however, Ruth didn't come barging into the room, shouting threats and dropping me to my knees in pain. And eventually, Jillian gave up the effort of peering in my direction. She turned back toward her brother, wearing only a slightly disconcerted expression.

"Nothing in this house is fair," she complained. Joshua began to laugh, which would undoubtedly have angered Jillian further had their mother's sharp command not silenced the entire room.

"Enough!"

Everyone, including me, turned toward the kitchen island where Rebecca Mayhew still stood. She nodded first to Jillian, then to Joshua.

"You, finish the salad. You, get upstairs and avert this crisis, before I make you."

With a groan of protest, Jillian spun back around to the counter and began furiously rearranging the salad, muttering something about fairness under her breath. Joshua gave his mother a quick salute and then ducked, as if to dodge the displeased glare she aimed at him. Behind us, I heard his father choke back a laugh.

When Rebecca directed the glare at her husband, Joshua used his parents' temporary distraction to catch my eye. He twitched his head to another archway on the opposite side of the kitchen. I took the gesture to mean we were leaving.

With as much grace as I could muster, I wove my way between Jillian and her father, careful not to touch either of them. Almost without thought, I paused next to Jillian, waiting for . . . what, I wasn't sure. When her eyes didn't flicker again in my direction, I crossed to the archway through which Joshua had already passed and turned to look at the kitchen one last time.

Rebecca had returned to setting the table, one hand continually brushing through her pretty hair. Jeremiah stood at the counter, staring down at his daughter with a surprising amount of patience as she finished the salad. When she began muttering angrily again, he picked a small piece of lettuce from the salad bowl and flung it at her. Jillian glared at him indignantly, but after only a beat, her expression softened. She smiled wryly and, without breaking eye contact, plucked the piece of lettuce from her shoulder and flung it back at him.

I smiled at them all and then gave them an impulsive little wave.

In that moment I wanted to join them so badly, it hurt. Aside from the ever-threatening presence of Ruth, the Mayhews represented something I craved, something I'd so obviously lost.

A family.

I pictured my own mother, sitting in that tiny house by herself; I pictured my father, wandering lost in the darkness of the netherworld. As I continued to watch the Mayhews, a melancholy fog started to sneak over me. My thoughts, then, were as sudden as they were dark.

*If Eli gets his way,* I told myself, *you'll never see these people again unless you're trying to ruin their afterlives. And if Ruth is*

*right, you've got less than forty-eight hours left with Joshua, any-*
*way. So, dead girl, you can totally forget about joining his family;*
*you weren't even around to keep your own together.*

I shook my head, hard, as if the movement could dispel
the bitter thoughts. I didn't want to think about those
things tonight, and I'd promised Joshua I wouldn't. So
I spun around through the archway, eager for Joshua's
face to clear away the sadness for a while.

As I'd hoped, Joshua waited for me, leaning against a
wall between the arch and a steep staircase. With a playful smile, he pushed himself off the wall and then crept
closer to me. I kept quiet and still, although the rational
part of my brain knew I didn't have to.

Now only a foot away from me, Joshua leaned in, very
close to my face, and hovered there for a second. After a
few deliciously tense seconds, Joshua leaned to one side.

Though I couldn't feel his breath on my ear, I closed
my eyes and imagined I could. Warm and feathery,
brushing along my skin. For the first time today, I shivered happily.

"Would you be offended," he whispered, "if I asked
you to come up to my bedroom with me?"

I opened my eyes and tried not to choke. I had no idea
about my past life, but I was more than sure a boy hadn't
asked me up to his room since my death. Of course,
there was a first time for everything. So I answered in

the steadiest voice I could.

"That doesn't offend me. And, yes, I'll come up. But just this once; don't expect it to become a habit or anything."

"I wouldn't count on it if I were you." Joshua moved back and flashed me a wicked grin.

I rolled my eyes, all the while telling myself, *Don't let your jaw drop. Don't giggle. Just be cool.*

"Let's go, Joshua," I sighed, trying my hardest to project an aura of total nonchalance.

He laughed and turned to climb the stairs. Whatever amount of "cool" I demanded from myself, it wasn't enough to stop me from shivering once more as I followed him.

*Chapter*
EIGHTEEN

The first step into his bedroom transformed me into a mass of giddy, spastic fidgeting. Although Joshua left the door slightly ajar, the whole room was a heavy black except for my creepy glow. So while Joshua fumbled around, I forced my hands together behind my back and prayed that my nervous squirming wasn't visible in the dark.

I heard a click, and the dim glow of lamplight bathed the room. Joshua stood across the bedroom from me, his hand on a small glass lamp that looked like an old miner's lantern. He looked up at me with an expectant smile, but his expression quickly turned amused when he saw my stance. I stood with my hands nearly glued together behind me, rocking ever so slightly on the balls of my feet.

I flashed him a tense smile. Likely, an unconvincing one.

"You all right?" he asked.

"Yeah." For some reason my answer came out as a high-pitched yip. I instinctively started coughing to cover the sound, and Joshua burst into laughter.

"You know, Amelia, I don't think I believe you."

"It's just . . . it's, well, my first time in a boy's room." Then I shrugged in a little gesture of qualification. "I think."

He laughed again; and, in just a few short steps, he crossed the room and wrapped his arms around me. He laid his hands upon mine, which were still clutched behind my back, and pulled me to him until we were pressed against each other.

We were now as close as we had been when we'd kissed. Maybe even closer. My whole body felt as if it might explode, gloriously and uncontrollably ignited. My breath quickened into a near pant; and when it did so, something entirely unexpected occurred.

I breathed in heavily and felt my head swim from the

suddenness of an actual, physical sensation.

Scent. A fantastic scent—sweet and musky—rushed at me. Not delicate, but appealing nonetheless. And vaguely familiar.

It took me a moment to realize the scent was the same one I'd encountered earlier today when I'd nearly collided with Joshua in the cafeteria.

I stared up at him in delight. His answering smile was surprisingly shy. Gently, he unclasped his hands from mine and released me.

Immediately, the scent disappeared. I dragged in another heavy breath. Nothing. Empty. Void. I exhaled slowly, trying to retain the memory of the scent while also trying not to let my breath sound like the disappointed sigh it threatened to become.

Luckily, Joshua didn't notice. He leaned back against one of the posts of his bed and crossed his arms against his chest. Once again he looked expectant, perhaps waiting on my assessment of his room.

I clutched my hands, this time less tightly, and began to look around me.

As one might expect in so old a house, Joshua's bedroom was small, but cozy. The room was mostly dominated by his dark, four-poster bed. Across from me, a large window faced south, looking out onto the night sky. Beneath the glass, a broad window seat, covered in inviting blue cushions, beckoned.

Then there was the most striking feature of the room: the columns of black, wooden bookshelves that lined the walls. The bookshelves filled the room so completely that I couldn't see an inch of wall space except for a bit above the bed and a narrow border around the window.

Despite the amount of furniture in it, the room felt strangely uncluttered. Its only real disorder came from within the bookshelves. The shelves were literally over-flowing. They were lined with rows upon rows of books, then books stacked on top of the rows, then more books in front of the rows. Leather-bound leaned against paperback. Creased and much-loved covers sat next to fresh, ready-to-read ones. A lifetime's worth of books crammed into the room of a teenage boy.

I walked over to the closest shelf and looked back at Joshua with raised eyebrows. He continued to watch me without speaking, but a slight smile twitched at his lips. The expression was as close to permission as I would get and so I let my fingers trace lightly across some of the spines.

"You have way more books than I did, Joshua."

He shrugged modestly. "Just a few."

"I *know* these titles," I muttered in amazement. "Lots of them."

"I had a feeling you might."

Something in his tone made me turn to look at him again. His expression had softened even further, especially his eyes. The way he now stared at me . . . it made me uncomfortable and happy at the same time. I couldn't think of a word to describe how I felt. Jubilant, maybe, came closest.

Before I could ask him what he was thinking, he cleared his throat and shifted his weight against the bedpost. He uncrossed his arms and tucked one hand into his jeans pocket while running the other through his hair: his classic, awkward pose. It was utterly endearing, as was the blush that suddenly flooded his cheeks.

"So, what do you think?" He gestured with one hand to the room. In turn, I gave him my brightest smile. I had just enough courage to make a confession of my own.

"Before I give you my opinion on the room, I really should tell you—the scenery doesn't really compare."

"Compare to what?" he asked, frowning. I ducked my head and sighed. Then I looked right into his lovely eyes as I spoke.

"You," I said, my voice surprisingly bold, even to my ears.

Joshua's face set again into that intent stare. Several moments passed, each one almost palpable in the charged atmosphere. Then, ever so slowly, he raised one arm and held out his hand. I reached out, too, and placed my hand into his.

The feel of his touch flared across my skin. This time the warmth spread faster, as if each renewed touch intensified the effect. And this time the fiery tingles now reached strange places on my skin, places that made my breath quicken until it was audible. Joshua must have experienced a similar sensation, because he closed his eyes and let out a low moan.

That sound was enough for me. I grasped his hand tightly, almost fiercely, willing the tingles to fade. Within only seconds I could feel his actual skin, rough and warm against mine.

I closed my eyes, too. Still holding on to him, I moved my hand across his and up his arm, to his shoulder. I began to draw closer to him until I stood only inches away from his body. Finally, I rested my hands upon his chest. Once I lost contact with his skin, everything went numb. But for once the numbness was worth it, to be this close to him again. I kept my eyes shut, even when he pressed himself closer to me.

"Amelia?" he whispered, moving his lips right next to my ear. "Can I ask you something?"

"Yes," I nearly gasped.

*Ask me to do anything. Anything!* I practically screamed the words in my head. *I'll kiss you again; I don't care about the risk.*

Joshua paused for a beat and then—

"Do you want to listen to some music?"

That wasn't exactly the question I'd expected. My head darted back, and I stared at him. He wore a mischievous smile, as if he'd read my mind and intentionally avoided the questions I wanted him to ask. I scowled a little.

"Tease," I muttered under my breath. Joshua simply grinned wider. I was more than ready to give him a soft smack on his chest for being so infuriating, but then I noticed his breath was just as uneven as mine. I sighed. As long as he seemed at least mildly ruffled by our contact, I could forgive him.

I carefully lowered my arms from his chest and backed away. Once there were more than a few inches between us, I made a show of stretching and yawning. The picture of utter boredom, totally blasé. Joshua obviously wasn't fooled, because he chuckled softly at my performance.

"So, you're finally going to entertain me? With music, I guess?"

Joshua sat down on his bed and patted a spot next to him on the dark blue comforter. I thrilled a little at the image of us sitting . . . on his bed . . . together, and then tried to accomplish the act as calmly as possible. I couldn't imagine how badly the mood would be ruined if I accidentally slid off the comforter and onto the floor.

"Actually," Joshua said, "the music is part of my devious plan."

I raised one eyebrow. "Your 'devious plan'?"

He nodded, and his face lit up with excitement. He tucked one leg beneath him on the bed and spun around to face me more fully.

"We need to figure out more about your personality, right?"

When I nodded, he went on.

"Well, what tells us more about your personality than your musical tastes?"

I twisted the corner of my mouth in disbelief. "Isn't that a little too simple?"

Joshua shook his head, still smiling. "Not really. Short of finding a time machine and going back to 1999, we aren't going to figure out who you *were*. So why don't we figure out who you are now? Isn't that more important anyway?"

I blinked in surprise. "That . . . well, that actually might be brilliant, Joshua."

He shrugged again. "Just because I can't do differential equations, it doesn't mean I'm totally useless."

I laughed, and then mirrored his position by crossing both of my legs under me.

"So, how do we do this?"

"I play DJ, and you tell me what you like."

"Got it," I said with a firm nod, fighting little jitters of excitement.

"And who knows? Maybe something will be familiar. As long as it's not death metal, I think we can rule you out as a potential Satan worshiper."

"Well, don't judge me if it is." I laughed.

He chuckled and then reached back to his nightstand to fiddle with something on it. I craned my head to get a better look at the object. It appeared to be a tiny, plastic box with a glowing screen sitting atop a small stereo.

"What is that thing?"

Joshua stopped what he was doing without letting go of the little box and threw me a quizzical look over his shoulder.

"You've never seen an MP3 player before?"

"A what?" A defensive note crept into my voice. "Died in 1999, remember?"

"Not a big deal." Joshua gave me a warm smile and went back to working on the machine. "I don't remember whether these things were big back then."

"Probably not for a poor girl from Oklahoma," I grumbled. Joshua simply nodded, too distracted by his efforts to answer aloud.

The machine made some soft clicking noises under Joshua's hands and then a few strains of perfectly clear music flooded the room. I assumed it came from the speakers, and the MP-whatever thing.

"Tell me what you think," Joshua murmured as he

leaned back against his pillow.

The song started with a soft guitar, strumming out a sad little melody. Then a young man's voice joined in, southern and a little slurry. As he sang, drums and a more insistent guitar merged with his voice. The song grew until it transformed into something soaring and plaintive: a sort of lament that managed to sound heartbroken and angry at the same time. Finally, the song began to fade, and I sighed a little

"Don't recognize it?" Joshua asked.

"No, I don't. But I like it."

"It's one of my favorites." Joshua wore a strange expression as he watched me listen to the last few chords of the song. He almost looked proud that we seemed to have the same taste. I smiled a little at the thought.

"What else have you got?" I asked.

"Let's see . . ." He adjusted the machine again and eventually found something appropriate. "This is from the early 2000s. Jillian likes to listen to it when we're in my car. She calls it 'old school,' which is kind of ironic, if you think about it."

Bass pumped from the speakers. After a few thumping drumbeats, a girl's voice warbled out, barely audible over the accompaniment. She wasn't the best singer in the world, but she sang in a throaty manner I guess one could classify as sexy. I wrinkled my nose each time she went off-key.

"Nope," I said after only a few repetitions of the chorus. "Don't know it, don't like it."

"Thank God," Joshua breathed, putting the song to a merciful, early end.

"Akin to death metal?" I asked with a sly grin.

"Close." He laughed. "If you'd liked that one, I might have had to get behind Ruth's 'pitchforks and torches' campaign."

"Har har," I said as Joshua tried to find something else on the MP3 player for us to analyze.

"Here we go. Late 1990s. This is a rock song from when I was a little kid. I actually really like it, but I was too young back then to remember whether it was popular." Joshua made one more click and then looked up again to watch me listen.

This song began much like the first, with a few repeated guitar chords. Then drums and a man's voice—older than the one in the first song but just as slurry—entered the song. When the man growled louder, so did the guitar. The sounds became raw and joyous. It made me recall the way I'd felt in Joshua's car while we drove to school. Free and flying.

And then it made me recall something else.

About halfway through the song, just at the point of its crescendo, my surroundings shimmered and changed.

When the image steadied, I was no longer in Joshua's bedroom. I was in some other room, standing at an open window and looking out over a sunlit yard. My hands gripped a wooden windowsill, its surface rough from the chips in its white paint. A warm breeze hit me from outside. There was just a hint of cool in it, promising fall but still tugging at the end of summer. Somewhere behind me, a radio played the same song I'd just been listening to in Joshua's room. As the man's voice wailed happily, I smiled and swayed to the beat. Free and flying.

Suddenly, the flash vanished.

The residue of light from the flash still ghosted across my eyes in weird black splotches, as though I'd been looking directly at the sun. It took a few seconds before I could see clearly—could see Joshua staring at me expectantly. When I finally could, a smile began to spread across my face.

"I know it!" I crowed. "I know the song! I listened to it once, inside some house . . . mine, I think."

"Excellent!" Joshua cried out, clapping his hands to his knees. Then he leaned closer and whispered, "You know, I don't think anyone who likes so much of the same music as I do can be evil."

"Let's hope not," I whispered back.

"I don't need to hope. I know."

I was simply playing—*we* were playing—and yet I

suddenly believed what he'd just said.

I wasn't evil. Ruth was wrong; Eli was wrong.

I didn't have much proof: only a few guitar chords, some disconnected memories, and a handful of moments with this boy. But I knew it, too, then. Believed it.

I focused harder on Joshua. Although he couldn't know what I'd just been thinking, he stared intently back into my eyes. After a few more seconds of this acute silence, Joshua ducked his head and looked down at the bedspread. He started to fidget, rubbing a loose fiber on his jeans. Mimicking him, I plucked at my skirt.

In our silence I read a few subtle changes. I couldn't speak for Joshua, but I felt as though we'd just shared something very intimate. More intimate than anything we'd experienced up to this point.

Joshua cleared his throat and moved to fiddle with the MP3 player again, maybe in an attempt to ease the tension. He turned on a song I almost immediately recognized: a soft violin concerto. Vivaldi. I smiled slightly as Joshua curled away from the machine and back onto the bed.

"I like this one."

"I figured, since I like it so much too." He gave me a timid smile. "Good music to sleep to."

At the word "sleep," I frowned and moved to get off the bed.

"Should I go now . . . ?"

"No," Joshua said, reaching out to me. "Stay. Talk with me."

I was more than happy to comply. I pulled myself farther onto the comforter and wrapped my legs back under me.

We talked for hours, sitting curled up together on his bed, quieting only when we heard another member of his family pass by the door. As we talked, we began to shift positions. At some point he removed his shoes and stretched out fully on the bed. I stretched out next to him, propped upon one elbow, watching as his eyelids slowly began to droop. Finally, well past two a.m., Joshua rolled over to click out the lantern light on his bedside table. He dropped his head back onto his pillow and shut his eyes.

I could still see his face in the dark, enough to watch him fading in and out of consciousness. Before he faded entirely, I wanted to ask him one more question.

"Joshua?" I whispered.

"Mm?"

"You never really explained why I'm supposed to call you Joshua when no one else does."

"I didn't?" His words came out muffled, mainly because as he said them, he rolled over to face me. It would only take a little movement for him to brush against me, to ignite the flames across my skin again.

I shook my head, trying to force some sense back into it. "No, you didn't."

Thank God Joshua was almost asleep, because he clearly didn't notice the ridiculous squeak in my voice. I scolded myself internally, telling myself to stop acting like an idiot every time he came close to touching me.

Joshua's mumble broke into my thoughts. "The people I care most about in the world . . . they get to call me Joshua."

"So . . . I'm one of those people? The ones you care most about?"

The stupid squeak snuck back into my hopeful whisper.

"Mm-hmm." A faint smile played on Joshua's lips. Keeping his eyes closed, he draped one arm over my waist. I couldn't feel anything more than a faint pressure, but . . . still. Joshua's arm was around me. *In bed.*

I coughed to rid myself of the squeak and then launched into the most inane follow-up question I could think of.

"Um . . . I've got one more question. A weird one."

"Shoot," he said without opening his eyes.

"It's really weird," I warned him.

He groaned and cracked open one eye to stare at me. He lifted one eyebrow lazily, as if he was too exhausted for even this minor gesture. I sighed, and hurried with the question.

"I was just wondering: can you smell me?"

"Huh?" He opened both eyes now, albeit narrowly.

"See, I—I don't usually smell things," I stuttered, embarrassed. "And I, uh . . . I smelled you today. Twice."

"Really?" The eyebrow rose again. "What was that like?"

"Nice."

"Huh. You know what else is weird?" He yawned the question, eyes drooping closed again. "I can't usually smell you, either. Only every now and then."

"And what's that like?" I repeated his question, trying to keep my tone casual while praying I didn't smell like ectoplasm or rotting trees or something.

"Nice," he murmured. "Sweet. Like peaches, or nectarines."

In the dark, with his eyes shut, Joshua couldn't see the smile radiating across my face.

"That *is* nice," I whispered before settling down beside him, still tucked under his arm.

# *Chapter*
# NINETEEN

While the night shifted into morning and Joshua slept on, my thoughts returned, unwillingly, to Eli.

I took Ruth very seriously when she'd said "We're coming for you." She and her friends—fellow Seers, no doubt—wanted to end my afterlife as I knew it. So I needed to find some way to defend myself against them, and soon. But I had the strangest feeling I couldn't do that until I gained more information about my ghostly nature. I needed to know how ghosts really interacted with the living world. I needed to know about my night-mares, and possibly my death. And I needed to know whether Eli had trapped my father in the netherworld with the other frantic, whispering souls.

Ruth had denied me this information yesterday, leaving me with only one remaining resource. As much as I hated to admit it, and as carefully as I would have to behave around him, Eli probably held the answers to some of my most desperate questions. Ones I *had* to obtain before Ruth and her friends made the task impossible.

The more I thought about it, the more my resolve solidified. Near dawn, I bent over Joshua's ear.

"Joshua?" I whispered.

"Mm."

Watching his peaceful face, I decided to risk an endearment. "Joshua, sweetheart, I have to do some-thing today."

"Mm?"

"I have to go find out a few more things. I'm not sure how long this . . . errand . . . will take, but I think it's important. We can't fight off the other Seers if we don't know as much as possible, can we?"

"No," he mumbled. Despite the assent, however, he was clearly still asleep.

"Glad to know you're on board," I whispered, smiling. "Can you meet me here tonight, around dark?"

"Mm-hmm."

I smiled wider as his forehead creased. The motion made him look as if he took the promise seriously, even in sleep. I stared at him for a moment longer and then leaned closer. Gently, I pressed my lips to his forehead, just above his eyebrow.

The heat of the little kiss spread across my lips, turning them into two smoldering coals. I closed my eyes for a moment, relishing the feel of it. Then I pushed myself off the bed. I crossed the bedroom and, pausing at the door Joshua had left partly open, looked back at him.

"See you soon," I whispered. I bit my lip; and, in a moment of sheer abandon, I added, "I think I might . . . you know . . . *love* you, by the way."

"Too," Joshua whispered back groggily. "Love."

He was asleep, and the words meant nothing, I knew. But the knowledge didn't stop me from stifling a shout of joy as I slipped out of the room. I tried very hard not to skip down the stairs and into the kitchen.

Only when I reached the back door did my mood sink. Actually, "sink" was too delicate a word. "Plummet," perhaps, better fit the situation.

Because, bent over a magazine at the kitchen island and casually flipping pages, was Ruth.

When I entered the kitchen, Ruth's head remained down, the dawn sun bright in her white hair. She looked as if she hadn't heard me approach. I hoped that if I just tiptoed very softly past the island to the back hallway, I might go unnoticed. I wasn't surprised, however, when Ruth's voice stopped me short.

"You know," she mused without looking up from her magazine, "I could have sworn I made my feelings on your relationship with my grandson quite clear."

I pressed my teeth firmly to my bottom lip, refusing to answer.

"Yet," Ruth went on without needing my response, "here you are."

She flipped the last page of the magazine shut and finally looked up, focusing those cold eyes upon me. For a moment I didn't move. Didn't react. Then, slowly, I nodded.

"Yes. Here I am."

Ruth sighed. "And why is that?"

I composed my face into what I hoped was a determined expression. "Because I was invited, Ruth."

"Not by the person who counts."

"I'm not scared of you." I gave myself a gigantic, internal high five when my voice didn't waver.

In an instant Ruth stood, her hands gripped to the edge of the island and a tight smile on her lips. "You should be scared," she whispered.

Suddenly, a vicious headache hit me, similar to the one

I'd experienced yesterday outside the church.

Similar, but not identical. Because this headache was far, far worse.

It exploded in my head, a searing pain that spread down my neck and crashed behind my eyes. I shut my eyes tight against it, but the effort didn't provide any relief. After a few more seconds, I couldn't help but drop to my knees and clutch both hands to my temples as if I could hold the ache at bay with sheer force.

The headache continued to expand as I cowered, blossoming in bright white flashes behind my eyes. The flashes pulsed like strobe lights in my brain, flaring in repetition until, abruptly, they changed.

Instead of white flashes, I saw the images, moving again in rapid succession against my eyelids. Like some kind of montage, switching so quickly from one image to the next that I could only catch one or two details from each: the crinkles around my father's eyes; tall, swaying grass; a strand of my mother's dark hair; the flash of lightning against something metal. The images sped and blurred until I could no longer distinguish any of their individual elements.

"Stop," I moaned, wrapping my fingers so tightly into my hair that my scalp ached too.

To my shock, the headache immediately ended. The images vanished, and the pain evaporated so fast, it may never have been there at all.

Without removing my hands from my head, I opened my eyes to peek up at Ruth. She still stared at me with the tense smile, but now her dark eyes danced with something powerful, and malicious.

"Life flashing before your eyes, dear? That's just a taste of what's in store for you tomorrow night," she whispered. She flicked her head toward the hallway behind me. "This house won't be open to you again. Now, get out."

I didn't need any further instructions. I scrambled to my feet, nearly falling over them in the process, and fled through the hallway.

I had a brief moment of panic, uncertain as to how I'd get out of the Mayhews' house without some sort of assistance. However, as my eyes scanned down the length of the back door, I found that assistance had already been provided.

On the floor, propped upright between the door and the jamb, stood an enormous book. Judging from its worn leather binding, the book was old and probably quite expensive. A wreath of drying herbs and flowers wrapped around the book, twining it shut. Scrawled upon its cover in gold I could just make out the words HOLY BIBLE.

Ruth's work, no doubt. Some talisman to protect

against anything sinister I might have planned. In its current position—wedged against the door in such a manner as to leave enough space for someone thin to pass through the doorway—the book also sent a clear message.

*Leave, dead girl.*

"Your wish is my command, Ruth," I muttered shakily, and slipped through the opening.

I stood on the bank of the river and paced, unwilling to walk too close to the water's edge but unwilling to stray too far away from it, either. The bank itself was empty of everything but me and a few chirping crickets.

"I'm here," I called out to the air, my voice echoing off the surface of the river. "You said I'd come back to talk, and you were right. So let's talk."

Only the rustle of the leaves answered me. I sighed and began to pace more forcefully.

"Hello? Anyone out there? Do I have to do a rain dance or something?"

"Only if you want it to rain."

Cold air swept over me in a wave, rolling up my body until it finally crested against the sensitive skin of my bare shoulders and neck. I wanted to shiver, but I wanted to present a powerful front to Eli more. So I kept my face expressionless, ambivalent, as I turned around.

Eli stood alongside the riverbank, where only moments before there had been nothing but tall grass and mud. He crossed his arms over his chest—mirroring the position I'd inadvertently taken as he approached—and leaned forward with a conspiratorial grin.

"Hey, Amelia."

"Hey, Eli," I answered, obviously in a less amused tone.

"So," he said with a barely concealed laugh in his voice. "What can I do for you on this fine morning?"

Looking at his smug grin, I lost a fraction of my confidence. But I forced myself to clear my throat and straighten my backbone. "I have some questions for you."

"Such as?"

The genuine curiosity in his tone, which was usually so smug, surprised me. Perhaps this wouldn't be as difficult as I'd anticipated? This unexpected turn disoriented me, and I blurted out the first question that came to mind.

"How did you get here so fast? This place was empty a few seconds ago."

Eli shrugged. "I materialized."

"You what?"

He slipped his hands into the pockets of his tight jeans and strolled closer to me. "Haven't you ever noticed, during times of stress or excitement, you're able to travel?

To move through time and space at will?"

I frowned. "Um . . . not exactly."

Eli stopped only a foot from me, *tisk-tisk*ing. "You really should take more time to notice these things, Amelia."

I scowled heavily. *There* was the smugness with which I was already so familiar. "Why don't *you* take time to be a little less condescending, Eli? Otherwise, I'm leaving."

He *tisk*ed again. "Didn't you invite me here?"

"Yeah, but I can just as easily uninvite you."

"I don't doubt you can." Then his smile faded, and he tilted his head to one side, giving me a quizzical sort of look. "You know, I'm very interested in seeing exactly what you can do."

"What do you mean?"

"Well," he said, "we all have abilities—and by 'we' I mean the dead. You're no exception, I'm sure."

"Abilities? Like being able to move through time and space at will?"

He nodded. "Yes, that's one of the more common abilities. But really, Amelia, this shouldn't be news to you. I've seen plenty of your materializations, each time you disappeared."

I blinked, taken completely aback. What on earth was he talking about? I'd never "materialized," whatever that meant.

Then proverbial lightning hit me.

The nightmares.

My nightmares were actually materializations? And they were something potentially controllable, through extreme emotion? Here was one of the answers I sought, then.

I looked up at Eli, unable to hide my excitement. "What else can we do?"

Immediately, I cursed my own stupidity.

Seeing the glimmer in my eyes, Eli grinned; and, at that moment, I could read it on every line of his face: he knew he had the upper hand. I wanted his knowledge, desperately, so I was his captive audience. At least for now.

"If you want me to answer your questions," he said with that smug note still in his voice, "my help obviously comes with conditions."

"Obviously."

Eli nodded, and I felt suddenly like this nod had sealed some kind of deal. One I wasn't sure I really wanted to make. Too late for me to recall my request, however; Eli clasped his hands behind his back and turned to stomp off into the woods.

"Wait," I called out despite my misgivings. "I thought we had a . . . deal?"

Eli laughed loudly but didn't stop walking. "Of course

we do. And our deal just became mobile. So keep up."

As he stepped into the trees, the riverbank instantly darkened behind him. With seemingly no command from Eli, the bank had shifted into the netherworld. But for now the flitting black shapes and whispering souls stayed away, leaving nothing but a cold, glittering landscape around me.

I tossed a wary look over my shoulder at the tarlike river dragging its way to the bridge. At first I thought the gaping black hole wasn't visible today. However, as I watched, a tiny spot of darkness appeared under the bridge and then began to swell, its black edges clawing their way upward and outward. Eventually, it stopped growing; but even in stillness, it seemed to move and shift like some crouching beast. Giving it one last, hesitant glance, I shuddered and faced forward again.

"Amelia Elizabeth Ashley," I whispered to myself. "You're an idiot."

Then I followed the creepiest thing I'd ever met into the deep, twisting forest of the netherworld.

*Chapter*
TWENTY

"Would you like to hear a story, Amelia?"

We'd been walking in the frost-covered woods for at least twenty minutes, weaving a crooked and seemingly directionless path through the trees. The scenery kept getting weirder and weirder—icy, clawlike shrubs clutched at my ankles; an almost purple moss covered every bare surface; and big gray flakes, like either snow or ash, had started to float down around us—but Eli had yet to tell me our destination.

In fact, Eli hadn't said a single word during this

excursion, even in response to my initial questions. As I watched his back—turned away from and always five feet ahead of me—I grew increasingly irritated. I threw around a few pointed sighs, even uttered a low "ahem" or two. My theatrics brought not so much as a peep from Eli.

So when he finally spoke, I actually jumped a little in surprise. It took me a moment to collect myself enough to answer his question, though when I was able to do so, my answer was rife with undisguised impatience.

"That depends, Eli. Is the story relevant?"

"What's your definition of relevance?" Eli countered.

I sighed so loudly, the sound came out like a groan. Eli stopped walking and turned to face me. He placed his hands into his pockets and met my eyes for only a second. Then he lowered his own gaze to my feet and slowly raised it, scanning my body. The appraisal made me squirm uncomfortably.

"Tell me the story," I said curtly, "to distract yourself from being so rude."

His head snapped up, and he looked me fully in the eyes. "Oh, I'm terribly sorry. Was I being rude?"

Still glaring at him, I twisted one corner of my mouth in disapproval.

"Fair enough." He appraised me again, although this time he did so with a less lewd stare. Then he nodded.

"Since I've embarrassed you, how about I apologize by telling you something about myself?"

"Only if it has something to do with what I want to know."

A smile twitched on his lips, and then he turned back around to march onward through the woods. I wavered, uncertain, before I began following him.

"Eli?" I prompted.

He remained silent for a moment and then called back, "Have you ever wondered why I'm dressed like this? What kind of profession I might have been in?"

I assessed the back of his fluttering black shirt. "Well, I had a feeling you weren't an accountant."

When Eli cast a quick, backward glance over his shoulder, he looked amused.

"You're right about that. You know, if I'd known what was going to happen the night I died, I might have changed into more comfortable pants. Or at least have buttoned my shirt."

Considering my own outfit, I had no room to judge. I swept an errant gray flake from my skirt—not ash but something like snow, I think—and nodded at Eli's back.

"When you've just come from a concert in 1975," he continued, "the last thing on your mind is changing clothes, I can assure you."

"You died after attending a concert?"

"Actually, Amelia, I died before *playing* a concert."

I stumbled in surprise and then stopped completely. "You did what?"

Eli stopped, too. After turning to face me, he gave me a lazy, self-assured grin. "In life I was the lead singer of a rock band. We were pretty good, too. Gaining a following . . . even negotiating with a record label."

Only my eyes moved, running over Eli's outfit once more: the impossibly tight pants, the wild hair, the cluster of necklaces on his bare chest.

"So . . . you were a rock star?"

"I was on my *way* to being a rock star. I even had my own groupies." His grin widened. "My band actually had a pretty big gig in Oklahoma City, but our tour bus broke down in Wilburton before we could get there."

"Wow," I said, begrudgingly impressed. I paused and then asked, "I'm guessing you never made it to that gig, huh?"

Eli didn't answer but instead raised one eyebrow for confirmation. Only now did his prideful expression falter. I couldn't be sure, but I think it was the first time I'd seen Eli regretful, as if he actually mourned the loss of all that impending power and fame.

"So . . . what happened?" I asked.

Eli grimaced, remembering. "Our bus driver insisted on taking a shortcut in the dead of the night, across a rickety old bridge." He frowned harder, as if trying to remember. "Of course, once the bus sputtered to a stop in the middle of the bridge, we decided to pile out and help the driver with the engine. We were pretty useless, though: a serious amount of drinking was involved, obviously, and maybe a few more chemicals. Soon things got . . . out of control. Eventually, someone had the brilliant idea to jump over the side of the bridge."

"You?" I gasped. "You *jumped* off High Bridge?"

Eli laughed vibrantly. The sound of it contrasted strangely with his story.

"Well, Amelia," he said, "I obviously didn't fly. And that was my messy end, so to speak."

We were silent for a few more moments as both of us digested his words. My distaste for Eli lessened slightly in light of his last revelation: we had died in the same awful place. And now we were both stuck between the living world and whatever else existed outside of this dark, icy limbo.

Frowning, I stared down at the icy moss beneath my feet. "You know, Eli, I don't remember much of anything. But I've got to be honest with you—I *really* don't remember any stories about a rock star dying on the bridge."

Eli sniffed imperiously, and I looked up. From the twist of his mouth, I could see I'd offended him.

"Like I said, Amelia, I was on my way to becoming a rock star," he explained in a clipped tone. "At the time I died, not many people knew me or followed me. But they were going to . . . I'm sure of it."

For some strange reason, I felt a little guilty about wounding his pride, at least on this issue. The story of Eli's human life was the only thing that made him seem . . . well, *human*. "Sorry, Eli. Really," I said, with only the slightest smile. "I'm sure you were going to be huge. A big star."

When he appeared somewhat mollifed, I pressed him again. "Keep going, Eli. Tell me what happened after you died."

He sighed, and the focused look settled upon his face again.

"Believe it or not, the initial years of my afterlife were far less peaceful than yours. Those years were my punishment, no doubt. I died angry—not at the world but at myself, for giving up all that success. All that power. I wanted to lash out at the living instead of beg for their help, as you did. I suppose I became a bit of a poltergeist. I found that, through strong emotions, I could affect things in the living world. Move them, even. I managed to break windows, overturn lamps. Make myself a general nuisance."

"Hard to believe," I murmured.

"Quit interrupting," Eli instructed, but he gave me a quick grin. "I went on like that for a few years. Until *they* came for me, of course."

Something about the way he said "they" made me flinch.

"I'm not sure what they saw in me that made me worthy," Eli went on, unaware of my sudden discomfort. "But one day, while I paced uselessly by the river, they appeared to me. They told me about all the things I'd hungered to know: my nature as a ghost, my powers, and my purpose. They told me I was special . . . essential, even, to their mission. Like I told you before, they then commissioned me for an important task and gave me control of this place. They gave me *power* again." He gestured grandly around him: to the crooked, shimmering trees and the flat black sky above us.

I shivered. "An icy tundra made for one?"

"The cold is a part of their world, Amelia. And ours."

"Yours," I corrected him softly.

"You're wrong about that," he said offhandedly.

"Oh? And what exactly am I wrong about?"

"About the loneliness of this place. It's meant to be shared, you know."

"By whom?"

"My masters have always wanted two ghosts to work together, pulling new souls into this world."

"Two ghosts?" I raised one eyebrow and looked meaningfully around us at the otherwise empty forest. I knew Eli wanted me to join him, but it struck me now that he had spent an awful lot of time on the job without help.

A strange look passed over Eli's face, one I couldn't quite place. A number of emotions might have explained that look: defiance, arrogance . . . and even a little bit of fear. Before I could decide whether it was one of those or all of them, Eli gave a curt reply.

"I had a mentor once. And now I don't."

He turned away quickly, so that I couldn't read his expression. Obviously, he meant to end this topic of conversation, and fast. I blinked back, startled by this evasion.

"Um . . . where's your mentor now, Eli?"

With his face still turned away from me, Eli shrugged. "Gone. And that's that."

I could sense there was more to it—much more. I had the sudden, overwhelming urge to find out what had happened to Eli's former mentor; if I had to guess, I'd have bet it wasn't anything pleasant. I opened my mouth to push the issue, but Eli's dismissive wave stopped me.

"I'm not going to talk about the time when I played apprentice, Amelia, so don't bother to ask. What I'm more interested in is the subject of my *own* apprentice."

"Oh, and I'm the current winner of that prize, right?"

I twisted my mouth disdainfully to show Eli exactly what I thought of *that* honor.

"Actually," Eli said, giving me another strange look, "you weren't the first helper I chose out of the souls I'd brought to this world."

"Huh?" I asked. "Who are you talking about?"

His face changed then, shifting from smugness to some other expression, one I couldn't identify at first. Then it struck me—Eli was sad. Not snide or condescending, or even angry. Just sad.

Slowly, he walked over to a low-lying tree branch—one that curved up, looped around, and then extended into the gray air like a misshapen *J*—and sat down on the makeshift bench it created. He removed his hands from his pockets and placed his palms on his knees. When he spoke again, he stared at a fixed point in the moss beneath his feet.

"Melissa." He said the name tenderly, mournfully, as if each of its three syllables was precious.

"Who's Melissa?"

"She is . . . was . . . my first real taste of life after death."

Eli's head suddenly jerked upward. He caught my gaze and held it, his own eyes glowing with a near-violent intensity. I felt as though I were hypnotized by the power of that stare. Eli didn't even blink when I folded my legs beneath me and sat down on the moss in front of him.

"The best night of my death," Eli whispered, still staring hard at me, "I stood on the bridge, preparing to collect a soul. Just business as usual; all I had to do was wait for her to fall off of it."

I made a small choking sound, but Eli didn't seem to hear me.

"While I waited, I watched her," he went on. "She was beautiful, with bright auburn hair that floated around her in a halo. She looked like an angel set on fire. I tried to reach out to touch her, but of course I couldn't yet. I was dead, and she was still living.

"Part of my mission consisted of listening, waiting until her heart thudded to a stop and then pulling her soul from the river so I could take her to the darkness. But the moment before she fell, I caught a glimpse of her eyes. They were green, and as bright as yours. She looked straight at me, and I could have sworn she *saw* me, even before she'd died. At that moment I was hers. Immediately and completely."

Eli paused for a moment, studying my face—for what, I wasn't sure. Then he went back to staring at the ground, the faraway look of remembrance in his eyes as he spoke.

"I had to have her. I had to. After she died, I pulled her from the river and begged my masters to let me keep her as an assistant. To my surprise, they agreed.

"Because I'd woken her immediately after her death, the girl never experienced the fog like you and I did. She retained all of her memories of life, and seemed more than willing to share them with me. She told me her name was Melissa and the year was 1987. In her life, Melissa had been a student, studying nursing at that little college off of the highway. And although she had died violently, she was still . . . cheerful. Sometimes joyful even.

"She was everything I wanted in a companion: smart, beautiful, full of fire. I loved her immediately.

"But, maybe because of her nature, Melissa quickly grew unhappy with our existence. Unlike you, I didn't exactly give her my detailed job description. Still, it wasn't long before she realized what my mission consisted of and expressed her distaste for it.

"For a few weeks she tried to convince me to give it up—to let go of my power and set all my followers free. When she saw that approach wasn't working, she began to disappear for days at a time, materializing away and then reappearing with little explanation for her activity.

"Then one autumn morning less than a year after her death, she came back to me looking . . . different. Her skin still glowed like ours; but it was brighter, warmer. Like real fire . . ."

Eli trailed off, frowning at the moss across which he

absently raked his shoe. Small sparks of ice drifted up in the air and hung there, stirred up by his feet. I waited for almost a full minute for Eli to go on, but my impatience eventually outweighed my empathy.

"What did she say to you then?" I pressed.

He shook his head. "She told me I couldn't trap souls in darkness for eternity. She said the dead are meant to decide for themselves where they go. She said that, by forcing them into this world to serve me, I wasn't helping them at all. I was supposed to let the newly dead wander lost, because only after they wake up from the fog should they choose which of the afterworlds they wanted to occupy."

"After*worlds*?" I breathed. "What other worlds are there?"

Eli shrugged, not fooling me with his forced nonchalance. "According to Melissa, she'd been someplace . . . else. Better. She asked me to go with her, but I refused. There's too much for me here. I'm too important. I'm *obeyed* here."

The prideful glint returned to his eyes, sparkling with an almost unnerving intensity. I could read his thoughts perfectly in those eyes: Eli was obsessed with this place. He would do anything his masters asked, capture and command any soul, to retain his supposed power.

"What happened to Melissa after that?" I asked carefully.

Eli sneered. "She vanished for the last time. I haven't seen her since, not that I'd want to."

As he spat out the final words, his lips curled into a snarl. He now looked savage, almost feral. But I saw human emotions skirting the edges of his mouth and his eyes. Buried beneath his sneer were desolation and deep, profound loneliness.

Lost in thought, I ran my fingertips in circles on the strange moss beneath me. So many details from Eli's story were important. So many things cast light upon what I was, and what kind of choices I had.

But another aspect of his story saddened me—the part of it that had absolutely nothing to do with me. Because, however much I might dislike him, I couldn't ignore an important theme in his narrative: despite Eli's fervor for this world and its dark imperative, he didn't want to be alone.

Seeing the misery in his face, I felt another surge of pity for him. I felt the strangest compulsion to help him, to pull him out of his mood, so I asked the only diversionary question I could think of.

"You kind of implied that you moved on after Melissa disappeared for the last time. So, what did you do next?"

His eyes flitted up to mine, and the ghost of his old smirk twitched at the corners of his lips.

"Well, I found myself another pretty assistant."

"Me, right?"

Eli nodded slowly, still smirking.

"So, what did you do: find me after I died and decide you wanted me to help you?"

"No, Amelia." His grin widened into something foreign and slightly wild. "I chose you *before* you died."

Chapter
TWENTY-ONE

I felt my vision narrow to a black pinpoint and then expand uncomfortably.

"You were there when I died?"

Eli moved suddenly, lurching off the tree branch toward me. His eyes were fierce, once again filled with that fervor. He spoke in a dizzying rush of words.

"I was, Amelia. I was there when you died, but I didn't wake you up like I did Melissa. I didn't even take you into the darkness like I do all the other souls. Don't you see what that means? Don't you see what I've done for you? I let you escape for a while. I allowed you your freedom. And you owe me for it."

Eli grasped for my hand, but I yanked it out of his reach. I couldn't think, couldn't breathe. Yet, somehow, I forced the words from my lips.

"What do you mean, you were 'there'? How . . . how long were you there?"

"Just like with Melissa, I was there even before you fell," he said with a tender smile that made me go cold. "I saw you hit the water and go unconscious. I saw your eyes open and saw you struggle against the current. And later I heard your heart stop. After the last beat, though, I left. I couldn't let you see me. I had to materialize somewhere else so your death would have meaning."

"Meaning? What meaning?" I stared at him, enthralled and horrified.

"Obviously, something went wrong with Melissa, otherwise I'd still have her. I had to behave differently with you in order to keep you. If I woke you up immediately, like I did with Melissa, then you might miss the significance of my mercy in letting you be my assistant; you'd have remembered your life, maybe even missed it. So you had to experience the fog to truly appreciate when I brought you out of it."

The image of Joshua's face flashed into my mind again.

"But you didn't bring me out of it," I whispered.

Eli smiled widely, his expression suddenly animated. "No, I didn't. I didn't even need to. You did it yourself."

I shook my head, uncomprehending.

"I was on High Bridge last week, waiting for a new soul to acquire," Eli explained, "when I saw you in the river beneath me. Just as a car approached, you started to flail, distracting the driver so I could spook him into the water."

I nearly gagged.

Joshua. Eli was talking about Joshua, and his car accident.

"You . . . you did what?" I finally managed to gasp.

"No, *we* did something. Together," Eli said with an excited gleam in his eyes. "Like a team. I mean, we obviously weren't successful, since I saw the boy make it out of the water. But even so, I watched you follow him, still trying to go in for the kill."

Eli beamed as if his misinterpretation of my actions actually made him *proud* of me. "You were a natural, Amelia. A perfect lure."

My head swam, and I had the strangest suspicion that I might just pass out if I didn't keep it together.

So . . . what? Eli thought I'd intentionally lured Joshua off High Bridge when I was really just reliving my death in the river? And then, while encouraging Joshua to swim for safety, Eli thought I'd actually been exhibiting some innate signs of evil?

I had to remind myself to focus on the most important detail of this revelation: all along, the real watcher—the real villian—had been Eli himself.

The thought of Eli playing an active role in Joshua's accident made me reimagine my own death scene, inserting Eli's figure above the greenish black swells of the river. Eli, watching me choke and struggle, grinning his arrogant grin. Perhaps a crowd of black shapes at the periphery, watching him watch me.

The reimagining made my death seem even more horrible, if that were possible. But really, I shouldn't have been surprised, considering what he'd just told me about his role in Melissa's death.

"You said . . . you s-saw my death too," I stuttered, swallowing back the great wave of rage that threatened to pour out of me. I had to. It was the only way I could learn about my death, from the only person—the only creature—who had witnessed it. "Did I jump, like you did? Or did I fall, like Melissa?"

He raised one pale eyebrow. "You don't remember?"

I simply shook my head.

Unexpectedly, Eli sat back upon the curve of the tree. The hint of fanaticism left his eyes, and the familiar smirk crawled across his face. Now I could see the expression for what it really was: the look of someone who believes he holds all the cards.

"Maybe I'll tell you about your death someday," he said. He leaned forward and traced his narrow fingers across the air above my cheek. "But I want that to remain a mystery for now. So you'll understand how much you need me."

I shuddered and then jerked away as if he'd tried to touch me with a branding iron.

"I'll never 'need' you again, Eli," I growled.

Eli's smirk vanished. "What do you mean, Amelia? We've been called together. We're fated."

"We. Are. Not. Fated." I pronounced each word carefully, individually, so he couldn't miss my meaning.

"But I . . . I saved you," he sputtered.

That one word—"saved"—demolished whatever small amount of self-control had been holding back my fury. I flattened my hands against the ground and shoved myself up into a standing position.

"*Saved* me?" I screamed. "You didn't save me! You did the exact opposite of saving. I know for a fact that you could have helped me. You could have done something before my heart stopped. But you didn't. You let me die."

Eli started to speak, but I went on, furious and loud.

"I don't care if it was part of your supposed 'mission.' Because that's not all you did to me. Even after your sick part in my death, you didn't stop there. You've been waiting the whole time I wandered lost and scared, ready to pounce on me. All because your masters told you I could be yours?"

"Amelia, I—"

"And I bet you didn't try to 'save' my father, did you?" I cut him off with a growl, my rage growing. "I bet you threw him into this forest with all your other victims."

Eli had the audacity to look confused. "Your father?"

"Spare me." I laughed. "You can't pretend to be innocent any longer. And I couldn't care less about whatever grand plans you had for our future. Oh, pardon me— my future. Whatever your plans are, they have nothing to do with *my* future at all."

"Our future," he snarled, the tenderness now absent from his voice.

"No. My future."

It was now Eli's turn to jump to his feet.

"You're mine!" he shouted into my face. His hand shook violently as he reached for me, but I took two quick steps backward.

I didn't even take a last look at him before I spun around on my bare heel and ran into the woods. I had no idea where my feet led me, nor did I care. I only cared that my feet slid across the icy purple moss with a speed they'd never shown before.

Unfortunately, no matter how fast or how far I ran, the

sinister landscape around me never seemed to change. I kept passing what looked like the same mangled shrubs, the same glittering trees.

As I ran, I saw other things too: dark shapes in the forest, flitting among the trunks and branches like wild animals following my path. Maybe I was so scared I'd begun to hallucinate, but I could swear the shapes had *faces*. Human faces, watching me run through the woods but not moving to stop me.

Were these the lost souls, biding their time until Eli gave them the order to attack? Was my father among them, watching me too? Part of me wanted to stop and hunt for him, but another part kept my legs moving, dragging me forward in terror.

Then, at the moment I was about to give in to full panic, the gray began to shimmer and shift. Like some massive drape over a theater set, the dark netherworld floated and fell away until I stood, panting, in the middle of the sun-filled woods of the living world.

Something about a hundred yards ahead caught my eye. I squinted and realized it was the river, glinting orange in what looked to be the late-afternoon sun.

I started running again, moving as though my very existence depended upon my speed. When I crested the hill above the river and stepped onto the asphalt of High Bridge Road, I paused only long enough to say a prayer.

"Please, God," I begged aloud. "If you like me at all, please, please, show me the way back to the Mayhews' house. I could really use the help."

I nodded once for an amen and then tore off again down the road.

My sense of direction would be the death of me. Metaphorically, at least.

By sunset I'd made one too many wrong turns, and my confidence unraveled a little more with each inch the sun dipped below the horizon.

At last, at the end of what felt like the hundredth road, I saw the front porch of an unmistakable house. I raced down its driveway toward the backyard, my feet flying over gravel. But as I left the gravel and crossed onto the grass, I found the Mayhews' backyard empty and dark. All the lanterns, now unlit, looked gray in the night. No light shined from the back windows of the house, nor did Joshua wait for me on the darkened porch. I slumped against the trunk of a cottonwood, exhausted and defeated.

"Amelia?"

The hushed voice came from somewhere farther back into the yard, away from the porch.

"Joshua?" I whispered. I heard a tiny click, and a small circle of light appeared more than fifty feet behind the house. Within the circle was Joshua, standing in the entrance of the gazebo I'd noticed the first night he'd brought me here.

Without another sound I was running across the back lawn, leaping up the gazebo steps, and throwing myself into his arms, all before Joshua could even move.

After only a second's hesitation, he pulled me to him, wrapping one hand around the nape of my neck and weaving his fingers through my hair. Just like when we'd kissed, I could feel it all: his arm around my waist, his fingers against my skin.

"Thank God you're here. It's late. I was worried . . . ," he murmured. He lowered his head to my neck and ran his lips across the skin just below my jaw, all but igniting a fire there.

"I'm sorry. I'm so sorry," I panted. "It took forever to do what I had to do, and then I couldn't find your house. I think I walked down about a million wrong driveways."

Joshua chuckled—a rough, low sound that reverberated off the base of my throat.

"You're not mad at me for kind of disappearing again, are you?" I asked hesitantly.

Joshua shook his head, the tip of his nose brushing across the soft skin of my neck. "No. God, no. I'm sorry about the other day, I really am. I was so stupid. If I'd just taken the time to think about what you are, and what you have to go through—"

"No!" I cut him off. "Don't blame yourself! It was my fault, too. I could have—"

Now it was his turn to interrupt me by moving his lips to my ear. "Let's just agree to make it up to each other, okay?" he whispered.

"I could live with that," I whispered back.

Joshua's fingers ran slowly up and down my spine, and I held him more tightly, relishing the tingles that seemed to have found their way over every inch of my skin. The sensation obscured every other thought in my head, made me trail off as I said, "You know, I really have so much to tell you about today. . . ."

"I want to hear it all, I do," he said fervently, pulling his head back and looking into my eyes.

In this position—one of his hands still woven through my hair and the other wrapped around my waist, both of my arms thrown around his neck and our bodies pressed together—our lips were only inches apart.

We must have noticed this fact at the same moment, because we simultaneously began to tremble. Joshua's breath sped; and I could actually feel it, warm and soft, on my lips. Our eyes were still locked, and I started to feel a little dizzy.

"I . . . I still want to kiss you," he whispered hoarsely.

"Me, too."

"Can I . . . ? Can we . . . ?"

"I think so," I nodded. "I just really have to concentrate, so I don't disappear."

Joshua's fingers tightened in my hair, and he pulled my face closer to his.

"Concentrate, then," he murmured, and pressed his lips to mine.

Just as it had before, our kiss threatened to melt every part of my body. Waves of hydrogen-fueled flames unfurled like petals in my brain.

But this time I paid close attention to more than just my passion. When I felt the blackness creep along the edges of my joy and when a tiny place in my core felt as though something were tugging on it with an invisible string, I fought back. I anchored myself to the present, holding on to Joshua and concentrating on the immediate feel of his mouth.

I didn't disappear. I didn't sink into the water. Instead, I kissed Joshua back, more ferociously than I could have imagined possible. I parted my lips and moved them against his, breathing him in, almost tasting him.

Eventually, we had to stop so he could breathe. We reluctantly pulled away but stayed pressed against each other.

"That was amazing," Joshua panted.

Even if I'd wanted to speak loudly, I couldn't. I could only whisper, "That was—"

"Beautiful," a voice spat from behind us.

Still wrapped in each other's arms, Joshua and I whirled around to face the same spot in the black tree line. The speaker remained invisible, hidden by the darkness.

"Who the hell . . . ?" Joshua began, but I already knew the answer.

"Eli," I said flatly.

"Who's Eli?" Joshua asked, turning back to me.

"My errand this morning."

"Oh, I'm an errand, am I?" Eli stepped out of the shadows, his skin oddly bright against the black of the night.

"That's far more than you deserve," I said through clenched teeth. "And you know it."

"I know no such thing," he hissed.

"How did you follow me without me knowing?"

"I stayed far enough behind you. Then, at the right moment, I materialized."

"I told you to leave me alone."

"And I do not now, nor will I ever, take instructions from you." As Eli continued to walk forward, the dead white of his skin left traces of light in the darkness around him.

"Amelia, am I seeing what I think I'm seeing?" Joshua

asked, frowning. "Is that . . . another ghost?"

Eli's eyes darted to mine. "The boy—he can't see me, can he?"

I shrugged angrily. "He's a Seer, Eli. That's what they *do*."

"Well, make him stop."

I couldn't have been prouder when Joshua pulled back his shoulders and fixed Eli in a steely glare. "I *can* see you. But whoever or whatever you are, I don't like how you're talking to Amelia. So get off my property."

Eli snorted. "Your property? How funny. Don't you mean your parents' property, *boy*?"

"Leave. Before I make you," Joshua growled.

"And how do you propose to do that? I'm dead. You can't even touch me." Eli smirked, folding his arms behind his back.

"Do you see this beautiful girl in my arms?" Joshua threatened softly. "She's dead, too. But I'm certainly touching her, aren't I?"

For the first time, Eli's expression actually scared me. Harsh lines crisscrossed his face, pulling his eyes into slits and tugging his lips up into a sort of rictus grin. In that moment, he truly looked dead. A malevolent dead thing that had suddenly locked his eyes on me.

"Amelia, I have to admit I'm impressed. You've been playing innocent, all the while trying to steal my things?"

"What are you talking about, Eli?"

Keeping that nasty smile, Eli jerked his head in Joshua's direction. "I thought we were working as a team when he drove off the bridge. I thought our joint effort was the reason you finally woke up. But now the boy is here—alive—with you. So . . . you want to keep all of him for yourself, do you?"

Eli's ability to think the worst never ceased to amaze me. Now he was implying that I intended to *own* Joshua, like Eli wanted to own me? Not likely. I sneered at the idea and opened my mouth to tell him so.

It was Joshua, however, who answered Eli first. "What Amelia wants is not your concern, because you're going to leave. Now. I'm not going to say it again."

"Please understand, boy," Eli said without looking at Joshua, "that when I speak now, I'm not speaking to you. I'm not even going to acknowledge you from this moment forward."

Eli's voice dropped a low, chilling octave as he then addressed me. "Amelia, you know what I want. And you can only guess what I am capable of. Materialization isn't my only trick. There are dark things in our nature, things you have yet to comprehend. I told you I control the dead, but I can do so much more than that. I have so many ways to . . . *hurt* . . . a living being, too." His eyes flickered momentarily to Joshua and then back to me.

"Especially one who can see the dead. I'm sure someone like that could be valuable. A nice addition to my little army."

A guttural sound bubbled out of my throat. With a little more power behind it, the sound could easily become a snarl.

Joshua blinked at me, but Eli just chuckled.

"Amelia, Amelia. I was there at your second birth—how could any little noise you make frighten me?" He raised one eyebrow, and then his expression unexpectedly relaxed. The strange, feral creases around his mouth and eyes smoothed, and his lazy grin slipped back into place.

"So," Eli drawled, slipping his hands into his pockets. "Think about what I've said. There's only one way you're fated to spend your future. That is, if you want the boy to have any future at all."

I began to snarl, but Eli cut off the noise.

"Tomorrow, at dawn. Your graveyard."

He gave me a final, hideous wink and then vanished, leaving nothing but the darkness of the night behind him.

*Chapter*

# TWENTY-TWO

Joshua hunched over his cup of coffee—the last remains of the pot he'd snuck inside to make several hours after his family had gone to bed. Neither of us felt comfortable falling asleep tonight, but unlike me, Joshua didn't have the luxury of almost-permanent sleeplessness. He would have to make do with caffeine.

"No, Amelia," he mumbled into his cup and then rubbed his tired eyes. He shook his head as adamantly as one could at four thirty in the morning. "I still think it's a terrible idea."

"Do you have a better one?" I snapped. I immediately regretted my tone, and I smoothed my hand down his arm in apology. "Sorry, Joshua, really. But I just don't see any other options."

If I spoke honestly, it seemed we were out of options in a lot of ways.

For starters, instead of lying curled up together on Joshua's bed, we sat huddled on the bottom steps of the gazebo in the backyard. After Eli disappeared, Joshua and I had tried to enter his house, but something kept me from doing so every time I'd tried. A quick check of the ground revealed our culprit: a layer of chalky gray dust now bordered all the entrances into the Mayhew house, probably sprinkled there today by Ruth. The chalk barred my entry like some invisible wall; even when Joshua swept away the chalk, the magical barrier remained intact. As if I needed another reminder of the painful—and maybe permanent—exorcism that awaited me tonight.

Unfortunately, Eli currently took precedent over my Ruth problem since I didn't doubt the sincerity of his threats against Joshua. I'd explained everything to Joshua: Eli's mad need to own me, his staunch insistence that I was fated to turn evil and serve him, even his role in Joshua's near-death.

Joshua, however, remained undeterred.

"How can meeting that guy—alone, in a *graveyard*— be our only option?" he demanded. "And how can you even think about giving in to what he wants?"

"How can I not?" I groaned as I flopped sideways onto the gazebo steps. I stared at Joshua, who had propped himself against a wooden post. "You know Eli's not going to leave us alone until I talk to him again."

"So? Just let him try and mess with us."

"Joshua, that's very brave of you and all, but could we please avoid pissing off a dead guy who can disappear at will? God knows what else he's capable of."

Joshua snorted. "Oh, disappearing. Real spooky."

But even through Joshua's sarcasm, I could hear a subtle hint of uncertainty. I pressed the point.

"Yeah, disappearing. At will. Something I can't do yet. And I don't think he was lying when he said he had even more tricks up his sleeve."

Suddenly, Joshua was alert. He lurched forward and grabbed my hips, pulling me closer to him. When our knees almost touched, he stopped pulling but left his hands clasped around my waist.

"Exactly, Amelia!" he cried. "Don't you see? That's why you can't go there by yourself to meet him. We have no idea what he's going to be able to do to you. Like you said: even my grandmother and her friends haven't been able to stop him from hurting people. So what makes you think *you'd* be safe?"

Joshua's concern touched me, far more than I let him see. But no matter how Joshua felt, no matter that today was the deadline Ruth had set for my exorcism, I had to end this skirmish with Eli; I had to clear him from Joshua's life before Joshua got hurt. I kept my expression rigid, firm.

"I'm not going to argue about this anymore. I'm going to the graveyard. That's that."

Joshua sighed heavily and closed his eyes.

"Amelia, Amelia, you are a stubborn girl." He sighed once more. "If you're going, then you're not going alone."

I opened my eyes and pulled myself from his arms. Joshua fell forward, too tired to react in time to my movement. He righted himself and gave me a baleful stare. I ignored him and shook my head forcefully.

"Absolutely not," I said. "You're not coming with me. We've already covered this, Joshua."

"But—"

"But no," I interrupted him. "I can't give in on this one, Joshua, I'm sorry. Eli wants me. Just me. He wants to love me, or own me, or whatever . . . but I don't think he'd actually hurt me. At least, not in a permanent way. He wouldn't hesitate to hurt you, though, if it meant getting to me. So you can't be there. Period."

"You're right," Joshua muttered. "I know you're right."

He frowned and stared down at his lap.

His apparent surrender surprised me, and it momentarily caught me off guard. But when Joshua looked back up at me, I could see that he wasn't surrendering. Not at all. His eyes showed nothing but absolute resolve.

"You *are* right, Amelia," he repeated with an air of finality. "Which is why I'm going to do my damnedest to make sure neither of us goes to see that guy."

Joshua clasped his hands back around my waist. I couldn't feel his arms, but I could see them tighten around me. His grip on me, and his hard gaze, made his point perfectly clear: he would do anything humanly possible to keep me with him, and away from that graveyard.

So I would have to resort to inhuman tactics.

I gave him a soft smile. "Can you promise me something?" I asked quietly.

"Not if it has anything to do with you trying to go out there."

I shook my head, still smiling. "Joshua, please. Just listen. I need you to make me a promise. If you don't see me again, I need you to promise you won't come looking for me, okay?"

"Amelia, what are you—," he began in a panicked voice, but I cut him off with a firm kiss.

This kiss was entirely different from our first two.

Now I kissed him roughly, moving my lips against his with a force that belied my desperation. Joshua was so surprised by this attack, he couldn't help but kiss me back. And, of course, his reaction just made me kiss him more fiercely.

Then, without warning, I jerked away and shut my eyes tight. Before Joshua could pull me back to him, I concentrated on difficult thoughts.

Thoughts of my mother, lonely and alone inside her worn little home. Thoughts of my father's face—a face I may never see again, in any of the afterworlds. And thoughts of Joshua. Not the happy thoughts of the last few days but thoughts of *forever*, as only my kind could understand it. Forever, spent without him.

On top of all these sad thoughts, I forced an overlay of one image: that of the graveyard in which I awoke after each of my nightmares. I squeezed my eyes tighter, burning the image onto the backs of my eyelids.

And suddenly, I couldn't feel the pressure of Joshua's arms around me.

My eyes shot open.

At first I couldn't feel or see anything. Everything was numb, and black. Then, painfully, my eyes began to adjust to their new surroundings.

Wherever I now sat, it wasn't entirely black, as I'd originally thought. This new place was just very, very dark.

A bird called out somewhere to my right, and my head jerked toward the noise. The movement brought into view dark shapes amassed all around me. As my eyes adjusted more, I could just make out the structure of the shapes. The tall ones were trees, drooping toward the ground. The shorter ones were less uniform: some of them, although wide at the base, narrowed into obelisks at the top; some formed squat half circles above a field of grass. Whatever their form, all of these shorter shapes were unquestionably gravestones.

I'd done it.

I'd willed myself into the graveyard a few hours before dawn.

A sharp, bitterly cold wind slammed into me, whipping against my cheeks and whirling my hair up in the air. When the wind died down, a dry voice slithered out from the darkness.

"You're early, Amelia Ashley."

"Well," I said shakily, trying my best to sound calm as I pushed myself upright. "What can I say? I'm a punctual girl." Then I paused and frowned. "Wait . . . you just said my last name, didn't you?"

Eli stepped out from the shadow of a tree, coming into dim view.

"Quite right, Amelia," he said. "How do I know your last name? And how do I know this is the graveyard where you wake up after your accidental materializations?"

I felt my stomach drop.

In my haste to get this over with, and to spare Joshua in the process, I hadn't even considered that detail. *Your graveyard,* Eli had said. He shouldn't have known about my graveyard. Unless . . . .

"You've been lying to me again, haven't you? You know more about my life than you let on."

"Only a little bit."

"How much is a little bit?" I demanded.

"Well, why don't you turn around and look at the gravestone you're practically lying on? That should provide some explanation."

I didn't want to look away from Eli's face. I didn't want to lose sight of him in the great likelihood that he had another nasty surprise planned for me. Yet my head seemed compelled by other forces. It turned slowly until I faced the grass and dirt just behind me.

I'd never wanted to stay in this graveyard long enough to study its headstones or search for my own grave. I merely assumed I'd been buried here, and the assumption was reason enough for me to run away from this place each time I entered it.

I also assumed that, should I stumble upon my grave, I would likely find it overgrown. I don't know why I'd made this assumption. But in the long years since my death, I'd forgotten my parents and their love for me. To my depressed, lonely mind, it only made sense that whoever I left behind wouldn't remember me or my grave.

The little, well-tended patch of earth I now faced proved this last assumption wrong. And despite that fact—despite the obvious love that went into the grave's care—its very appearance broke my heart into a million pieces.

Behind me, a concrete slab lay flush to the ground. Concrete, I suppose, because my parents couldn't have afforded much else. Someone had carefully cleared away the grass from the slab and wiped it clean of dead leaves. A ceramic pot filled with silk daisies sat at the base of the stone.

Simple block letters were imprinted on the stone's surface. Apart from the epitaph, the letters read much like my senior yearbook inscription:

AMELIA ELIZABETH ASHLEY
APRIL 30, 1981—APRIL 30, 1999
BELOVED DAUGHTER FOREVER

Seeing those words, all I could imagine was my father's face as he chose that headstone at the funeral parlor and my mother's hands as they gathered up those daisies in the fabric store.

My dead and unbeating heart could still ache with grief, so it seemed. Fiercely so. I wiped at the one tear that had coursed its way down my cheek and turned back around to stare up at Eli. Even his unpleasant face would be better to look at than the last gifts my parents had left me.

Meeting my eyes, Eli nodded grimly. "So, now you see why I know your last name, Amelia Ashley."

"How did you find this?" I asked.

"I was here myself only a month ago, wandering a bit and thinking. When, lo and behold, who did I see appear out of thin air? My little Amelia, choking and gasping right on top of that grave. You must have materialized here without meaning to. By doing so you solved a great mystery: where does Amelia go when she disappears? After answering that riddle for me, you ran away, not seeing or sensing me."

I nodded absently, processing this information. So, Eli had watched me wake up from a nightmare. That explained how he knew about "my" graveyard and how he'd discovered my last name. Yet, another question remained.

"Why were you here in the first place, Eli?"

Eli frowned heavily. "It may surprise you to know, Amelia, that I find this place as distasteful as you do. But, just like you, I return to it occasionally, for reasons even I don't fully understand."

My eyebrows knit together in an unspoken question. In answer, Eli held out his hand.

"Come on. I'll show you."

I stared warily at his outstretched hand. Eli sighed impatiently and waggled his fingers at me.

"It's not a snake, Amelia. It won't hurt you."

"No, but you might."

Eli sighed again and pulled back his hand. "Fine. Would you at least follow me, then?"

I thought about the request for a moment, then rose to my feet, trying to repress the thought that I currently stood on my own grave. And that I actually walked across my own grave as I followed Eli deeper into the cemetery.

Eli strode slowly through the grass for a while until he came to a weathered headstone. He stopped at the foot of the grave and, expressionless, stared at it.

"This," he said, gesturing to the stone. "This is why I come here."

The writing on the marker was plain and nondescript, perhaps intentionally so. It merely read:

ELI ROWLAND

1956—JULY 11, 1975

CLIMBING THE STAIRWAY TO HEAVEN

"Yikes," I murmured.

Eli snorted in agreement. "My band mates obviously couldn't remember my birthday. I don't even think they contacted my family about my death. But the Led Zeppelin inscription's a nice touch, isn't it?"

"Heartfelt." I turned back to him. "So . . . this means we're buried in the same cemetery?"

He nodded, and then the tiniest smile crept over his features. When he spoke again, his tone had lost some of its bitter edge. "More proof that we're fated to be together, don't you think?"

"If that were the case, Eli, I'd have a whole graveyard full of choices, wouldn't I?"

Eli chuckled darkly but then turned his eyes back to his headstone without further comment. He didn't even watch me when I walked away from him.

I picked my way through the weeds, back to the relatively manicured area in which my own concrete slab lay. Once there, I knelt at the foot of my grave and pressed my hands to the low grass. It seemed firm enough beneath my hands. This plot of earth was no dream, no nightmare.

I had an instant, sickening thought: what lay in the grave now, just six feet below my fingertips? I didn't know, but I could guess. An unbidden picture flashed into my mind, and I gagged. I turned my face to my shoulder so I wouldn't have to stare at this suddenly repulsive stretch of grass.

Unfortunately, I realized only too late that I shouldn't have turned. In doing so, I brought another headstone into my line of sight: the one right next to mine.

The early-morning sun had crested the horizon, and it now threw its soft pink rays from behind the neighboring headstone. The rays were almost strong enough to shadow the headstone and obscure its letters. Almost, but not quite.

On a tall stone, only slightly fancier than mine, the following letters glared out at me:

TODD ALLEN ASHLEY
JUNE 5, 1960—MARCH 29, 2006
WE'LL MEET AGAIN

The breath simply whooshed out of my lungs. As I sat there trying to reclaim it—hands pressed to the ground, eyes fixated on my father's epitaph—the faint tunes of a song echoed in my ears. I closed my eyes and imagined the scene that had always seemed to go along with it.

My father and mother, on one of their happier days. One of those days when money worries or job insecurities didn't bother them as much, and they each remembered the other's presence. On those days my father would barge into our tiny kitchen and scoop my mother into his arms. It wouldn't matter if she was covered in flour from making our dinner or suds from the dishes. She would wrap her arms around his neck and lay her head upon his shoulder while he crooned an old tune to her, one that promised they'd meet again, sometime, someplace.

The song was so loud in my head, I didn't hear Eli walk up behind me.

"You don't have to be sad about your death anymore, Amelia." Eli's voice cut off the song just at its crescendo. "I'm here to share it with you," he added, placing one hand upon my shoulder.

I brushed Eli's hand away, perhaps with unnecessary force. "I'm not sad about my death, Eli. I'm sad about his." I pointed to my father's grave, my finger jutting out in a rigid accusation, as if to blame the grave itself for my misery.

"Oh. And who is this?"

"My father," I whispered.

"This stone?" Eli leaned over me to read the stone. "Todd Ashley? This is your father?"

"Y-yes."

The word broke apart as I spoke it. I pressed one hand to my lips in an effort to hold back the torrent, but it was too late. My enormous, gasping sobs ripped through the dawn air, wrenching out of me not only my breath but also a great flood of tears.

I sank, then, at the foot of my father's grave. I left my hands on the grass and lay my head upon them. I let my tears fall from my face, onto my hands and then onto the ground.

"You're . . . crying," Eli breathed in wonder.

"Yes," I moaned, but then barked out a bizarre little laugh. I pushed myself back up into a seated position, wiping ineffectually at my cheeks and my chin. "I've been known to do that from time to time."

Eli grabbed my waist, and, before I realized what was happening, he pulled me to my feet and whirled me around to face him.

"You'll never have to cry again. Not while you're with me."

His fingers dug into the fabric of my dress. With one huge breath—for courage, perhaps—he wrenched me to him and pressed his lips to mine.

His mouth muffled my cry of protest. I shoved hard against his chest, but my struggles only made him pull me tighter.

As the kiss continued, I cried out again, but not in protest. This time, I did so in fear.

Because, while Eli kept his mouth crushed to mine, I felt a piercing sensation there, like something had ripped the delicate skin of my lower lip apart. The corners of my eyes prickled from the pain.

When Eli loosened his grip in an attempt to cup my cheek, I was finally able to break free. As I pushed myself out of his arms, I had to retreat several steps back onto my own grave. Even without the pressure of Eli's mouth to mine, my bottom lip still throbbed painfully, rhythmically. My tongue darted to the tender spot on my lips and, inexplicably, I tasted copper.

"What did you just do to me?" I gasped, bringing my fingers to my lips but not yet touching them.

Eli had the decency, at least, to look confused. "I'm pretty sure I kissed you, Amelia."

I dragged the back of my hand across my mouth and then looked down at it. There, smeared across the skin of my hand, was a streak of something bright red.

Blood.

"Y-your teeth," I stuttered. "I think they cut me. I . . . I'm *bleeding*."

Eli shook his head, uncomprehending. "No. No, that's not possible."

"Oh, it isn't?" I said, wiping again at my mouth where I could still feel a hot swell of blood. "Then what's this on my lips?"

"I don't know. But whatever it is, you're wrong," Eli protested. "I wouldn't hurt you, Amelia. Not like that. Besides, I couldn't if I tried—we're both dead."

"It doesn't matter." My voice rose to a near shout. "You won't be kissing me again anyway."

"Oh, I think I will, Amelia. We're fated."

"Quit saying that," I hissed.

"I'll say whatever I want to you. You're fated to serve me, remember?"

I laughed and shook my head. "Oh, I remember, Eli. And thanks for reminding me: I should have known better than to trust you, even for a second."

Eli's mouth twisted as if he'd bitten into something sour. "And who do you trust, Amelia Ashley? That *boy*? That living boy?"

I thrust back my shoulders. "That's none of your business, Eli Rowland."

His scowl deepened into a disdainful smile. "Exactly what do you hope to do with him? Live a long and happy life?"

"I'll do whatever I want with him," I shouted, but Eli merely laughed at me. The cruel sound crawled over my skin.

"You're missing one very important detail, Amelia," he said. "You can't share your future with that boy, because there is no future for you. He'll age, but you'll stay the same, forever, dead—unchanging. Futureless."

"I don't have to stay here and listen to this," I spat. "And I'm not going to."

I spun on my heels to leave, to go anywhere but here, and fast. Before I could run away, though, Eli grabbed one of my wrists and whirled me back around to face him.

Immediately, I became aware of a rough burning upon my wrist at the place where Eli's fingers gripped me. I looked down at my arm and gasped. Just beneath Eli's fingers, pale pink streaks appeared on my skin: abrasions, caused by his too-tight grip.

As Eli had said, it wasn't possible. Yet as I struggled, the marks beneath his fingers grew brighter, more irritated.

"Eli, my arm!" I looked back up at him in panic. Eli, however, didn't seem to hear me. His eyes, bright and frenzied, bored into mine. I tried in vain to yank my wrist from his grip while I clawed at his fingers with my free hand.

"Stop it!" I shrieked. "You're hurting me!"

Eli ignored my demand and tugged me closer.

"But maybe I'm forgetting something too, Amelia. After all, isn't your death one of the reasons you came to see me? You *did* want to know about your death, didn't you?" That malicious smile changed into something darker, something wilder. "Well, *honey*, let me fulfill your wish."

"No! Let me go," I cried out just as I lost the tug-of-war

with my arm. Eli finally pulled me to him, his face only a few inches from mine.

"Too late, Amelia. Too late."

"Please," I gasped. I couldn't quite catch my breath, and the bones in my wrist strained under his grip.

"Don't beg. It's unbecoming," Eli whispered. Then he jerked me even closer to him, pressing his body to mine. "Now, I'm going to tell you something very important and then I've got to get to my second appointment today. I don't have much time, so listen carefully: you didn't fall off that bridge."

"No," I moaned. "I fell. I know I fell. I didn't jump."

"Shut up," Eli commanded. "You didn't fall. And you didn't jump, either."

"W-what?" I shook my head, unable to think clearly, unable to understand.

Eli leaned in until his cold lips brushed my earlobe. Softly, almost too softly for me to hear, he whispered, "You were pushed."

Without warning, Eli let go of my arm.

I hadn't stopped struggling and so I flew backward from the momentum. I fell toward the ground, staring wildly up at Eli's twisted face.

The last thing I heard, before my vision went black, was the loud crack of my head against my own tombstone.

*Chapter*
# TWENTY-THREE

It was the same as always.

I opened my eyes to the terrible, familiar water. It churned and frothed around me, whether from the river's current or my struggles, I couldn't be sure. The water obscured my vision, battered against my weakening limbs, and pried at my lips, trying to open them and inundate my lungs.

My lungs ached for air, and my arms ached from flailing. Black spots—the by-products of a lack of oxygen—began to dance across my eyes.

Another nightmare. I was in another nightmare.

The rational part of my brain recognized this fact. It spoke softly, quietly telling the rest of my brain that this horror would end soon, that I always awoke from this wretched scene even if I did so as a dead girl. I knew this much: if I stopped struggling, the nightmare would eventually end and I would wake up in the graveyard.

And after I woke up, I would be able to return to Joshua. The very thought of his name gave me hope. It gave me a reason to let go of the fight no matter how much it went against my somewhat ironic survival instinct.

So I stopped struggling. I let my arms and legs go slack. I let the current pull at them, let it catch them and drag them. I closed my eyes just so I wouldn't have to watch this part of the nightmare happen, and I opened my mouth to breathe the inevitable air of the graveyard.

Yet water instead of air rushed into my open mouth. I choked on it, inadvertently allowing in more water. I opened my eyes, but I still saw the dark river around me, not the sunlit cemetery.

Something was going horribly wrong.

I'd never choked before. In no other nightmare had the water actually entered my lungs. I always woke up just before the point of death. Always.

But not now, it seemed.

My lungs screamed in my chest since the water burned

them far worse than the lack of air had. My whole body moved in a frenzied response to the burning in my chest, arms flapping and legs scissoring beneath me.

I flailed, I flailed, and then—

Impossibly, I rose. Within seconds, my head emerged from the water.

I felt wind, and the heavy pelting of rain against my skin. The rain came from all directions, pouring down on me in a torrent and then splashing back off the river and into my face.

My body began to react again. I coughed twice and choked up some of the water from my lungs. My hands slapped weakly against the surface of the river, mostly ineffective in their battle to keep me afloat.

While I floundered, I felt the strangest sensation along my wrists, under my jaw, in my chest: a heavy thumping that reverberated throughout my body. Without being terribly cognizant of what I was doing, I clenched one hand to my heart.

Only then, with my hand pressed against my chest, did I realize what was happening: my heart was beating. That was a pulse, thumping at my wrists and under my jaw.

I was alive.

I opened my mouth to scream—from fear, from joy. And for help. If I was truly alive, I needed help, fast.

But another noise cut off my scream: laughter, loud

and crazed, from somewhere high above me. Individual voices blended together in their frenzy, with only the occasionally distinct shriek.

Despite the uniformity of the laughing voices, they all sounded so familiar. Who were they? Where were they?

I squinted up through the rain. Far above me I could just make out the shape of High Bridge and the crowd of figures standing at its edge.

*Don't you remember this scene, Amelia? Isn't everything awfully familiar?*

The silky voice—a darker version of my own—whispered in my head. I frowned as I continued to cough and choke up more water. What was happening here?

I looked back up to the bridge and the figures on it.

"Help," I pleaded. The word came out as a feeble moan, barely loud enough to reach the bridge.

At the sound of my voice, one of the figures moved away from the pack. Its head whipped away from the other figures, and it met my gaze. Even through the rain, I could see that the figure was a boy.

I may not have been able to make out his features. But I could, at that moment, have easily described his square jaw, his perfectly straight nose, and his short blond crew cut.

Because I *knew* the boy now staring down at me from High Bridge.

I'd only known him for a short time, really, before my death. Only for my senior year, the one I'd practically forced my mother into letting me attend at Wilburton High School. The boy now watching me would have been in my graduating class, if I'd had the chance to graduate.

I remembered him. I remembered everything about Doug Davidson.

Doug, the most popular boy at school. The one with the most friends, the fastest car, and the richest parents. The one who had befriended me the minute I stepped into Wilburton High. The one who had . . . had . . .

I struggled with the memory, trying to grasp at it, when another figure joined him at the edge of the bridge and flung its arm around Doug's neck. When it leaned forward, I could see its face.

It was Serena Taylor.

Serena had been my best friend since childhood. The girl I'd met during endless hours of homeschooled soccer, forced on us by our parents in an attempt to make us socialize. The girl who'd taught me how to apply lipstick, sneak sips from the bottles in my dad's liquor cabinet, and charm my dad into letting me go to public high school shortly after she'd entered it. The girl who was as blond and as beautiful as Doug and who, once I'd introduced her to him, had tried various schemes to seduce him, including forcing him to help her organize a party.

The one they'd thrown together for my eighteenth birthday.

The day on which I'd died.

My head jerked up to Doug and Serena again. They were both bent over the railing of the bridge, their faces more visible now. Even from this far away and through the rain, I could tell something was wrong with them. Their nearly identical blue eyes looked too dark, too unfocused.

Inexplicably, I started to shake. Staring up at their familiar faces—faces that shouldn't still look eighteen, should they?—I felt dizzy.

At that moment Serena cried out to me. Her shrill voice pierced the night air, sounding slurry and drunk and completely out of control.

"Amelia! Amelia. Happy, happy birthday, baby!"

She reached an arm out to me and, with an absurdly wide smile, gave me a frantic wave.

Before I could answer her, or scream at her to help me, for God's sake, I had a sudden, uncontrollable flash.

It happened much like the other flashes I'd been experiencing since I'd met Joshua—the sights and sounds of the past, the memories I'd forgotten since my death, came rushing back into my mind.

Without warning, I was standing in front of my locker

in the brightly lit hallway of Wilburton High School. Taped to the front of my locker was a small card decorated with cartoon balloons. I didn't need to open it to know who had taped it there. Nor did I feel any real surprise when the card giver squealed out a greeting behind me.

"Happy birthday, birthday girl!"

Grinning widely, I spun around. "Serena, you've had about ninety tardies this semester. Don't you think you should be in homeroom by now?"

She grinned back and then blew one blond strand out of her eye with a puff of breath. "Not on my bestie's b-day." She flopped against the bank of lockers, banging their doors with the paper bag in her hand.

"What's with the bag?" I asked. "And the trench coat?"

With her free hand, Serena tugged at the belt of her khaki overcoat, and it fell open. Underneath, she wore a pink dress that narrowly towed the line between sexy and sleazy. Its tight bodice plunged just a little too low for my taste, and its hemline crept just a little too high.

"Hello, hot stuff," I crowed.

"Glad you approve." She tossed the bag at me, and I caught it in midair. "Here's yours for tonight. Hope you like strapless."

"Serena, I can't—"

"Yes, you can," she growled with mock ferocity.

"Okay, okay." I laughed. "But what do you mean, 'tonight'?"

"You didn't think you'd get out of one of my famous parties, did you? Especially for your eighteenth birthday. It's, like, mandatory."

I groaned, more out of concession than protest. *"Fine. When and where?"*

She flashed me a wicked grin—one that, for some strange reason, made me uncomfortable.

"Not telling you, Amelia baby. I'm just picking you up at eight and escorting you to the best party of the year. After I talk your mom into a very irresponsible curfew, of course."

"You're going to start another one of our epic fights if you do."

Serena, however, just shrugged, unconcerned about my family drama.

I laughed again, but more shakily this time. "Really, Serena. I need to know where the party's going to be."

She shook her head and winked. "Nope. Now, shut up so I can go find Doug and see if he approves of the dress too."

Suddenly, the flash skipped me forward several hours. Images blurred all around me until my vision cleared and I found myself standing in a large crowd.

A *huge* crowd, actually. Tons of people surrounded me, smiling and laughing and converging around what looked like a small keg of beer. Some of them were my friends, from homeschooled extracurriculars as well as from Wilburton High. Most of the partygoers, however, were total strangers.

"Serena," I said through clenched teeth. "Who are all these people?"

Serena bounced next to me, hyperactive and probably a little tipsy. She handed me her cup, and I took a nervous swig from it.

"Friends," Serena giggled. "Or, like, all of Wilburton High. So . . . potential friends?"

"Is this Doug's doing?" I asked, handing her back the cup and then smoothing imaginary wrinkles from my white dress.

Serena's choice for my birthday outfit hadn't really surprised me. The dress was absolutely gorgeous—strapless and tight on top, with layers of delicate tulle below—but also totally inappropriate. I flushed with embarrassment as I stared down at it. It probably made me look like I was on my way to the prom.

A thick arm slung across my shoulder, making me shriek in surprise.

"Of course it is," Doug said, pulling me closer to him. He took a sideways peek at me. "Nice dress, by the way."

I shrugged out from under his arm. "You know you like Serena's better."

"Possibly," he mused, and then pushed past me toward Serena. Within seconds the two of them had linked arms and disappeared into the crowd, leaving me alone, in a beautiful but embarrassing dress, at my own birthday party. I peered into the crowd, searching for my friends without success.

A loud boom distracted me from my search, and I looked up. Above me, the night sky appeared dark and blank, but I knew better; thick gray clouds had covered the sky all day, threatening storms. Now lightning sliced across the black, glinting harshly off the metal girders of High Bridge.

I hated this place, I really did. It was too rickety and too old, and it had seen far too many car accidents and suicides for my taste. But I had a good idea why Serena had chosen this bridge for my party: its bad reputation had left it pretty abandoned as a roadway, making it the perfect spot for wild parties. In fact, I may have been the only person in Wilburton who *wasn't* inclined to booze it up on High Bridge. Tonight was no exception.

Thinking like this, however, hardly improved my mood. So I glanced at the faces around me, trying to find someone to talk to.

Everyone, however, ignored me completely. Well, all

but one person ignored me. A boy, far into the crowd and only partly visible, caught my eye. He looked startled for a second, as if something about me surprised him, but then he smiled and gave me a slight nod. The gesture should have made me happy, but it actually unnerved me. I'm not really sure why since the boy was so attractive: oddly luminous skin beneath his long blond hair; bright blue eyes; and a black shirt, open provocatively over his bare chest to reveal a cluster of necklaces. But something about his smile seemed more like a smirk.

I leaned over to a girl who looked vaguely familiar and shouted above the noise. "Hey, you see Mr. Rock Star over there? What's his story?"

"Who?" she yelled.

When I turned back to point him out, I could no longer see him in the sea of faces. Maybe he'd moved?

I frowned and began to shove through the crowd, suddenly and inexplicably intent on finding him. The crowd swayed and surged around me, sometimes blocking my way and sometimes pushing me forward. I studied each partyer but had about as much luck finding Mr. Rock Star as I'd had with Doug and Serena. As I elbowed my way across the bridge, raindrops began to fall, slowly at first and then gaining in speed.

"Perfect," I muttered, wiping at a fat droplet from the corner of my right eye. No matter how furiously I wiped, though, the droplet wouldn't go away. In irritation, I swung my head violently to the right.

That's when I saw them. They must have hung at the edge of my peripheral vision, almost but not quite out of sight: black shapes wafting through the crowd, circling around people's heads. The inky, insubstantial things moved like liquid, undulating and swirling. Yet they looked dense, almost like clouds, or . . .

"Smoke!" I screamed, pressing against a particularly out-of-control boy.

I kept screaming the word and shoving against people, but the crowd responded to my screams with nothing but shrieked laughter and unfocused stares, as if they couldn't see me, much less the strange shapes moving above their heads.

I started to panic. My adrenaline surged, and I tried to elbow my way through the thick mass of unresponsive bodies.

Suddenly, my arms broke through the crowd. My hands flailed in the air for a moment until they caught something solid: the cold, wet smoothness of metal. I grasped it tightly and used it to pull myself free from the wall of bodies.

I looked down and saw my hands clutched to the edge of the metal guardrail of the road, a flimsy one meant to keep cars from plummeting off the bridge and into the river below.

With the crowd writhing behind me, I hugged the railing as if to escape them. But escape to where, honestly? I spared one glance below me, to the river.

The water rose up to me, swelled by almost three weeks of Oklahoma's spring storms. I'd never seen the water so high or so churned by the speeding current. The river seemed to foam at the edges, frothing like a rabid dog. The sight of it sent a deep, piercing chill through me.

And yet . . .

What if I just . . . jumped?

I leaned farther over the rail, staring into the water. Sure, I was a few stories up, and the river looked more dangerous than I'd ever seen it. But maybe I could get away from the party if I leaned forward just a little more . . . ?

I gasped and pulled myself back from the guardrail, shaking my head in fear. What on earth had given me that impulse, made me think I could just jump down and swim away? Where had that so obviously lethal idea *come* from?

At that moment I'd never felt so strong an urge in my life: I wanted to be away from this place. Away from this crowd of strangers and the bizarre smoke hovering—seemingly without a source—above them. Away from this river.

I stared back into the crowd, desperate to find someone I knew. Someone who could get me out of here.

At that moment I caught his eye again. Mr. Rock Star. He watched me from behind an array of faces, now wearing an unmistakable smirk. I don't know how I knew, but instantly, I just *did*—he could see the fear in my eyes. And he was enjoying it.

Before I could call out to him, to tell him to leave me alone, another face popped in front of his. When Serena gave me a broad grin, I nearly fainted with relief. She brushed aside the partyers until she broke through to stand in front of me.

"Serena, thank God—"

"Amelia!" she interrupted with a happy cry, and then threw her arms around my neck in a fierce hug.

The motion was too forceful, and it nearly rocked me over the railing. I grabbed onto the edge of the curved metal, clawing desperately against its smooth surface.

"Serena, let me up!" I screamed.

Immediately, she dropped her arms, and I was able to plant myself against the railing once more. But instead of checking my safety or even calming me down, Serena turned back to the swaying mass on the bridge.

"Hey, all you people," she said, slurring each word. I'd never heard her so drunk. "Did you know it's Amelia's eighteenth birthday?"

In response, the entire crowd shifted its focus to us. The effect was disturbing, as if hundreds of eyes had simultaneously riveted on me. Now I could just make out Doug's blue eyes, no more than twenty feet away. Mr. Rock Star's eyes also reappeared, sparkling coldly, close to Doug's. Above all of them, the black shapes still floated, slipping over and around each figure.

Suddenly, the partyers all began to speak again, but this time they spoke only one word. The same word, repeated over and over again in a hundred different voices.

My name.

Still staring at them, Serena leaned back against me, and her weight pushed me farther over the rail. My feet actually lifted up off the asphalt and swayed slightly in the air.

The motion should have horrified me. Yet when Serena spun back around to face me, I found myself transfixed by her eyes.

They were unfocused, as anyone's would be if they were drunk enough. I'd seen her eyes affected by drink before, plenty of times. But whatever clouded Serena's eyes now, it certainly wasn't alcohol. Her eyes seemed too wide and vacuous, the pupils so enlarged that only a thin line of blue circled them.

Serena looked possessed.

When she leaned in to me this time, I flinched. But my fear didn't deter Serena. She closed the space between us, pushing me farther and farther over the bridge until I was parallel with the river. Then Serena grasped my shoulders and, in a raspy whisper, said, "Happy birthday, bestie."

With a strange, too-wide grin, she let go of my shoulders. That movement was all it took.

My scarce balance upon the guardrail vanished. I rolled backward and hovered for what seemed like an eternity on the edge of the railing. Then I fell, tipping over the metal. Beneath, I could hear the water, foaming and slavering as the river rushed up to meet me. Just before I hit the water, I could hear a chorus of shouts above me.

At that moment the flash ended.

For a while I'd almost forgotten I was experiencing a flash. But the past blurred and faded, and I was once again back in the river, staring up at the bridge.

A terrible realization dawned on me. I didn't know how or why, but when this latest flash ended, it didn't take me back to the present and the relative safety of my graveyard. Instead, the flash left me still flailing in the river, still experiencing what I'd initially thought was just another afterlife nightmare.

So, the flash hadn't ended. Not really. Because this was the present, in a sense. I was still here, in the river, on the night of my eighteenth birthday. And, suddenly, Doug and Serena were still staring down at me with wild eyes.

"Doug, she sees us!" Serena shrieked. "Amelia sees us!"

Doug didn't respond to her proclamation, nor did he break eye contact with me. He just grinned like a crazy person and, as Serena had done before the flash, waved at me.

I could still see the shadows, dark and swirling around my friends. I knew what they were now. Those shadows could be nothing other than the trapped souls from the netherworld. Eli's minions. The mindless orchestrators of this entire evening.

"Doug, Serena, please. I can't . . ."

My voice came out even fainter than it had before the flash. I could feel myself losing the fight against the current. I was far too weak to swim out of the stormy waters now; I knew it. I would need their help.

Help they didn't necessarily seem inclined to provide me. Doug and Serena looked like statues, standing stock-still on the bridge.

"Please," I called out once more, as loudly as I could.

At the sound of my watery voice, Serena turned toward the crowd of partyers behind her. She called out to them, her voice rising to a hysterical octave over their laughter.

"Hey, everyone! Let's sing 'Happy Birthday'!"

I shook my head feebly. I wanted to scream out to the crowd, to beg them not to listen to Serena. To tell them they were all being controlled by dark spirits, driven wild and out of their minds. But my voice, like my arms, seemed to be on the brink of failure. Instead, I stared at Serena and pled silently with my eyes.

Serena looked back at me with a suddenly determined stare. I breathed a huge sigh of relief. Her expression could only mean one thing: she'd decided to call for help. The police, an ambulance, maybe even my parents. Whoever came, I didn't care so long as someone pulled me out of this water.

But when Serena finally spoke, she did so calmly, warmly. With no sense of urgency at all.

"This one's for you, Amelia, baby," she said, and then turned toward the crowd. "Ready, everyone? Okay!"

A unison of voices surged from the bridge, like a choir. *"Happy birthday, dear Amelia . . ."*

"No!" I screamed, trying to struggle once more against the waves.

But of course, my scream never rose above a hoarse whisper, and my struggles were nothing compared to the control the current now had over my body. I was fast losing my ability to stay afloat, much less escape the drag of the current.

With horrifying clarity, I realized what was happening.

The people above me were too crazed, too lost, to help me. I wouldn't regain my strength. And I would continue to weaken in my fight against the river.

There was only one way this scene could end.

*No!* I screamed in my head. *This doesn't have to happen again. I can change this. I don't have to die this time, I don't!*

"Help!" I screamed aloud, but my energy was almost completely gone and the scream echoed only in my mind. My head bobbed underwater and stayed there for a few seconds. When the current bobbed me back up to the surface, I gasped in fear.

The gasp didn't have much of a lifespan, because the current almost immediately yanked me back down. Once under, I continued to gulp for air, swallowing more water in the process. The current spun me around and finally pulled me to the other side of the bridge before it lifted me out of the water again.

Coughing and sputtering, I looked up at the bridge, now from the opposite side from which I'd fallen. I could just make out the rain-blurred figures of Doug and Serena running to this side of the bridge. I tried to reach out to them, but I couldn't even bring my arm above the surface of the river.

Only then did I notice Serena hold something out to me. It was her hand, once again extended over the railing toward me. She gave me another cheerful wave, flailing her arm joyously in the thick rain.

Her bright smile was the last thing I saw before my head bobbed back down for the third, and final, time. I didn't see anything after that.

*Chapter*
TWENTY-FOUR

I woke up, still wheezing and gasping. My fingers twitched frantically, grasping around me.

At first I couldn't feel anything, which only terrified me more. Then I felt the dull pressure of something beneath me—something solid. I turned my head as far to the right as it would go and saw dusty yellow, just inches from my face. As I squinted, the scene came into greater focus. I could see dark brown threads woven through the yellow. It took me a moment to realize the brown was my hair, fanned out upon the dried grass beneath my head.

Above me, all I could see were stars. I pushed myself up and scanned my surroundings. Far off to the west, the sky had turned a faint violet, wherein the sun had just set behind the mountains. Elsewhere, the night had already begun to darken into deep purples and blues.

And yet, even in the darkness, I recognized the curves and twists of the familiar headstones around me. I was in my graveyard again.

I reached around and tenderly touched the back of my head, at the place where it had connected with my gravestone. Nothing. No dried blood or wound, although, inexplicably, my head still throbbed slightly. I pressed my hand to my chest, just above my heart. No thumping there. No pulse.

I was dead again. For the first time that fact made me happy.

Still seated, I turned to my gravestone. Even in the dim light I could see the enormous crack now running down its center. If the gravestone hadn't really hurt me, then I had certainly hurt it.

*Well, Dad had always said that I had a hard head.*

At the thought of my father, I glanced quickly at his headstone. It was still intact; and, for some reason, I sighed in relief.

Then my head shot back up and I searched for the

next most important menace in my afterlife. A cursory scan of the graveyard, however, let me know that Eli Rowland had disappeared.

I looked down at my arm, where a slight bruise seemed to have formed around the place Eli had gripped me. Gingerly, I touched my bottom lip and found a thick cut there. Neither injury hurt. Yet, despite their impossibility, they were very real.

I sighed again and sat backward, pulling my legs to my chest and wrapping my arms around them. I needed to leave this place, and soon. But right now I needed to think.

First things first, I remembered my death, obviously. Every horrible moment of it. I could see now where my nightmares always began. They started at the moment I first fell into the river; at the moment the river sapped me of my energy, before I surfaced just long enough to watch my friends, controlled by some dark—and definitely evil—power, watch me die.

In some ways, then, my nightmares had been merciful. The universe or fate or even my own mind had forced me to reexperience my death many times but hadn't, until now, put me through the worst of it.

These new, disturbing memories brought something else to light, as well.

Eli had been there, watching, waiting with malicious

glee. Mr. Rock Star, with his knowing smirk and cold glare. Serena hadn't pushed me, nor had Eli, obviously. But Eli certainly had something to do with my fall. He controlled the black shapes (so much like the ones in the netherworld, I couldn't doubt their origin), which had surrounded the partygoers and possessed them, prevented them from helping me.

As I rubbed my wrist absently, I couldn't help but wonder what Eli had done: angered me so much, worked me into such a frenzy, that I would transport myself back to the very memory he'd referenced?

If so, then the strength of this forced materialization gave me another idea. Clearly, I was able to move through time and space, if not yet entirely by will. But I also felt sure I had additional, undiscovered powers. I now believed Eli's claim that ghosts could do the extraordinary, particularly when we entered into a state of heightened emotion. My injuries provided one item of proof.

I thought then of the chair that had screeched backward when I'd stood up too quickly in the Wilburton High School library. That chair had moved just after I saw my in memoriam senior photo, just after I'd experienced a great surge of emotion.

And what about my years of nightmarish materializations, or the new crack on my gravestone?

Apparently, Eli wasn't the only one with poltergeist-like powers. I too could materialize and affect stationary objects. But could I do more? How much of the ghostly and living worlds could I influence?

Asking such questions made me recall the best part of the living world I'd experienced so far.

Joshua.

If I could affect things in both worlds, maybe I could protect Joshua from Eli. If I could keep Eli from touching me—from hurting me, or angering me into an unwanted materialization—then I might have some power against him. Could I possibly hurt Eli? Make him bruise or bleed, like he'd done to me? Just enough to stop him from harming Joshua.

Maybe, if I focused hard enough, I could do . . . something. Whatever that something might be.

"Amelia!"

The unexpected shout made me leap into a crouch, clenching the grass and snarling in the direction of the voice. At the thought, the very insinuation, that Eli had reappeared, I went completely feral.

I must have looked completely crazy, too, when Joshua, not Eli, came running up to me. Seeing my wild stance, Joshua skidded to a stop.

"Amelia?" he asked again, more timidly.

I dropped out of the crouch and onto my knees. I felt

humiliated, terrified, confused. Joshua's eyes were also wide with fright.

"Are you really here?" he whispered. "I'm not crazy, right? I'm not, like, imagining you?"

"No," I said, uncurling and reaching out to him with one arm. "You're not crazy. I'm as real as a ghost can be."

Joshua surprised me by diving across the grass, dropping to his knees, and pulling me to him with dizzying speed.

"Oh my God, Amelia," he murmured in my hair. "Is it possible to be really mad at you and really relieved at the same time?"

"Probably." I laughed, hugging him close. I pressed my face against his pale blue shirt and sighed. "I'm sorry, Joshua. So sorry. I mean, I'm glad I did it alone, but I'm not glad I did it the *way* I did."

"What did you do, exactly?"

"I materialized in the graveyard. I met with Eli, and some stuff happened—bad stuff, including a nightmare—and then I just woke up. I'm sorry I didn't tell you what I was trying to do. I just didn't want you to follow me, if it worked, because I didn't want you to get hurt. But obviously you did follow me, because here you are, and here I am—"

Joshua cut off my babbling with a tense laugh. "Do

you know how many graveyards there are in Wilburton? Way too many."

"Oh, God, I'm so sorry," I moaned again.

Joshua grabbed my face with both hands, gently but firmly lifting it until our eyes met. "Amelia, you can't ever do that again, okay? Not unless you want to kill me, too."

"I'm sorry," I repeated once more. Then I shook my head. "I just keep having to apologize to you, don't I?"

"If you promise you'll at least tell me before you do something like that again, then you don't have to apologize."

I held up one hand in a pledge. "I promise. I will always, always tell you before I do something stupid from now on."

Joshua nodded, looking slightly mollified. "Okay. Now a second promise: you'll never go see Eli without me."

"How about if both of us never see him again?"

Joshua blinked. "Well, that would be more than fine with me. But how's that going to happen?"

"I learned a few things today," I said. "I have so much to tell you. But first, I think I have some powers too, just like Eli does. I'm not sure which ones yet, but I think if I get worked up enough, I can use them against him."

Joshua arched one eyebrow. "So, you think he'll show back up again?"

"Definitely, but who knows when . . ."

I trailed off, frowning and staring down at the grass without really seeing it. As I thought back over my early-morning conversation with Eli, something struck me as odd. For the first time, I processed something Eli had said, just before he'd told me I'd been pushed off High Bridge. Something about having another appointment today.

A song suddenly filtered through my head, tinny and faint.

*We'll meet again. . . .*

I felt an eerie tingle race across my skin, and it had nothing to do with Joshua's touch.

"Joshua, Eli wasn't at your house today, was he?"

"Not that I know of."

"Are you sure?"

He laughed. "Pretty sure, yeah."

"Have you checked on everyone in your family?" I insisted.

Joshua's laugh faded. "Well, no, but—"

"How long was I gone?" I interrupted.

"You've been gone all day. It's still Friday. But it's Friday night now."

"Where's the rest of your family?"

"Mom and Dad are out for their date-night. And Jillian's taking advantage by going out, too."

"Out?"

"Jillian came home from school all excited about this party tonight. She made fun of me for not wanting to go—I didn't, because I figured I'd be looking for you all night—and then she invited all her stupid friends over to get ready. I guess I should have followed them, but I was worried about you."

The story bothered me, particularly the part about the party. My head snapped up, and I met Joshua's eyes again.

"I . . . I think we need to go check on Jillian," I said. "Sooner would probably be better than later."

Not yet attuned to my mood, Joshua chuckled. "Jillian wouldn't appreciate me pulling the big-brother card on her, you know."

"Still," I mused, biting my lip and carrying on an internal debate. Finally, I nodded. "Joshua, the night I died, I was at a party on High Bridge for my birthday. The party . . . well, I'm pretty sure the party is the reason I died. And Eli and his minions made it all happen."

I could practically hear Joshua's thoughts shift in tone. "What exactly does that mean to us now?" he asked quietly.

"I have no idea. Maybe nothing. But I have a weird feeling about this. What if Eli tried to get to us another way? Like maybe through this party, and what he could do to the people there?"

"Do you really think he'd do that?"

"I don't know—nothing seems beneath him at this point."

A sudden, chirping electronic noise interrupted my worrying. Joshua also seemed surprised by the noise, because he jerked upright too quickly and jostled me in his arms.

The noise chirped again, insistent, so he reached into his pocket and pulled out his cell phone. He flipped open the tiny device and began clicking away at its keys.

"It's a text from Jillian, inviting me to the party."

"A text?"

"It's like an email, but on your phone," he murmured, clearly not interested in explaining technology to me at this moment. I couldn't blame him. Nor was I surprised when, after he read the text, his mouth tightened into a grimace and he loosened his hold on me.

"Where's the party supposed to be?" I asked, shutting my eyes in dread. I felt a strange, sudden ache at my temples as if in response to my fears.

"High Bridge Road."

Everything screeched to a halt. Nothing had moved, and nothing had changed; but I felt as though I were sitting at ground zero at the exact moment before a nuclear bomb detonates.

"Joshua?" I whispered.

He frowned deeply before looking up at me. I easily read the emotions in his eyes: uncertainty, yes, but also a deep, growing fear.

We continued to stare at each other, both of us momentarily frozen. In mere seconds a barrage of thoughts ran through my mind. How fast could Joshua get to the river? Did Eli have something to do with this? And if he had, what could I do to make him stop?

My head started to throb in earnest now. Only Joshua's voice broke through its buzzing.

"Want to go to a party, Amelia?" he whispered, panic edging into his voice.

"I think that's a good plan," I whispered back. Without another word the two of us were up and sprinting toward the entrance of the graveyard.

"I'll drive," Joshua called back to me.

"Then drive as fast as you possibly—"

A burst of fire, bright and less than fifty feet away, ended my sentence and stopped both of us short.

*Chapter*
TWENTY-FIVE

For a moment I thought something inside the graveyard—possibly a tree—had caught fire, but then I realized that the sounds accompanying the light weren't fiery hisses. They were human murmurs.

Chants.

The fires glowed brightly and the sun had nearly set, so I had to squint just to make out the dim figures of the chanters standing just inside of the iron cemetery fence. At first, the scene made no sense. But when I looked up at the darkening sky, to the waning crescent moon that hung there, the pieces began to fit together until—

"Joshua, the exorcism!" I gasped. "It's supposed to be tonight."

In my rush to deal with Eli, I'd completely forgotten about the exorcism. But Ruth and the other Seers obviously hadn't. They probably followed Joshua here tonight, knowing he'd lead them right to me.

Now the ache at my temples pulsed in time to their voices; it must have started when they began to chant, before we noticed them.

Joshua groaned and grabbed my hand to drag me through the cemetery, to the small hill near its gates. There, about ten people had gathered. Except for Ruth, each held a lit torch and had taken his or her place in a ring around what looked like a circle of gray powder—identical to the kind now bordering the Mayhew house—sprinkled onto the grass. Through the ring of people, I could just make out a small, square object lying on the grass. Ruth's herb-wreathed Bible, probably.

All of the Seers but Ruth stared intently into their makeshift circle. Ruth, however, stood off to one side and looked at Joshua and me.

Joshua gave his grandmother a curt nod. "Torches, Ruth? Wouldn't flashlights have been a bit less heavy-handed?"

The corner of Ruth's mouth twitched in irritation.

"The torches add a touch of ceremony, Joshua."

At the sound of voices, the other Seers finally glanced in our direction. I was surprised by their faces: mostly elderly but a few young ones, not much older than Joshua and me. But only a few of them—mainly the older ones—stared directly at me. As Jillian had done outside the school and then in the Mayhews' kitchen, the younger Seers seemed to peer with difficulty at the space in which I stood.

"Why isn't everyone looking at me?" I managed to whisper, although everything in my body, including my vocal cords, felt paralyzed.

"Not all of them have had a triggering event," Ruth explained, turning her sharp eyes on me. "Some of them can't see you . . . yet."

"Then don't let them," Joshua pleaded.

Thank God he did, because I didn't think I had the strength to choke out another sentence. I didn't know whether this group of Seers had enough power to cast me into oblivion, but I knew this headache (not yet debilitating, but getting there) wasn't a sign of good things to come. Whatever the Seers intended to do to me, I certainly didn't want to go through it.

Nor did I want tonight to be my last in the living world. My last night with Joshua.

Ruth, however, shook her head at Joshua's request.

"That's not possible. If she's wandering among us, unclaimed by one afterlife or another, then she's evil. And we can't take the risk of letting her join the other spirit in hurting more people on that bridge."

Joshua lurched forward, inadvertently yanking me with him. "You have the wrong ghost, I swear." Ruth shook her head again; but Joshua continued, cutting her off. "No, listen to me, Ruth. Amelia has nothing to do with all the deaths on High Bridge. In fact, she was a victim of the guy you've been hunting—Eli. I know. I've seen him myself, and he's seriously creepy."

Ruth took a hesitant step away from her grandson as if his words confused her. Joshua took advantage and moved forward, fumbling with his free hand for something in his pocket. He produced his cell phone, flipped it open, and shoved it in front of Ruth.

At first she avoided looking, but soon her eyes were drawn to the phone's glowing screen. She frowned, still staring at the device.

"What does this mean, Joshua?" she asked.

"It's a text from Jillian," he said, pushing the phone closer toward Ruth. "She and our friends are at some party on High Bridge, and we're pretty sure Eli's lured them there."

"How do you know?"

"I just do," he nearly shouted, his patience running

thin. Each second of delay might cost his sister, and Joshua knew it.

Ruth still looked skeptical, with her mouth twisted with disbelief. Her eyes, however . . . in her eyes I could see doubt. I could see it each time her gaze flickered over to me.

"Ruth," I said quietly, stepping forward with Joshua's hand still clasped in mine. The pain at my temples grew in intensity the nearer I got to her, but I kept moving. "Ruth, I know you don't trust me; and all things considered, I don't blame you. But you're right about one thing: Eli Rowland is bad news. He controls that river, and I'm almost certain he's behind this party tonight, after what he showed me about my death today."

I could still see uncertainty in Ruth's eyes, so I leaned closer. "Please," I murmured. "Just hold off on this exorcism for now. At least long enough for me to do something about Eli, and to make sure Jillian is safe."

Ruth looked back at her group of Seers, each of them watching us intently, and then she turned back to us.

"Please," I repeated.

Slowly, so slowly I wasn't sure she even moved, Ruth nodded at me.

"I can hold them off for a while," she whispered. "I'm not promising any length of time—a day, two weeks, who knows—but you have to make sure my granddaughter is safe. If she isn't . . ."

Ruth trailed off, but I didn't need her to finish the thought. If I didn't save Jillian, nothing could save me. I bit my lip, nodding as well.

I turned to Joshua, who still looked pale, afraid. "Joshua?"

Finally, he stirred, moving his eyes from his grandmother to me. Once I had his full attention, I gripped his hand hard, sending fire racing up and down our arms.

"Joshua, you've got to go," I commanded him. "Now!"

Those words were all the motivation Joshua needed. He dropped my hand and began to dash to his car, jingling his keys out of his pocket. He had made it almost to the door before he noticed I wasn't behind him. Only then did he spin back around to me.

"Amelia?"

"Go on without me. I can get there a lot sooner if I materialize."

"Great idea." Joshua nodded. "Do whatever you can. I'll drive fast."

His expression told me that he was too distraught to question what exactly I could *do* once I beat him to the river. Within seconds he had ducked into the car and started the engine.

As he skidded off across the gravel, I turned back to Ruth.

She stood motionless, still watching me. Her eyes flickered briefly to her Seers, all waiting expectantly—almost angrily, it seemed—for her to take some kind of action. When Ruth's eyes flickered back to me, I could see the emotions warring in them: worry for Jillian; frustration about the position in which she'd just been put; and, of course, unadulterated hatred.

Of me.

Her blatant hatred angered me, especially since the headache still throbbed along my temples and threatened to break into that awful, incapacitating montage of images. I was about to risk myself, my own afterlife, just to save her granddaughter; a little gratitude, or at least a little less intentional infliction of pain, couldn't have hurt.

Despite my irritation, however, I didn't feel intense enough emotions yet. I would need to get much more agitated before I tried to materialize.

So, instead of Ruth, I thought about Serena Taylor and Doug Davidson. My best friends in life. The two people, outside of my family, about whom I cared most in the world. I pictured their crazed, possessed faces on the night I died: horrible distortions of the good people they truly were. Pawns, played with indiscriminate cruelty by Eli in his little game to procure souls. None of them—not Eli, nor his dark masters—had ever considered that our own volition should have something to do with our futures.

Hence my current lack of a future.

Immediately, I became angry. Violently so. The emotion began to simmer somewhere in my stomach. It threatened to bubble up into my throat and break out in a growl. The force of it made me dizzy. I reached out but found nothing except empty air to steady myself.

While I grasped, I felt an unexpected sensation brush along the skin of my palm: air—as cool as if it had come blowing in off water—shifting with the movements of my arm.

I opened my eyes and stared down at my hand. It still flailed, clenching nothing but darkness and hovering several feet above asphalt. Out of my hand's reach, the asphalt ended in grass. Not the grass outside the cemetery, however, but a thicker, coarser grass that sloped steeply down into rushing water. Into a river.

High Bridge Road—I was now standing on it.

I could have spent some time congratulating myself on this second materialization, and marveling at the fact that my headache had suddenly vanished, had my attention not been drawn elsewhere by a chorus of voices. My head jerked toward them.

A huge crowd of young people—Wilburton High students, by the looks of their purple shirts and hoodies—clogged the road across High Bridge. Someone had parked a car in the middle of the bridge, and loud music blasted out from its open doors. Just next to the car I glimpsed the shining metal rim of a beer keg.

A normal enough scene. Just a high school party on a Friday night, one full of people having a great time. And one held directly over the mouth of what I no longer doubted was some cold, pitiless outpost of hell.

I wove my way through the mass of bodies, searching the faces of the students but not finding anything unusual. Aside from the effects of the beer, everyone looked relatively normal: no blurry, possessed eyes, no maniacal laughter. Maybe I'd overacted? Maybe there was no danger here, except for a few possible hangovers?

Ahead, a few yards between me and the bridge's newly repaired guardrail, were some familiar faces. O'Reilly stood closest to the keg, with one arm around Kaylen, sloshing beer from his cup as he gestured to Scott and Jillian. Although Kaylen looked mildly bored, Scott kept sneaking glances at Jillian, who blushed each time his eyes met hers.

I sighed in quasi relief, mostly because none of them looked crazed. Maybe I *had* overacted.

"All's quiet on the western front," I muttered, shaking

my head at my own foolish paranoia.

A familiar whisper, so close to my ear that it felt like a cold caress, made me shriek.

"Oh, I wouldn't say *all's* quiet, Amelia."

*Chapter*
TWENTY-SIX

I should have known, from the first moment I spotted all these people on the bridge. I should have made the connection and trusted my instincts.

Because Eli would never let me go free without a fight. Not after today's argument in our graveyard. He wanted another confrontation with me and as he had done in the past, he'd used as many pawns as he needed to provoke one.

"Hello, Eli," I whispered.

Keeping uncomfortably close, Eli circled around me

until we stood directly face-to-face. He smiled, obviously pleased with himself.

"Nice party," I said. "Looks a little familiar though."

Eli's grin widened. "Ah. So you remember."

"Yes. I remember now."

As I spoke, I took slow, cautious steps toward Jillian and her friends, trying to circle Eli so I placed myself between him and them. With each step, I prayed Eli wouldn't notice until I was close enough to do . . . who knows what.

Eli kept grinning, still oblivious to my movements. He probably thought I was just trying to avoid him, which, on some level, I was. Then his eyes flickered to my feet. I stopped moving, but too late. Eli caught my movements, and his face darkened.

"Stop," he commanded.

"Or what?" I asked, trying to sound brave.

Eli gave me another grin. "Or else, obviously."

The smug glint in his eyes made me want to wipe the grin off his face. I tried to straighten my spine, to ignore the shivers running along it.

"I don't believe you, Eli."

"Well, you should, Amelia." He twitched his head to something behind me. Without letting him out of my sight, I peeked over my shoulder to Jillian and her friends.

I was horrified to find that, in the few seconds I'd been distracted, the entire scene had changed. O'Reilly still had his arm around Kaylen, but the expressions on both of their faces had shifted drastically. Each of them wore an idiotic grin, and each had those unnaturally wide, unfocused eyes. Even Scott's sweet glances at Jillian had become vaguely maniacal.

Of all the people in the small crowd, only Jillian remained unaffected. She glanced nervously from friend to friend, clearly unnerved by their sudden, hysterical giggles. All around her, the party had grown wilder, more uncontrolled. She sensed it, just as I had on the night of my death.

And there, woven throughout the party, were a few new guests; the inky, shapeless forms had arrived, weaving and oozing between the partygoers like smoke. Each time one of these dark souls brushed past a partyer, the living person would stiffen and then began to laugh louder, more vacantly.

I turned around fully to Eli. Although I already knew the answer, I asked, "Who's the latest victim?"

"Well, Amelia, it's none other than Little Sister over there."

"What makes you think she's Joshua's sister?" I asked, disdainful. The bravado in my voice sounded too shaky, however. Unconvincing. Eli smirked in response.

"Because I've been stalking Big Brother's house all afternoon. And wouldn't you know, I eventually found the perfect candidate to invite to a party. A few whispered suggestions in some teenage ears, a few promises to my masters, and voilà—the party of the year." Eli gestured grandly to the throng of people around us. "I could have chosen to inspire a suicide like I did with Melissa, or caused a car accident like I did with your lover boy, but—considering my audience—I thought I'd put on a repeat performance instead. The exact same thing I did more than a decade ago when I needed to find a new assistant."

I wanted to choke, or even scream, upon hearing what Eli had just revealed: that he'd intentionally killed Melissa, that he'd purposefully lured my friends to a party on this bridge so that one of them could die. Or maybe so that I could die? Had he engineered the whole party more than ten years ago just to capture *me*?

"You should know, Eli," I said in a still-shaky voice, trying to distract not only Eli but myself, "that Jillian Mayhew is a Seer, like her brother. They're exorcists by birth, and their family has a long tradition of sending ghosts to hell."

Eli snorted, undeterred. "Not scary, Amelia, considering the girl obviously can't see me right now."

"But she will," I insisted, "if you keep up with your

plan tonight. And her Seer grandma isn't the forgiving kind, trust me."

Eli just smiled, totally disinterested in my threats. Disinterested in the Seers who'd been hunting him without success for so long. When his eyes briefly flickered back to the crowd, mine followed. As I saw the increasingly glazed expressions on the partygoers' faces and listened to their shouts of laughter, I realized how little time I had left. I had to think, think, *think* of some way to make Eli stop.

"A trade!" I cried out suddenly.

Finally, Eli looked back at me, his grin fading. "A trade, Amelia?"

I took a quick peek at Jillian, only to find her being propped up on the guardrail by O'Reilly, with Kaylen and Scott giggling and bending over to hold her legs. One could have easily interpreted this scene as harmless play among friends.

But I knew better.

O'Reilly had his arms around Jillian, but he seemed to be struggling *forward*, as if he was making an effort not to prevent Jillian from falling backward, but to keep her from sliding down off the railing, onto the safety of the road. The same went for Kaylen and Scott, who both looked as if they were trying to pin Jillian's legs to the rail, not keep her steady. As for Jillian, her fingers had clenched into white claws, dug firmly into the skin of O'Reilly's arms.

"Guys," she said with a seemingly casual roll of her eyes. "This has been a real riot and all, but it seriously stopped being funny about twenty seconds ago."

Her friends merely laughed and pressed her more firmly to the guardrail.

I spun back around to Eli.

"Yes, a trade," I said, now desperate. "Me, for them. My life, for theirs."

Eli blinked, obviously surprised by my willingness to negotiate.

"And you answer a question for me first," I added hurriedly.

"Well . . . I might be able to do that," he sputtered. Then his face grew serious, almost reproachful. "As long as you'll hold up your end of the bargain, of course."

"Of course." I nodded.

"And that entails you, staying with me. Forever."

"Yes, yes," I said impatiently, "for however long forever lasts."

Eli blinked again. Then a wide smile began to spread across his face, one that had only a touch of incredulity to it.

"What's your question, Amelia?"

I hesitated for a moment, knowing that now wasn't

really the time for this, but I couldn't help myself.

"Why me?" I asked.

Eli tilted his head to one side, confused. "What do you mean?"

"Why did you kill *me*? What about me was so . . . special, you just had to have me join you? I mean, other than the fact that you thought I was trying to kill Joshua."

To my surprise, Eli laughed. "I could just tell we were meant to be together. I knew it from the first moment I saw your green eyes across the bridge at your birthday party. I didn't even know you were the guest of honor until I started pressing my army to chase you. I only knew your eyes were like hers. Like Melissa's."

My mouth dropped open in shock.

My *eyes?*

My death, my afterlife, my struggles with Ruth and Eli—they had nothing to do with my supposedly evil nature? The whole, tragic thing had started with my *eyes?*

I shook my head, stunned, trying hard to remember my purpose here. To remember my promise to help Jillian.

"Oh," I finally managed to say.

"What on earth made you come to this decision anyway?" Eli asked, unaware of how much he'd shaken me. "Not that I'm disappointed."

I shrugged as nonchalantly as possible under the

circumstances and fought to speak again. "Well, if you'd stop behaving like this—if you'd stop trying to hurt the Mayhew family—then I guess I could see you in a better light. Maybe I could learn to feel like we're meant to be together. After all, you're dead, I'm dead. It makes a weird kind of sense, doesn't it?"

"Of course it does," Eli said. "But what about the living boy?"

"What about him?" I tried to feign a smile.

"Well, obviously, if I let this girl go, if I leave her and her brother alone, then you have to give me your word you'll never see him again. Even in his own hereafter, whenever he becomes like we are now. Can you promise me that, Amelia?"

"I—I promise."

Not only did I stutter, but my voice cracked at the word "promise." Without thinking, I winced at the sound. Eli's eyes automatically narrowed into dark slits. He obviously saw through my ruse, and fury began to brew upon his face. Without another word, Eli flung out his arm toward the group of people clustered around Jillian Mayhew.

Suddenly, their laughter took on an animalistic quality, like the howls of an attack. The black, shapeless souls began to gather around them and writhe frantically. In response, Jillian's captors began to shake their arms, rocking Jillian back and forth against the railing. Her eyes widened in terror, and her mouth open in a silent scream.

"Let her go!" I shrieked. I launched myself at Eli, grabbed the arm he'd extended, and sank my nails into his dead flesh.

For one silent moment, Eli stared down at his arm and the small half-moons of blood my nails had drawn from it. We both knew he shouldn't—*couldn't*—bleed. And yet, as he'd done to me in the graveyard, I'd hurt him now.

"What the hell?" Eli began when a strange, groaning noise erupted under us. It sounded like metal against metal, protesting as it began to fold.

Eli jerked his arm from my grip, and we both looked in wonder at the road beneath our feet. There, zigzagging through the thick asphalt between us, was a narrow fissure. It ran from one side of the road to the other, as if some impossibly large force had cracked the bridge itself.

"Amelia, what did you just do . . . ?" Eli murmured, but the sound of squealing tires cut him short. All of our heads—Eli's, Jillian's, and mine—whirled around to the sound.

At first, all I could see were the negative images of two headlights, flashing black spots against the backs of my eyelids. As I tried to blink them gone, a car door opened, and I heard a wonderfully familiar voice.

"Let them go, Eli, or I swear I'll kill you a second time."

"Joshua!" Jillian and I cried simultaneously. I turned to Eli with a triumphant smile.

Eli looked past me to Joshua. "Your knight in shining armor?" he asked me softly, dangerously.

"Yes," I whispered, suddenly fervent. I grasped his open shirt. "Please, Eli. I love him. I do. And I don't think you're evil, either. Just . . . misguided. So prove me right and let Jillian go. Let them all go. *Make* me care about you, Eli."

For one unbelievable moment, Eli wavered. I saw the war of thoughts on his face, the battle between his need for power and his desire for something else. . . .

"Amelia," he whispered, and reached out with one hand to cup my cheek. But the moment before his fingers brushed my skin, I pulled away from him.

Eli grunted, in both anger and—I was sure—hurt. "I can't stand this anymore," he muttered to himself.

All at once the partygoers straightened and froze. They stood absolutely still, their wide eyes suddenly immobile, vacant. Then, in unison, they began to twitch and convulse.

Almost at once the wraiths pulled back from the living

people as if the force of their involuntary movements had frightened the spirits. The partygoers trembled so hard they appeared to shimmer, the lines of their bodies wavering like the air above a hot tar road in the summer.

From what I could see, all the living people convulsed, with no exceptions. Which would also mean . . .

My head whipped back to Jillian and her friends just in time to see O'Reilly slump like a puppet whose strings had been cut. Both of his arms went slack at his sides, including the arm that, until now, had been one of the only things holding Jillian upright. When Kaylen's and Scott's convulsions caused them both to fall backward, they also lost their tenuous hold on Jillian's legs.

Everything after that seemed to happen in slow motion.

Jillian's eyes briefly flickered to her brother, who was still pushing through the twitching crowd, and then flickered back to her friends. Her arms lifted from the railing like a trapeze artist's as her body shifted farther backward.

She screamed, just once. The noise was muffled and dull in my ears, as was Joshua's shout behind me. But I heard the next sound clearly, the one that cut Jillian's scream short.

A sharp crack rang out, followed by a low, vibrating twang as Jillian's head connected with one of the support beams that extended up from the bridge.

Instantly, her mouth went slack and her eyes rolled back until only their whites showed. Her head slid away from the beam, leaving a dark red smear on the metal. For less than one second, Jillian's entire body relaxed. She looked peaceful. Lovely. Then, without another noise, she toppled over the railing and into the darkness below.

I rushed to the guardrail, but I was too late. Before I'd even gripped the metal, I heard a loud splash from beneath the bridge. Right afterward, Joshua slammed into the railing next to me, and we leaned over together. Only a circle of white foam gave us any clue as to where Jillian had fallen.

Joshua howled wordlessly. Through the howl I heard a timid, boyish whimper from behind us.

"W-what just happened? Mayhew?" O'Reilly moaned. "Dude . . . I think I'm gonna puke."

I ignored his pleas and pulled Joshua down from the railing over which he'd begun to climb.

"No, Joshua, don't! You'll hurt yourself."

"I don't care," he shouted, trying to brush my hand off his shoulder.

"And how will you help her then?" I pleaded. He tossed me the briefest of looks. The misery in his dark eyes made me cringe.

"Go down the hill," I commanded. "It'll be safer for you to get in the water from there, and then you can swim to her. I'll jump in and try to find her this way."

"No. Not you too."

"I can't die, Joshua," I cried, shaking him. "Now, hurry, please, before it's too late."

He twitched for a moment as though he might scream again. But then he spun around and ran away from me. I saw him bring his cell phone to his ear, presumably to call for help as he ran. Only when he disappeared down the grassy hill did I turn back to the crowd.

O'Reilly's face was now a light shade of green, and he'd dropped to his hands and knees on the pavement. The poor boy looked as if he couldn't quite catch his breath. Beside him, Kaylen and Scott panted, clutching at their sides.

"O'Reilly, man," Scott groaned. "What's going on here? Why do I feel like this?"

I looked over his hunched back at Eli. Judging by the expression on Eli's face, the party was no longer going as he'd planned. He seemed to have folded in upon himself in the middle of the moaning crowd, his eyes darting this way and that as he tried to figure out what to do. My lip curled up in distaste.

"I'll deal with you later," I growled. Then I spun away from him and bent over the metal railing again. Far below, I could just make out Joshua's figure on the dark riverbank as he struggled to pull off his shoes.

Free of his sneakers, he waded into the river. When he reached a sufficient depth, he began to swim furiously against the current, toward the place where Jillian had fallen.

Now it was my turn. It should have been a simple enough task. I would use the metal girders to climb up onto the railing. Then I would dive.

*Piece of cake.*

Instead of climbing, though, I shivered. I couldn't lie to myself: the idea of jumping off High Bridge petrified me, no matter what the circumstances were. I looked over the railing once more, down to the black water. It seemed to spin in strange, dizzying circles, moving closer to and then farther away from me.

I had vertigo. Powerful and debilitating.

I gasped and leaned back, letting go of the railing. I

closed my eyes and tried to force my breath back into an even rhythm. I had to do something, I had to. But it seemed as though I couldn't force myself over the edge of this bridge. I couldn't make myself plunge down into the river where, in another world, an evil darkness waited; where, in another existence, I had died.

Then an idea struck me. I had a far easier way to travel, one that didn't involve me falling off High Bridge for the second time. I could go to Jillian immediately, if I desired it strongly enough.

*Materialize.*

I repeated the word in my head while picturing Jillian's face. To my endless relief, it worked, and much faster than it ever had before. Only seconds later, I opened my eyes to the familiar, greenish black darkness.

This time I didn't panic at the sight of the water undulating around me. Thank God I was becoming an expert at navigating this river, because I now had a clear purpose in being here. I twisted myself around, searching.

Finally, I saw a blurry figure floating several feet from me, its thin arms and long hair waving in the water. Jillian. She resembled her brother as she floated, unconscious and dangerously peaceful. A dark streak of what could only be blood trailed in the water just above her.

I whipped my head around, looking for Joshua. I knew from experience that I could do nothing for her, and I wondered why this thought hadn't fully occurred to me before, when I'd told Joshua I would get to her first.

"Joshua?" I called out, my ghost's voice perfectly clear and unaltered by the water.

No one responded. As I looked back at Jillian, her head bobbed lightly in the current. The motion shook loose a few bubbles, which raced from her lips to the surface. I frowned, uncertain of what to do.

Then I heard a faint noise. A *thud, thud, thud* a few feet from me. A rhythmic, pumping, living thud.

The thud of Jillian's heart.

The sound of her heartbeat could mean only one thing if I heard it: Jillian Mayhew would die, and soon.

"Joshua!" I screamed, frantically whirling around again in the water. After several spins I found him, although I realized he wouldn't provide us much help.

I could see him, submerged but high above us. He had his head above the water and was therefore unable to hear my screams. More disturbing, however, was the fact that he was swimming in the wrong direction, moving away from us and upriver.

The current had probably carried Jillian at least twenty feet away from the place where she'd originally fallen—the place to which Joshua now swam. If he stayed on course, Joshua would have no way of finding us. Not in time to save Jillian, judging by the audible thud of her heart.

I swam the short distance to Jillian and began to clutch at her, trying in vain to grab the folds of her light jacket. Unable to grasp that, I reached for the hood at the back of her neck and prayed that my ability to touch her brother would manifest itself now.

It didn't. My hands grasped at nothing. I felt the numb pressure of her clothes, but not the clothes themselves. It was as if Jillian was surrounded by an invisible shield against my dead hands. However much I could touch Joshua, or hurt Eli, I couldn't move Jillian.

I couldn't help her.

The truth of it crushed down upon me. I wanted to throw back my head and scream at the dark water. To howl at my own uselessness.

"Please!" I called out into the dark water. "Please help me. I . . . I don't know what to do. Please help me."

Jillian sank a little farther in the water as her heart continued to pound, its beat noticeably slowing but growing louder in my dead ears. I brought my hands to my face, covering it in a cowardly attempt to shield my eyes from the sight of Jillian Mayhew dying.

At that moment something—or someone—answered my prayers.

At first I didn't really see it; I was too involved with my sorrow, too wrapped up in my misery. But something began to glisten red in my eyes, bright and insistent, distracting me. I pulled my hands away from my face and frowned at the small light that seemed to have formed in them.

The glow moved like a little tongue of flame, pulsing and flickering upon my skin. It looked as if I held the flame as it danced in my palms. This idea made no sense, of course. Yet the light continued to dance, spreading out to my fingertips and up my arms. Soon my arms glowed red and orange, bright like fire beneath the water.

What was happening? Had my terror for Jillian finally found its way to the surface, bright and suddenly visible?

Possibly. I wasn't just scared, though. I was frustrated, sad, even hopeful that I could still help Jillian. An entire range of emotions burned inside of me. They were powerful. Painful.

But the fiery light on my skin wasn't. It didn't hurt at all. It just shined.

I twisted my hands up and then down, watching the light spread past my elbows and up to my shoulders. I kicked one leg into my line of vision and saw the glow there as well. Soon I could see my entire body radiating the glow.

I'd become a luminous beacon in the dark river.

And then, like a miracle, Joshua was there, treading water beside me. For the briefest of moments, he stared at me. His eyes, wider than I'd ever seen them, sparkled with the reflection of red and orange. He gestured back and forth, between his eyes and my glow; apparently, he'd seen the glow from above the water and swam down toward us. Now his expression was one of awe and, possibly, a little fear.

The moment passed with a quick shake of Joshua's head. Neither of us needed a reminder of why we were in this river again. The light on my skin could wait.

Joshua wrapped one arm around his sister's waist. Grabbing my hand, he began to tug us both toward the surface. I squeezed his hand before casting it away from me; without me they could rise faster. I followed them up, pushing Jillian whenever I could though I knew my efforts accomplished nothing.

It felt like hours had passed—though it may have only been seconds—when Joshua lifted Jillian above the water. Only after she reached the air did Joshua himself rise, coughing and gasping. He pulled his sister to him as he paddled to stay afloat. Unfortunately for Joshua, she was as close to deadweight as a living girl could get. Her head flopped lifelessly against her brother's shoulder; and, almost as lifelessly, her heart thudded slower with each passing second.

"Joshua," I shouted over the rush of the water. "I can hear her heart."

"Good," he yelled.

"Not good, Joshua. If I can hear it, that's not good at all."

"Why?"

"I heard your heart, just before it stopped. That's how I knew you were dying."

Joshua didn't answer me, but he began swimming more furiously toward the shore.

I impotently watched him struggle, both to drag his sister toward land and to keep her head above water. All the while I listened to Jillian's faltering heartbeats as they grew louder.

I could still hear them when our feet touched the river bottom and we stood upright to run upon the shore; they beat so loudly I hardly noticed the shouts from the people on the bridge as they began to flee the scene of their disastrous party.

Although he couldn't hear his sister's heart, Joshua also ignored the cries from the bridge. He laid Jillian upon the shore and then dropped to the ground beside her. I bent next to him in the mud, still tracking those loud beats with a dull terror.

I only stopped tracking them when Jillian's eyelids fluttered open.

Joy swelled inside me in response to this small sign of life. I turned to Joshua to celebrate, but the sound of

Jillian's weak voice stopped me short.

"Who are you?" she whispered. I looked down at her, and, unbelievably, she looked back at me. Her hazel eyes stared directly into mine.

My mouth gaped open. I looked back at Joshua, but he didn't seem to have heard Jillian. He checked her pulse and then leaned over to listen for breath, thoughtlessly stroking the fan of her hair on the mud. When he did so, Jillian's eyes fluttered closed, and her heart started to stutter more unevenly.

My head began to spin. *If she saw me . . . if she can see me now . . .*

"Joshua," I cried, "you have to do something fast. I don't think she's doing too well."

"Oh, God," Joshua moaned. He looked up to the road, which was still empty of any emergency vehicles. Then he bent back over Jillian's motionless body.

"I used to know some CPR, if I could just remember it." He tilted her head back and began to murmur. "Is it, breathe then push or push then breathe? Which is first? Which is *first*?"

Watching Joshua press his hands to Jillian's sternum—obviously, without a clue how to save her—I felt a hard, painful clench in my own chest. I ignored it, and decided to do the only thing I could think to do. I pushed my hands into the mud and leaned in close to Jillian's ear.

"Jillian," I whispered, "I know you don't know who I am. But I love your brother, and I know you do too. So . . . do you think you could wake up? Do you think you could at least try?"

For far too long she gave me no response. I'd just about given up—hung my head and prepared myself for the inevitable, impossible job of comforting Joshua—when Jillian whispered back.

"I guess. Since you asked so nicely."

In spite of everything, a quiet laugh escaped my lips. "Thank God. Because I have a feeling you'd be a huge pain in the ass if you died."

The faintest smile twitched upon Jillian's lips. Then she coughed.

The effort was feeble, and it didn't even part Jillian's lips. But Joshua must have heard it, or at least felt the vibration of it, because he jerked away from Jillian's body and stared down at her intently.

"Jillian?" he asked.

In response, she coughed again. This time the cough wrenched itself out of her, loud and clear across the riverbank. Her back arched from the force of it, and her hands squished into the mud beneath her. She coughed for a third time, rolled to her side, and began to choke up the river water.

"Yes!" Joshua crowed. He pressed one hand to Jillian's

back and grasped for me with the other. I clutched myself to him, entwining my fingers with his and wrapping my free arm around him. I laid my forehead against his shoulder and felt it shake from his laughter.

Our laughter came in sharp bursts that verged on hysterical. I can't imagine what Jillian must have thought of the noises coming from her brother, if she could even think clearly. The poor, bedraggled girl continued to cough, although—miraculously—I could no longer hear her heartbeat.

I tilted my head as far back as it would go. "Thank you," I mouthed to the night sky. "Thank you so—"

The sound of another voice, high above me, cut off my prayer.

"You see, Amelia? She's safe, like I said she would be. We can finish our trade now—your life for hers."

My head snapped around to the sound. I could see Eli, standing on the now-empty bridge, calling out to me. Claiming me.

Though the riverbank lay too far below the bridge for me to see Eli's face clearly, I knew it well enough to identify his expression. I didn't need binoculars to see the confidence in his wretched smile.

However much Eli had doubted himself earlier, he obviously didn't now. In fact, he looked more self-righteous than ever. As if Jillian had survived merely through his own will and generosity. As if Eli's own hand had played no part in her near-death. As if he hadn't taken a massive crowd of innocent people hostage in his play to capture me.

For some reason I couldn't take my eyes off Eli's smug face. The sheer loathsomeness of it held me in thrall. I released my arms from around Joshua's neck and slowly rose to my feet.

I was vaguely aware that the strange glow within my skin had dimmed, sometime between finding Jillian in the water and watching her come back to life upon the shore.

Yet as I stood to focus upon Eli, the radiant light burst forth again. It seemed to erupt from my skin, blooming in violent reds and oranges and yellows. I'd never seen colors this fierce, or lovely. Maybe their light had been dulled or obscured by the water. Or maybe I'd never felt this angry before . . . this protective.

Whichever the case, my body now illuminated the entire riverbank.

"Amelia?"

Joshua spoke from behind me. Obviously, he could see the glow again, because his voice broke in a fearful tremble upon my name.

I wanted to turn to him, to tell him *Don't worry, sweetheart. I'm sure burning like a human torch is normal for dead people.* But before I could do so, Eli spoke to Joshua first.

"Don't you dare address her directly, boy," Eli snarled. "She's a servant of this place now, and she is *mine.*"

And that was all it took.

With that one little word—"mine"—the world exploded all around me.

*Chapter*
# TWENTY-EIGHT

I thought I'd burned them all, incinerated the living and the dead together in a final, inescapable blast.

From my perspective, the explosion looked like what I pictured when I thought of hell: fire billowing everywhere, obscuring my vision. I couldn't see anything but bright orange waves, and I had the oddest notion flames poured out of my eyes and fingertips. Instinctively, I clenched my hands and shut my eyes tight.

I stayed like that for a moment, praying, *willing* that

everything would be okay.

With my eyes still closed, I relaxed my hands and slowly stretched my fingers far apart from each other. Then I opened my eyes to stare down at my hand.

I could finally see again, but to my shock, the fire was still there. It glowed upon my skin, just as bright as ever. Yet the explosion hadn't incinerated anything. Everything looked as it had before: no charred trees, no twisted metal, no embers dancing on the wind.

I was the only thing that looked aflame, just as I had on the riverbank. There hadn't been any explosion at all, it seemed.

My location was the only thing that had changed since the explosion-that-wasn't. Instead of standing on the shore beside Joshua and Jillian, I now stood back on the bridge—materialized here, I supposed, by the force of the glow on my skin.

My eyes darted immediately to my right, toward the riverbank below me. To my endless relief, Joshua still crouched in the mud unharmed, and he'd propped Jillian up in his arms. Perhaps he'd positioned her this way so she could more easily cough out the dangerous water in her lungs. Whatever his motives, Joshua had momentarily forgotten his mission. He stared up, wide-eyed and openmouthed, at the bridge. At me.

From my peripheral vision, I could see another

wide-eyed and openmouthed observer standing just a few feet from me on the road. Only now that I was certain Joshua and Jillian were safe could I force myself to turn and look fully at Eli Rowland.

His blond hair fluttered from the breeze, and his already pale face had turned a new shade of ashen white. Though he looked awed—stunned, even, by the glow on my skin—he still wore his earlier, smug expression. As if he had absolute confidence that, despite this new ability of mine, he *owned* me. The sight of his horrible face made me want to snarl, to growl at him like an animal. It took all of my self-control not to do so.

I turned away from him to view the rest of the empty road. In front of me, a pair of fresh tire marks crossed the asphalt. Behind me, the black rubber zagged to one side of Joshua's car and then streaked off across the dark road.

It appeared that, in the few minutes of chaos I'd witnessed from below the bridge, the owner of the loud car stereo had fled the scene, as had the rest of the students of Wilburton High.

I shook my head at the tire marks. I couldn't blame any of them for running away, including O'Reilly, Scott, and Kaylen. I didn't imagine that they would remember anything, or that they would want to, for a long time.

They shouldn't have had to play any role in this twisted

supernatural game. Nor should Jillian, who would likely carry the frightening memory of this night with her always.

Then there was Joshua. The one for whom I feared the most during this ordeal. The last—and, to me, the most important—of the living people who would have suffered horribly, had Eli's plot ended in a darker way.

So much fear, and so much potential tragedy, all because Eli Rowland wanted me.

Nothing but outright ownership would satisfy Eli. Even now Eli had a glimmer of it in his eyes—not only the need to obey his masters' orders, but also that mad, unstoppable need to own. To possess.

And because of some passing resemblance to his dead lover, I was the current object of his fixation. I might always be, if I didn't act now. This knowledge burned within me, much stronger than any fire ever could.

I took one last look at Joshua's shadowed face. Joshua had once more pressed his cell phone to his ear. He still cradled Jillian in his arms; and, every few seconds, he cast worried glances down at her and then back up at me.

When Joshua's eyes met mine across this wide distance, my vague plans solidified. I had to stop Eli immediately if I ever hoped to spend this hereafter in peace. I had to make Eli fear me more than he did now. More than he feared anything on this earth. Only then would I stand any chance of existing without his constant, dangerous interference.

Eli only added to my resolve when he finally spoke.

"Whatever this is, Amelia," he said, gesturing to the glow, "I think it could be very useful to me."

I turned back to him. Eli didn't meet my eyes, however, because he was still too busy watching the glow. Studying it intently.

"Oh, you think so, do you?" I asked softly.

"Of course." Eli nodded, and I could almost see the ideas forming in his head. "You'd be my best servant yet. Just imagine what that light of yours could do— how many new souls it could help me gather; how many people would be drawn to it, like moths to a flame."

I tilted my head to one side. "And if I don't want to serve you?"

He started and met my gaze. A slow, incredulous smile spread across his face. "'Don't want to?'" he repeated. "Do you still think you have a choice in all this?"

I pressed my lips tight, fighting the surge of fury inside me. Only once I had a better handle on myself did I respond.

"We all have choices, Eli. I don't care how often I have to say this: I have a choice too. Even if I'm dead."

Eli shook his head. "That's what I've been trying to tell you all along: *I* chose *you*. That should be enough."

I too shook my head. "It's not enough. Because I don't choose you."

He sneered; and as if on cue, the crowd of long, black shapes gathered around him. They seemed to appear out of thin air, swarming into view. They moved restlessly, constantly shifting so that I could hardly recognize their almost human forms, much less their faces.

Eli didn't look at them, but his grin widened. "You sure you want to put up a fight, Amelia?" he whispered menacingly.

I stifled my gulp and clenched my fists at my sides. "I'm sure."

Eli nodded again. Not to me, I realized, but to the black wraiths around him. In response the wraiths surged forward, surrounding me with a speed I didn't know they possessed. They clustered around me, pressing together until they blocked out almost all the light and then began slinking closer.

Now enclosed by their dark forms, I whipped my head first one way and then another, seeking some sort of break in their ranks. Some beam of light in between them. My arms, extended from my sides, whipped around with me. When one of the shadowy souls reached out to grab me, I shrieked.

The soul didn't trap me, however. At the moment it tried to wrap, snakelike, around my arm, the glow on my skin brightened and intensified. It shined powerfully against the wraith, cutting through the black shadows around it and revealing its almost human form. The wraith yanked back for a moment, shifting angrily among the dark periphery. Then as if to retaliate, the other wraiths moved at once to converge upon me.

Before I could fight back, before I could even scream, the glow flared around me. Instead of its previously warm oranges and yellows, the light shined so white and pure that I had to shield my eyes from it. This light was unlike anything I'd ever seen, more intense and fierce than the glow my skin normally gave off in the dark; this new glow was glorious and terrifying at the same time.

Finally, the light dimmed enough so that I was able to lower my hand in time to see the wraiths break apart, flying back across the road and away from the protective white glow around me.

Once they cleared, I could finally see Eli, waiting in the same spot he'd been standing earlier. He had his arms folded casually over his chest, and he wore an expression of near boredom. Waiting for his servants to finish his dirty work, no doubt.

But when he saw his minions scatter and flee over the side of the bridge, his expression changed. He frowned at them, his scowl deepening as each one disappeared. Only after the last black shadow had left the bridge did

Eli look up at me. Now he looked savage. Vicious.

Meeting his furious eyes, I felt the ghost of a grin skitter across my lips. "What else have you got, Eli?" I murmured.

With a deep, wrenching snarl, Eli lunged at me.

*Chapter*
# TWENTY-NINE

I should have been scared. And I was. But instead of cowering, or even lunging to meet Eli head-on, I closed my eyes.

I may not have known the source of the supernatural light around me or how to control it, but I knew one thing that could certainly stop Eli. So, with my eyes shut tight, I pictured a series of images: the chair in the library flying back, away from me; the jagged crack that now marred my headstone. I pictured the bridge, bending under the force of my anger.

Then I pictured it breaking in half.

At the sound of metallic groaning beneath me, my eyes opened. I looked down and saw the fissure in the bridge widen. Above me, the metal cables between the girders began to swing wildly, and the bridge groaned again, shouting under the strain of movement.

Turning my attention back to the road, I held out my arms and braced myself.

Eli, however, was caught unprepared. The moment the bridge itself began to shake, he stumbled and fell, midlunge, to his knees. I locked my eyes on Eli, still concentrating as I watched the road crack and buckle around him. I gave a tiny flick of my head, and the asphalt split into a gaping hole through which I could see glimpses of the river below.

Eli scrambled to get on his feet but couldn't. As he struggled against the shaking road, his eyes met mine. Finally, I saw in them what I'd been seeking: fear.

At this, my most powerful moment, our surroundings plunged into total darkness. The darkness hovered, heavy and thick, before lightening to reveal the familiar colors of the netherworld forest below me.

Here on the bridge, however, things were much different from what I'd expected. I'd never seen the netherworld version of High Bridge this closely, and the sight momentarily shocked me. Upon the bridge, and so close to the evil black hole beneath it, the colors of the netherworld were almost violent and wild. Bloody reds against glittering blacks; livid purples blossoming on top of bruised grays. The place looked stunning, beautiful. But also horribly wrong. Like an enormous, wounded animal.

The structure of this netherworld bridge looked worse for the wear, too. Its girders angled unnaturally together; and its surface showed deep, irreparable cracks. Whatever I'd done in the living world, it must have altered this bridge as well.

I frowned, ready to shake this place into glittering rubble, when a hissing sound made my head shoot up, toward the bent girders. High above me, two black shapes swooped and circled the girders, moving nimbly around the structure of the bridge. Their movements hissed softly into the darkness.

At first I thought they must have been more trapped souls, forced by Eli to confront me. As I stared harder, though, I realized that they weren't black but a deep, arterial red. They also moved too deftly, too freely, as if they, unlike Eli's minions, had their own wills.

I glanced down at Eli to gauge his response to these creatures and blinked back in surprise. He now looked even more terrified than he had before. He had actually curled up into a ball and ducked his head beneath his arms when, with a quiet sort of whoosh, they took form and landed on either side of him upon the cracked surface of the bridge.

Now where the two creatures had hovered stood two people. At least they *looked* like people.

Both of the figures wore dark clothing: the man, a well-cut black suit; and the woman, a stylish black dress. They both had white-blond hair: his cropped short and hers long and free across her pale shoulders. Something about them gave off a sort of funereal air. Creepy, certainly, but no creepier than anything else I'd seen tonight.

It was their eyes, though—their eerie, inhuman eyes—that made me gasp and take an involuntary step backward across the cracked road. Those disturbing eyes, black and pupilless, studied me for a moment longer; and then, simultaneously, both figures smiled.

"Well, isn't this an interesting little thing?" the male mused.

"Eli," the female purred without taking her eyes from me, "where have you been hiding this treasure?"

Eli kept his head ducked as he answered her. "I've been trying to claim her for you, I have, but—"

"Stop making excuses." The woman cut him off, her voice suddenly sharp. "Are you telling me she isn't under your control yet?"

Her eyes landed on him; and, although Eli couldn't see

her with his head down, he still shuddered. "I didn't . . . she hasn't . . . ," he stuttered, but couldn't finish the protest.

"I think Eli is telling us *exactly* that, my dear," the man said, still watching me. "And so I suppose, like his predecessors, Eli has outlived his usefulness."

The man twitched his head toward the woman. "Take him away."

Upon hearing her counterpart's command, the woman smiled again. I too shuddered at the sight. Despite her cold, beautiful features, she looked *dead*. More dead than Eli and I ever could.

Eli raised his head from his arms, and his eyes briefly shot to mine. Seeing the unadulterated horror in them, I felt something clench in my chest. Despite everything he'd done tonight, despite everything he'd done to me in the past, my heart suddenly ached for Eli.

"Don't—!" I cried out, but I was too late.

In one swift motion, the woman melted back into a reddish black shape and enveloped Eli. Before another word escaped my lips, they disappeared together over the side of the netherworld bridge. For a few seconds I heard a primal, wrenching shriek. I realized, with a jolt, that the sound was Eli as he cried out in terror. Then, abruptly, the scream cut short.

I spun back around to the man. "Where are you taking

him?" I demanded, my tone forceful in spite of the very real danger I was obviously facing.

The man lifted his eyebrows in mild surprise. "To our home, of course."

"'Your home'?" My eyes flickered briefly to the edge of the bridge as if I could see through the ruined surface to the dark, gaping expanse below.

As I did so, the man watched me closely. When I looked back at him, he tilted his head to one side. Studying me, even when he spoke.

"I'm referring to the place where my companion and I live, obviously," he said. "The entrance to it lies beneath this bridge."

"Why there?" I asked, still not sure what had given me all this courage. "Why live in that darkness?"

The man laughed without smiling. "You could hardly expect us to live up here with those pathetic, shadowy creatures. Or with the living in their world. Besides, we prefer to remain among our kind."

I tried not to shudder, imagining what kind of beings would choose to live in that vile blackness. Although I kept my expression impassive, I had to swallow fear as it started to well up inside me.

"And what are you going to do with Eli, now that he's in your home?"

"We're going to implement punitive measures." He

sighed and shook his head, the picture of bored irritation. "We've had to take such actions before. It's a shame we'll have to do the same to Eli now."

Well, that explained what had happened to Eli's former mentor, and why Eli had acted so cagey about the subject yesterday in the forest. Not that the discovery provided me much comfort, especially when I considered the fact that, judging by the dark man's cold expression, he wouldn't have known shame if it slapped him in his creepy face.

The man studied me for a moment longer and then, in a genuinely curious tone, asked, "Do *you* care what happens to Eli?"

Part of my brain was raving, screaming at me to stop acting like a lunatic and run. Another part of my brain made me straighten my back and answer.

"Yes, I do. I care about everyone you've hurt. Everyone you've trapped here. Even Eli."

The corner of the man's mouth twitched with amusement. "How . . . interesting. What's your name, girl?"

I shook my head, my bravado wavering slightly. "Doesn't matter. What matters is that you need to let all the souls in this place go, including Eli . . . and my father."

His eyebrows lifted again. "You think your father's in here?"

"I . . . I'm not sure. But if you let them all go, I can probably find out."

He laughed, but the sound was too brittle for real humor. "How about I do something better? How about I offer you a job?"

I balked. "You mean, what Eli does for you?"

He nodded. "Judging by that light of yours, and by the redecorating you've done to this place, I think you could prove quite valuable to us. Besides, the position is now open."

I bit back what I really wanted to tell him he could with his offer and instead asked, "What exactly does that job entail?"

"We need an intermediary to build our world: a human soul who hasn't moved on yet. One who can still go between worlds at will and influence the living . . . make them join us, one way or another."

I frowned, examining the smooth contours of his perfect, inhuman face. "Why can't you just do the job yourselves? Why would you need Eli, or me?"

"We have no desire to leave our home, to perform such tasks—we have everything we need in there. Every creature comfort." He gave me a small, skin-crawling kind of grin and then went on. "We don't condescend to come up here unless we must do something out of the ordinary. Like punish. Or collect."

At the word "collect," he titled his head, once again studying me. Assessing me and my usefulness to him, no doubt.

I tried not to gag at the thought of serving someone like this. No, not some*one*—some*thing*. Some demon, I was sure of it.

I had to get away from him. Immediately.

But even if these dark beings had no desire to follow me out of this world, I had no idea how I would leave it, either. Something told me that this man—this creature—wouldn't just let me wander off toward the exit.

I tried to stall, tried to think my way out of this situation. My voice shook as I asked, "Why do you have to build your world at all? If you have everything you need in your . . . home?"

The man gave me a disdainful smile. "You don't *really* think that's how the afterlife works, do you? Is that what you've been taught about the whole cosmic game: that heaven and hell just sit back, waiting?"

At those two names, so deeply laden with meaning and myth, I finally shivered. I felt certain that I wasn't standing over one of the entrances to heaven right now.

"So you want to do what?" I asked. "Win the game?"

"Yes," he said, his smile growing wider until his teeth looked unnaturally sharp and bright, like a cluster of knives. "My side wants to win. And you're going to help us do it."

His eyes suddenly sparkled, dancing with a cold, soulless glow as they moved up and down my body. The appraisal chilled me—an actual chill, one that brought goose bumps to my arms.

As if it sensed the danger I was in, my light brightened suddenly, flaring with my fear, shining out toward the man as if it meant to protect me. I could see its glow reflected in the dark depths of his eyes and the glinting edges of his teeth.

The whole netherworld must have felt my fear, because the road beneath us began to groan as it split farther apart, just behind the place where the man stood. Unlike Eli, however, the dark man didn't respond in fear to the display. His eyes flickered down to the damaged roadway, then back to the light that insulated me from him. When he met my gaze again, he looked pleased—no, overjoyed—by what I could do.

He took one step toward me, then another. His eyes widened with manic excitement, and he stretched a pale hand out to me. To catch me and drag me into the darkness with him, no doubt. To keep me here forever.

My eyes darted to the tree line of the netherworld forest, where my father might be trapped, pacing with all the other condemned souls. The sight held my gaze for one brief, regretful second and then I closed my eyes tight.

"Materialize," I whispered desperately.

The bridge groaned again under my feet. Then, just beneath the groan, I heard the soft whoosh of air flying past me.

My eyes flew open. At first all I saw was the blinding white light. As it faded, however, I could make out the faint outlines of my surroundings. My vision became progressively clearer, and I searched frantically around me. But I saw no demonic man, no glittering netherworld. Just the bent metal and churned-up asphalt of the real High Bridge.

I stared at the black patch of air where the dark man had just been. I didn't trust that darkness; I didn't yet believe it was empty. But when I realized that he was gone—truly gone—I sighed. At my sigh, the glow around me extinguished with a soft *pop*.

"Huh," I muttered, raising my arms and looking down at my body. "Well, how about that."

I didn't have a mark on me. No cinders, no singeing, no streaks of soot on my white dress.

*Does this make me flammable, or inflammable? Or are they the same thing?*

Despite the horror of this evening, I heard a small, hysterical giggle escape my lips.

The sudden wail of a siren, however, broke into my

reverie. The noise reminded me of where I wanted to be, and it certainly wasn't on this bridge. I closed my eyes, and, mere seconds later, I reopened them to the sight of Joshua and Jillian at my feet. The siren still sounded, now above me.

My easiest materialization yet, it seemed.

Joshua hadn't seen me arrive, so I knelt beside him and gently placed one hand on his back. At my touch he whirled around with one fist clenched. The violence of his reaction startled me, and I moved to step backward. Before I could take the step, however, Joshua's eyes lit up with recognition. He grabbed my hand and pulled me down to him. While keeping one hand clasped around one of Jillian's, Joshua draped his free arm across my shoulder. I leaned into him, closing my eyes and dropping my head against his chest.

"I have no idea what just happened," Joshua said. "And I want to know everything. But we don't have much time to talk before the EMTs get here."

I opened my eyes and looked up at the grassy embankment above us. The ambulance had come to a stop at the edge of the ruined bridge, and a handful of emergency responders now moved carefully down the steep hill toward the river.

"I'm glad they're here," I said, looking down at Jillian's wan face. Joshua must have stretched her out upon the riverbank again, because she lay in the mud again, close eyed and pale.

"Yeah. She'll be okay, I think." Joshua stared down at his sister, frowning heavily. Then he abruptly chuckled and turned back to me. "She'll probably just wake up really, really pissed off."

I laughed with him, but our laughter felt somehow out of place. Joshua must have sensed this too, because his face once again grew serious.

"Are *you* okay, Amelia?" he asked, his eyes searching mine.

"Yeah." I sighed, and, for some inexplicable reason, I dropped my face back to his chest and sank farther into him. Maybe it was the sound of his rough voice that broke down my defenses, or maybe it was the simple act of resting for the first time this evening. Whatever the case, I was suddenly and overwhelmingly exhausted.

Joshua moved his arm up my shoulder to wrap his hand around the nape of my neck, where he then threaded his fingers through my hair. Not for the first time, I thought about how much I absolutely loved the way that felt. A slight smile crept over my face, and I sighed again.

"We don't have to talk about it right now," Joshua murmured. "But I've got to at least ask: did you . . . save us?"

"I wouldn't call it saving per se," I said, pressing my

face harder into his chest. "I would call it . . . spooking, maybe."

"So, you spooked Eli away?"

I smiled grimly, although Joshua couldn't see my face. "*I* didn't. But he's definitely been spooked away. Pretty effectively too, I think."

"Good."

The sound we heard next surprised both of us. A soft voice—hoarse from exhaustion and too much river water—croaked up at us from the bank.

"Amelia?"

I looked down at Jillian. She'd leaned up a few inches, onto her elbows, and she now stared directly at me. Her hazel eyes—almost feverish in the dark—met mine. The intensity of her stare seemed to hypnotize me.

"Yes," I whispered back, more out of compulsion than anything else.

"Is he gone?"

"Yes, O'Reilly's gone."

"No, not O'Reilly. The blond one."

I blinked in surprise. Jillian meant Eli. How had she known about Eli? She hadn't even seen him, had she?

"Y-yes," I stuttered. "The other one's gone too."

"Then . . . thank you."

She gave me one weak nod. Then she closed her eyes and laid her head back down upon the muddy bank.

# EPILOGUE

"I'd stop asking you if you'd stop being such a stupid jerk."

"Well, I wouldn't have to be a stupid jerk if you'd stop being a weirdo freak."

I sighed heavily, leaned back against the wall, and splayed my fingers in front of me to study my nails for invisible dirt. I'd heard this argument so many times in the last two weeks that I could have had it alone, debating each ridiculous side by myself.

Yet Joshua and Jillian seemed intent on having it at least one more time.

While I hovered at the top of the stairs—more than ready to end this pointlessness and leave—Joshua stood in front of Jillian's room with his hand clenched tight against the doorframe.

"Look," he growled. "Considering everything Amelia did for you, you're being . . . rude."

Jillian simply gave her brother a cold smile and folded her arms across her chest.

"As far as I'm concerned, Josh, nobody but *you* did anything for me; and I'm not going to show you how grateful I am by pretending some imaginary person exists."

"Oh, for the love of—!" Joshua released the doorframe and threw both of his hands up in the air. "Amelia is not imaginary. You saw her, the night she saved you. You *talked* to her, Jillian. And you can see her now, just like I can."

Joshua pointed to me. Jillian's eyes followed the line of her brother's arm, all the way up to my face. I only had the briefest second to smile at her before her eyes flickered away again.

"Nope, nobody there." She chanted the words in a singsong voice.

I groaned and rolled my eyes. "Joshua, this is useless. Just like it was useless last night, and three nights ago, and on and on . . ."

"It's not useless, because Jillian's going to come with us tonight."

"I don't know how many times I have to tell you this," Jillian said through clenched teeth. "I'm not going to spend my Friday nights with you and Casper the Friendly Girlfriend."

Joshua opened his mouth, in all likelihood to yell again, but I interrupted him.

"Look, Joshua, she clearly isn't going to give in tonight, so can we please, please just go?"

"Yeah, Josh, listen to your imaginary friend and get out of here," Jillian spat.

Joshua immediately began to crow, laughing and slapping his hand in triumph against the doorframe.

"Ha!" he cried. "I knew it! You *can* hear her, you big liar!"

Jillian's mouth gaped like a trout's. She glanced right at me again for a second. Then she shook her head violently, as if the motion would make me once more invisible to her. She grabbed the edge of her door and, with one last scowl, slammed it in Joshua's face.

Even with a door in his face, Joshua continued to chuckle. He turned to flash me a broad grin.

"See? I told you she'd give in."

"Sweetheart," I said with another roll of my eyes, "she didn't give you anything you didn't already know.

Besides, she's a full Seer now, whether she likes it or not. And I'm pretty sure she's not going to start making Save Amelia from Exorcism T-shirts whenever Ruth finally ends the truce. Even if Ruth *did* let me back in the house."

"Doesn't matter," he insisted. "Jillian and Ruth will like you. Eventually."

Despite my strong doubts, I laughed too. "Joshua Mayhew, ever the sunny optimist."

"Because my plans always work. You'll see."

"Speaking of mysterious plans . . . ," I prompted, and then slipped my arm through the crook of his elbow. Joshua's grin widened as he pulled me closer to him and led me down the stairs.

"I told you—it's a surprise."

"What, are you going to try to bring me back to life or something?" I pretended to sound hopeful. Well, at least, I sort of pretended.

Joshua, however, just laughed. "Give me time, Amelia. Give me time."

I shook my head. "Joshua, normal people surprise each other on their birthdays, which we both know I no longer have."

"All right. Then instead of giving you a present, how about I just ask you to destroy some public property again?"

I grimaced and squirmed uncomfortably against him. "Hey, I told you I don't like talking about that."

Joshua's eyes sparkled mischievously. "I'm just saying, it's probably going to take the county *years* to fix High Bridge."

"I hope they never do," I murmured. Then I smiled, shrugging. "Anyway, I told you, not going to talk about it. Period. End of discussion. Finis."

What I didn't say was that there were more than a few topics I now avoided. Such as Ruth's thinly veiled hostility to my nightly presence in her home; Jillian's impending induction into the Wilburton Seer community, which I basically saw as inevitable; or the near-constant worry I felt for my father when I thought about where, and by whom, his soul might be trapped.

And, of course, I wasn't exactly ready to bring up all the impossibilities facing my relationship with Joshua himself, either. After all, we were, collectively, a Seer and a potential target for exorcism. A vibrant, living boy and a dead girl.

Not exactly an obvious, or easy, match.

Unaware of the dark thoughts that plagued me, Joshua gave me another mischievous grin. By now we'd reached the back door of the kitchen, and he playfully shoved me out the doorway.

Soon he had me safely deposited in his new vehicle—a

used truck, painted a shiny black—while he drove us to some undisclosed destination. Upon his orders I slid all the way back against my seat (after muttering my protests for a solid five minutes) and pressed my hands against my eyes. Each time I tried to peek between my fingers, Joshua caught me and threatened me with the punishment of an entire trip spent listening to Jillian's hip-hop playlist.

Eventually, Joshua rolled the truck to a stop. We sat in silence for a moment, and a strained air began to settle over the cab. I could feel Joshua's hesitancy radiating out from him like the vibration of a tuning fork.

"Joshua? You're awfully quiet."

"I guess I'm nervous about the surprise. I want you to like it, but I don't want it to make you sad."

"Sad?" I asked. "Why would I be—?"

I stopped my sentence short, letting the question hang in the air. I did so because that very air brought with it a familiar but long-forgotten scent.

Honeysuckle.

No matter where we'd parked Joshua's truck, I shouldn't be able to smell the plant. We were now into the chill of fall, and early frosts had already laid waste to most of Oklahoma's flowering plants. Yet the scent hit me now, strong and floral and sweet.

The Mayhews didn't grow any honeysuckle in their

yard, nor did I remember passing any in my afterlife wanderings. But I recognized the smell instantly, mostly because it had grown in thick, amber-petaled vines all along the fence line of my childhood home.

I turned my head toward the passenger side window and dropped my hands from my eyes. Sure enough, I faced the little clapboard house, the one in which I'd spent my first—and only—eighteen years of life. The honeysuckle vines around the house weren't in bloom right now, but their flowers had blossomed for so many years that the smell must have permeated the very air of this place.

"My home?" I whispered.

"I had an idea," Joshua explained, "of how you might see your mom. Just for a little bit. Do you think you'd want to?"

I stared more intently at the house. A rusted sedan now sat parked in the driveway. The light of the TV flickered out from the front window, shifting from yellows to blues in the dusk.

I thought about Joshua's suggestion for a moment longer and then nodded.

Joshua got out of the truck and came around to my side, opening the door and pretending to pick something off the floorboard in case my mother was watching us. I slid out of the truck, my eyes never leaving the front door of the little house.

Joshua and I didn't speak as we made the short walk across the yard. We tromped over the porch, only Joshua's steps echoing against the floorboards. Joshua raised one hand and, with a reassuring nod at me, rapped upon the door.

I heard shuffling from inside the house, and my head began to swim. A few seconds later, when the door swung open, I thought I might faint.

There she stood in the doorway, backlit by the hall light. Elizabeth Louise Ashley. Liz to her friends. Mom to me.

She'd aged horribly, much worse than I'd expected. Yet beneath the new wrinkles, and the ten extra years of sadness, my mother's beauty still shined. Anyone could see that.

Her dark hair glistened in its ponytail, with only a few grays for decoration. Her large brown eyes—still fringed with thick lashes—assessed the young man on her porch before she gave him a full, gracious smile.

"May I help you?" she asked in that lovely voice, the perfect one that had read me every bedtime story I knew. The one she'd fought not to raise during each and every stupid fight we'd had—fights I wished, more than anything, I could take back now.

"Mom," I moaned, unable to catch the word before it

spilled out of my mouth.

From the corner of my eye, I could see Joshua clench the hand closest to me. I could tell he wanted to reach out to comfort me. I loved him for it, even if he couldn't act upon his impulse right now.

Instead of clasping my hand, Joshua cleared his throat and answered my mother. "Yes, ma'am. I'm here on behalf of my church youth group. We're . . . um, passing out Bibles, door-to-door."

I arched one eyebrow at Joshua. To my surprise, he pulled a tiny green Bible out of his coat pocket and held it out to my mother. You have to give it to him—the boy came prepared, New Testament and all.

My mother smiled, her incredulity mirroring mine; but she reached out and took the book from Joshua. She looked down at it, and her smile softened. Keeping it in one hand, she ran a thumb across its surface.

"You know," she mused, still staring at the book, "my daughter had a little one just like this. Same color and everything."

That struck Joshua silent. Even I didn't know what to say. I swallowed, feeling an odd thickness in my throat.

My mother must have sensed Joshua's discomfort, because she finally looked back up at him. For a moment I thought I could see the glitter of tears along the rims of her eyes; but she turned her head, and the shadows covered her face.

"I'm sorry. That was . . . random."

"Not at all, ma'am," Joshua insisted. "I'm sure your daughter is wonderful."

"Was," my mother said quietly. "And yes, she was. Wonderful."

Guilt twisted in my core like a spasm. The thickness in my throat hardened, and I tried not to choke on it. But the cough I suppressed still threatened to spill over my eyes in the form of tears.

Unaware of the little drama I carried out in front of her, my mother turned to glance over her shoulder at something inside the house. A shaft of light illuminated her face, and I took a last, precious look at it. When she turned back to Joshua, my view vanished.

"You know, Mr. . . . ," she prompted.

"Mayhew. Joshua," he offered, and then cringed. Perhaps he'd wanted to give her a fake name, although there was no real need for subterfuge. She would never know the connection between Joshua and me.

"Well, Joshua," my mother went on. "It's only eight o'clock. I have some sweet tea, if you want to come inside, or something."

Joshua's eyes flickered over to me, but I shook my head no. Although part of me desperately wanted to sit beside her for hours, listening to her voice and trying to catch a whiff of her perfume, another part of me did not. Possibly, it was the part of me that focused on self-preservation. I'd come back later, I knew; but I couldn't be here right now. I had the suspicion that, if we stayed here much longer, I might fall apart entirely.

"No, ma'am," Joshua said, shaking his head. "But that's awfully nice of you. I'd better just go . . . pass out the rest of the Bibles."

"Sure," my mother said with a nod.

Even in the dark, I could see her faint smile.

"It's been a pleasure, Joshua Mayhew," she said, extending her Bible-free hand. "A brief one, but a pleasure nonetheless."

Joshua laughed quietly. With a smaller version of his usual grin, Joshua took my mother's hand and shook it.

"It's been a pleasure for me, too, Mrs. Ashley."

Then he blanched and dropped her hand. I could almost hear the screamed regrets in his head: she hadn't told him her last name, so he shouldn't have known it. How would he explain this? How could he?

My mother, however, didn't call him out on this error. In fact, she didn't say anything further. She simply raised one eyebrow and flashed him that half smile of hers before turning to close the door.

"The mailbox—," Joshua began feebly. But my mother had already shut the door, effectively leaving Joshua with the secret of why this eighteen-year-old boy knew her last name.

Joshua and I drove in silence for a while, although he didn't take us home.

I didn't need to ask where we were going as he pulled off onto a steep, pine-thick road. Although he'd never taken this route before and the night had fallen dark and heavy around us, I instinctively knew our destination.

After winding his way up and around the sharp curves that the road cut through Robber's Cave Park, Joshua parked the truck next to a small clearing. He left the truck running but turned off its lights and then exited to help me out of the cab. I stood to one side while he leaned back in and fiddled with the MP3 player, which he'd attached to the truck's stereo.

My favorite song—the one to which he'd introduced me and that I loved for its slowly soaring guitar—drifted out of the open door. Joshua pulled away from the truck and, without a word, took my hand. He led me to the middle of the clearing, just to the right of our favorite park bench. Then he pulled me close to him. I draped my arms around his neck, he wrapped his arms around my waist, and we began to sway in time to the music.

Soon the song ended and another of my favorites began. I suspected Joshua had created this list of songs just for me, but I didn't ask if this was the case. There was romance in the mystery.

Eventually, I sighed and looked up into his eyes, which were almost black in the darkness.

"Thank you for tonight," I murmured.

"You aren't . . . sad, or upset with me?"

"I'm sad, for sure. But I'm happy, too. For lots of reasons. Seeing my mother. And then . . . well, *you*."

"Me?"

"Yes, you. You're constantly giving me the best gifts, even if I don't realize it at the time. Like tonight. Or when you brought me to see my home for the first time. Or when you woke me up." I slipped one arm from around Joshua's neck and placed my hand upon his cheek. "So, Joshua, how could I ever be upset with you?"

He laughed quietly, taking my hand from his cheek and wrapping my arm back around his neck. "Well, I haven't given you your final surprise yet, Amelia."

"Life?" I asked with a small grin.

Joshua grinned, too—broad and charming and so completely perfect—before leaning in close to me.

"No," he whispered, shaking his head. "This."

And then he pressed his lips to mine.

I tightened my arms around his neck and kissed him back with all my might. Tingling fire spread through me, though it was far less fierce and all-consuming than the light I could create by myself.

But this fire was better. Much, much better.

As Joshua and I kissed, I made a list of the things I didn't have: a pulse, for one, but also a family I could talk to, including my missing father and my lonely mother; a future—one free of dark spirits and vengeful Seers, one I could share with the boy in my arms.

Then I made a list of the things I did have: a wakefulness I'd long forgotten but could now enjoy again; maybe the occasional scent of honeysuckle, or Joshua's cologne.

Then, of course, there was Joshua himself.

As I reviewed the lists, I found that, were I given a choice, I would always choose the second list.

In an instant. In a heartbeat.

I always would choose the hereafter, when it was a hereafter spent with him.

# ACKNOWLEDGMENTS

Enormous thanks to my editor, Barbara Lalicki, for her warmth, insight, and encouragement. Also to Maria Gomez, Alexandra Bracken, and the entire team at HarperCollins Children's—I can't say thank you enough.

I'm eternally grateful to my agent, Catherine Drayton, who took a huge chance on me. I don't know where I'd be right now if it wasn't for that first international call and my mad scramble to find a spot in my house with good cell reception. (Or that first cup of tea when I realized it was all real.) Also, kudos to the staff at InkWell

Management for their extra help in getting this book rolling.

To my parents, thank you for so elegantly doing the impossible: keeping me grounded while telling me to reach for the stars. To Robert, thank you for your patience, humor, and endless ability to deal with the crazy. You're proof that, sometimes, we win big.

To my amazing sounding board: Melissa Peters Allgood, Beth Prykryl, Krissy Carlson, as well as Andrea, Sarah, Tonya, Brandy, Jason, and a myriad of other cheerleaders. You're ridiculous. I love you all.

And finally, to Melissa Thompson and Mandy Haskins—this book would not have happened without you. Hands in, forever.

Management for their extra help in getting this book rolling.

To my parents, thank you for so elegantly doing the impossible: keeping me grounded while telling me to reach for the stars. To Robert, thank you for your patience, humor, and endless ability to deal with the crazy. You're proof that, sometimes, we win big.

To my amazing sounding board: Melissa Peters Allgood, Beth Prykryl, Krissy Carlson, as well as Andrea, Sarah, Tonya, Brandy, Jason, and a myriad of other cheerleaders. You're ridiculous. I love you all.

And finally, to Melissa Thompson and Mandy Haskins—this book would not have happened without you. Hands in, forever.